"I spent some pretty good times here."

Beau motioned to the small cubicle between the windows.

"The kissing cubbyhole." Clary recalled the infamous locale.

"It was everybody's favorite place when I was in high school. The trick was to wedge yourselves in just right."

"I never knew there was a technique."

"Here, I'll show you."

Turning to Clary, he took her by the shoulders and guided her into a corner of the small space. Then he squeezed in in front of her.

He was so close, and her heart was beating so fast and hard that Clary wondered if he could feel it against his chest. His body ran the whole length of hers without a hairbreadth between them, his forearms resting against the wall on either side of her head.

She glanced up into his face. "Are we stuck?"

That made him smile. "No, we're not stuck. We could get out right now. If we wanted to."

Dear Reader,

Welcome to Silhouette **Special Edition** . . . welcome to romance. Each month, Silhouette **Special Edition** publishes six novels with you in mind—stories of love and life, tales that you can identify with—romance with that little ''something special'' added in.

This month, we're pleased to present the conclusion of Nora Roberts's enchanting new series, THE DONOVAN LEGACY. *Charmed* is the story of Boone Sawyer and Anastasia Donovan—and their magical, charmed love. Don't miss this wonderful tale!

Sherryl Woods's warm, tender series—VOWS—will light up this Thanksgiving month. *Honor*—Kevin and Lacey Halloran's story—will be followed next month by *Cherish*. The vows that three generations of Halloran men live by create timeless tales that you'll want to keep forever!

Rounding out the November lineup are books from other favorite writers: Arlene James, Celeste Hamilton, Victoria Pade and Kim Cates. This is truly a feast for romance readers this month!

I hope that you enjoy this book and all the stories to come. Happy Thanksgiving Day—and all of us at Silhouette Books wish you the most wonderful holiday season ever!

Sincerely,

Tara Gavin
Senior Editor
Silhouette Books

VICTORIA PADE

HELLO AGAIN

Silhouette®

SPECIAL EDITION®

Published by Silhouette Books New York
America's Publisher of Contemporary Romance

SILHOUETTE BOOKS
300 East 42nd St., New York, N.Y. 10017

HELLO AGAIN

Copyright © 1992 by Victoria Pade

ISBN: 0-373-09778-6

First Silhouette Books printing November 1992

All the characters in this book have no existence outside the
imagination of the author and have no relation whatsoever to
anyone bearing the same name or names. They are not even
distantly inspired by any individual known or unknown to the
author, and all incidents are pure invention.

®: Trademark used under license and registered in the United
States Patent and Trademark Office and in other countries.

Printed in the U.S.A.

Books by Victoria Pade

Silhouette Special Edition

Breaking Every Rule #402
Divine Decadence #473
Shades and Shadows #502
Shelter from the Storm #527
Twice Shy #558
Something Special #600
Out on a Limb #629
The Right Time #689
Over Easy #710
Amazing Gracie #752
Hello Again #778

VICTORIA PADE

is a bestselling author of both historical and contemporary romance fiction, and mother of two energetic daughters, Cori and Erin. Although she enjoys her chosen career as a novelist, she occasionally laments that she has never traveled farther from her Colorado home than Disneyland, instead spending all her spare time plugging away at her computer. She takes breaks from writing by indulging in her favorite hobby—eating chocolate.

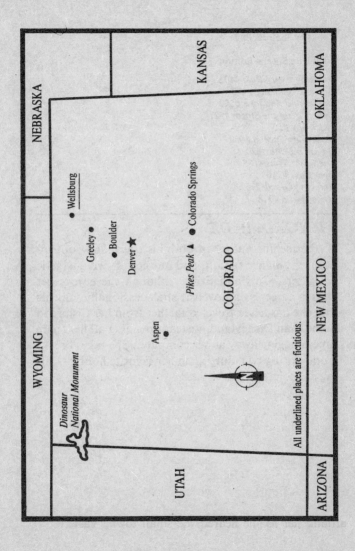

All underlined places are fictitious.

Chapter One

Clary Parsons glanced at the dashboard clock on her rental car, as if she had an appointment to keep.

Force of habit.

But there was no hurry and she let up on the gas pedal; after all, she was not in California anymore. She was on a highway in the middle of farm country, Colorado, on a lazy Sunday afternoon. And she was on vacation, not on her way to work or any of the other hundred-and-one things she rushed to every day.

She hooked her very long, very curly milk-chocolate-colored hair behind her ears and took a deep breath, willing herself to relax. If anyone had told her even a few months ago that she'd be spending a vacation in her old hometown of Wellsburg, she'd have told him he was out of his mind. But that was where she was headed.

The late spring countryside north of Denver lay open all around her as she neared the small town. Vast fields of young green cornstalks lined either side of the road, the sky was the color of a blueberry Popsicle, and in the distance, occasional silos pointed like giant arrows to heaven.

Hers was the single car on the road, after she passed an old couple obviously out for a Sunday drive doing fifteen miles under the speed limit. The only other people she saw were a scant one or two sitting on the front porches of the scattered farmhouses, and two men idly chatting in the sole service station she drove by as one of them pumped gas into a pickup truck.

Clary felt like a streak of lightning, shooting through a communal nap.

But, then, that was how she'd always felt about herself in this part of the country.

An efficient green road sign was the first announce-ment of the county line, three miles before there was any sight of Wellsburg itself. Two miles beyond that there was another marker, this one weathered wood, its white paint naturally antiqued, its stenciled letters grayed. Wellsburg. Population: 823. Welcome.

Eight hundred and twenty-three people. There were probably more than that living in Clary's Los Angeles condominium complex. And here, she knew, that census counted not only townies but families on the outlying farms, too.

The white brick building that housed the town hall, post office and tourist bureau was the beginning of Wellsburg proper. That was where Clary turned off the two-lane highway onto Front Street, the small town's main drag.

She had to smile at the thought of a tourist bureau; what was there to see? The new convenience store that had fi-nally been lured here? And where were tourists supposed to stay, without so much as a motel or even a boarding-house?

"Come to Wellsburg! Pitch a tent in the park square, feast on chicken-fried steak at Sylvia's Kitchen and tour the new convenience store!" Clary hawked, with a laugh, as she started up Front Street.

In the middle of farm country, where sunshine was so important but could beat down without mercy, Wellsburg sat under enough trees so that the whole town and its few surrounding blocks of houses were shaded by a canopy of leafy green branches like an umbrella on a beach. Only dapples and patches of sunlight poked through even now, before summer lushness had set in.

Clary knew there would be a big difference in the temperature, so she turned off the car's air conditioner and rolled down the window.

The air that drifted in was lighter than what she was used to in L.A., and it smelled the way she remembered. Of fresh-cut grass and peach blossoms. And the town was still just as quiet; the sound of her car seemed to echo like a loud voice in an empty room.

How she'd hated that quiet as a teenager, she thought, remembering long afternoons of wishing evil would rise out of the sewer system like in a horror movie, just to shake things up in the sleepy town.

And yet.

Somehow it felt good to be back, she admitted. But, then, knowing that her stay was only temporary was probably why she could enjoy it. A short visit to tie up some loose ends and spend a little time with her cousin and childhood best friend, Isabelle, before Izzy's baby was born. Clary had neglected that relationship longer than she should have. She meant to make amends and catch up.

The whole of Wellsburg's business district was six blocks of aged brick and crisply painted wooden buildings. They were lined up along a sidewalk that bordered a street wide

enough for cars to park nose-first at the curb and still leave
a two-lane width in the center. Being Sunday, there were
almost no cars there at all.

There weren't many people, either. Just two teenage
girls—one making a phone call outside the library, while
the other waited against the building; a young boy looking in the auto-parts window; and three elderly women
with covered dishes in hand, headed into a storefront that
had been turned into the bridge club even before Clary had
left.

At the end of the six blocks was the park square that divided the business district from the homes of the townies.
Clary took off her sunglasses as she rounded it. Three
small boys were playing some sort of game with toy
swords, one of them wearing a green cape that looked like
a turtle shell. They raced around turn-of-the-century
street-lamp poles and hid behind tree trunks, charging out
with cries that wouldn't even be heard in L.A. but seemed
loud in the stillness of Wellsburg's afternoon.

Clary had a sudden memory of hunting for Easter eggs
and running sack races on Fourth of July picnics on that
greenway as a kid. Was it still safe for a woman to be there
alone at night? It seemed like a million years ago that she'd
slept half the night on one of the park's wood-and-
wrought-iron benches to cool off after an argument with
her grandmother.

Not far past the park square, Clary turned right onto her
grandmother's old block. The Tylers sat on their front
porch like white-haired fixtures that hadn't moved an inch
in the fifteen years Clary'd been gone. She waved and they
waved back, but she could tell they didn't know who she
was.

All eight houses and yards on the block were as well-
tended as they had always been, lived in by the same peo-

ple—unless Izzy had failed to mention that someone had sold out. But Clary doubted it. After all, nothing much ever changed in Wellsburg, and when it did, it was news enough to spread.

At the end of the block her grandmother's house came into view—Clary's house, technically—along with the empty acre lot beside it. A plain one-story clapboard with a big wraparound porch, her childhood home was painted lemon yellow and trimmed in white, just the way it had always been. The steep shake-shingled roof and carved posts made it look like a Victorian farmhouse, if there was such a thing.

Her maternal grandmother had raised her there, after Clary's teenage mother had joined Clary's teenage father in a great escape from the confines of the small town and the baby neither of them was prepared to care for. Clary had inherited the house and the adjoining two-acre plot of ground when her grandmother had passed away seven years ago. She would have sold it then, but the will had stipulated that she couldn't dispose of anything until she turned thirty-three.

Her birthday had been two weeks ago. So here she was.

Clary stopped the car in front of the house and got out, taking a look at the place for a moment before heading toward it. There hadn't been shutters around the windows before, and where her grandmother's nasturtiums had outlined the porch, marigolds were just beginning to bloom. But the porch swing was still hanging between the big picture window and the wooden screened front door, painted a crisp white to match the house trim.

Izzy, Clary's cousin on her father's side, and Izzy's husband, Jack, had taken good care of the property in the seven years they'd rented it. Clary was glad to finally be able to sell to them..

Her cousin from one side of her family living in the house that belonged to her grandmother on the other side. Thinking about that made Clary smile again. Everything and everyone all twisted up together, that was Wellsburg all right.

She went to the back of the car and opened the trunk to take out her suitcase. The sound of the trunk slamming closed brought Izzy out of the house.

Even without being pregnant, Izzy had always been a big woman. She stood five-ten without shoes and carried a man's weight on a big-boned frame. But there was nothing masculine about her, in spite of her size. Her chin-length blond hair was soft and full as it curved around her jawbone. The long bangs that reached her eyebrows made her look younger than her thirty-three years. And just seeing her was like being home, no matter where Clary was.

"Look at you! Trim and gorgeous, while I'm the Whale of Wellsburg. I hate you," her cousin said, as Clary brought her suitcase up on the porch and they managed a hug.

"You look great."

"For a blimpo."

"For a big ol' pregnant lady," Clary teased, grateful for the closeness that still existed between them even though they'd only seen each other half a dozen times since she left Wellsburg for Los Angeles fifteen years ago. The letters and phone calls had helped, but Izzy got more credit for keeping up with those than Clary did.

"Come inside," Izzy said, holding the screen door open for her to bring in her suitcase. "Jack's not here or I'd make him carry your bag. He had some paperwork to catch up on at the post office, so he went in for a while. I hate it when he works on Sunday, but sometimes I just can't stop him."

"That's okay. This has wheels," Clary assured her, setting the suitcase down on the hardwood floor of the entryway.

"Does it seem strange to come back home?" Izzy asked as she followed Clary in.

"Do you mean to Wellsburg or to the house, now that it's yours?"

"Both."

"Wellsburg is just Wellsburg," she said with a shrug.

"And the house?"

Clary thought about it for a moment, glancing around at how different the place looked on the inside. To the left of the entrance was the living room. Izzy's country-style furniture had a more cozy, welcoming appeal than Clary's grandmother's ornate Chippendale reproductions had. Cream-colored wallpaper with tiny sprigs of flowers replaced the dark maroon flocked that had dimmed the room before. All in all, Clary thought this fresher style was a big improvement. "It does seem a little strange, I guess. But not bad-strange, just familiar and not, at the same time. I like what you've done with the place."

"Oh, good. I'm so glad. Come and see the rest, then." Izzy turned sharply to the right and the room that opened off the entrance. "I'll bet you can't tell what this is."

"Let me see if I can figure it out—balloons and teddy bears—this must be Jack's den."

"Right. And he crawls into the crib for all those moments when he's desperate to get into a fetal position and suck his thumb."

"I know a lot of men like that, but I never thought Jack was one of them."

They both laughed, as Izzy led the way farther down the hall. "This is your room," she said at the door to what actually had been Clary's room growing up but was now obviously for guests.

Clary's scandalous water bed had been replaced with a four-poster, the gigantic fluorescent flowers she'd painted on the walls were covered with blue-and-mauve striped wallpaper and an oak dresser replaced the orange crates she'd used as catchalls.

"Much better," Clary said, as she set her suitcase on the antique trunk at the foot of the bed.

"And Jack and I took your grandmother's old room," Izzy went on to the bedroom at the far end of the hall, decorated in hunter's green and white.

Clary poked her head through the doorway and then backtracked to peek at the bathroom that divided the master suite from the guest room. "You guys have done a lot of work around this place," she said, glad to find the pink-and-black plastic tile gone, and a new sink, tub and toilet replacing the old.

"Wait till you see the kitchen. We completely remodeled it."

Another hallway at a right angle to the main one led straight there and Clary followed her cousin. New cupboards, new appliances and a breakfast nook completely revamped what had been a very old-fashioned, outdated kitchen. But none of the charm had been lost in the process.

"I'm impressed."

Izzy smiled broadly and looked around as if seeing the room for the first time herself. "We like it," she said in a tone that made the words an understatement. "Now sit down and let me fix you some lunch." She motioned to the breakfast nook.

"I stopped in Greeley on the way and had a sandwich. But iced tea would be good."

Clary slid into the nook as her cousin went to the refrigerator. When Izzy joined her a moment later, it was with a pitcher of tea and two glasses full of ice.

"What? Do I have mustard on my nose?" Clary asked, when Izzy sat across from her and stared.

"I was just thinking that I don't know what finally made you come home, but it's so good to have you here."

Clary accepted the glass of iced tea her cousin poured for her. "You know I came to close on selling you and Jack the house and Beau the acreage next door."

Izzy put two generous spoonfuls of sugar in her own tea from a bell-shaped sugar bowl in the center of the table that was spotted like a cow. "You could have done the closing by proxy," her cousin pointed out.

"But then I wouldn't have gotten to see you. I wanted to spend some time with you before the baby comes." It sounded so simple. So commonplace. Only Clary knew just how strong was her own need to touch base with her cousin again. How strong it had been in the last month. How much Clary wanted to make up for lost time with Izzy.

"What about Biminis? Can your restaurant do without you?"

It couldn't have seven years ago, when Clary had opened it, but it was successful enough now not to miss her. "I have a good manager—Marta. And Wolf has promised to keep an eye on things, too. The law firm he works with has offices a block away and he eats there a dozen times a week anyway."

"Wolf." Izzy repeated, clearly trying to place the name.

Clary filled her in. "Wolfgang Schmidt—my attorney, neighbor and bosom buddy—I've written you about him."

"Right. The guy I keep wondering why you don't get involved with."

"And ruin a good friendship? Why would I want to do that?" In truth, there had been a slight attraction between them when they'd met at a party fourteen years ago, but it had fizzled before they'd even finished their first date. "Wolf is a wonderful guy and I love him dearly, but he's so much of a perfectionist he has his underwear ironed. He'd drive me crazy, as anything more than a friend."

Izzy's pale eyebrows arched. "How do you know what he does with his underwear?"

"I caught him pitching a fit to the woman who does his laundry one day, and besides, the times we've traveled together, he complains when it gets wrinkled."

"You travel together and talk about his underwear, but you aren't romantically involved with him?"

Clary fought a smile. Her cousin was the principal of Wellsburg's only school, a woman who had a master's degree in education, oversaw grades kindergarten through twelve and enjoyed a high standing in the community. She was intelligent and better-educated than Clary. And yet her small-town thinking was coming through. A relationship such as the one Clary enjoyed with Wolf just wouldn't exist in Wellsburg and Clary knew it. Still, she couldn't resist teasing her cousin. "I'd travel with you and discuss your underwear, if you wanted. It's no different with Wolf."

"Whatever you say, Clary," Izzy answered.

Clary laughed. It had been a long time since anyone used that tone that said they thought she was an oddball but loved her anyway. "Well, what I say is that Wolf and I are just friends. That's all we've ever been and all we ever will be."

Izzy refilled Clary's glass and got up for more ice. "I wish you had a man in your life who wasn't just a friend. I worry about you being all alone."

But Clary chose not to answer that. Instead, she addressed what she felt was more important. "I don't want you waiting on me, Izzy. I won't stay, if you treat me like a guest," she said as her cousin sat down again.

"Not a chance. I have plans to work you like a dog."

"Whatever you need."

Izzy laughed, in a confused sort of way. "Don't be so serious. You made that sound like I was asking for one of your kidneys and you couldn't wait to give it to me."

Clary smiled and joked, "Sorry, I'm keeping both my kidneys. But I'm signed on for anything else you might need—housecleaning, ironing, painting, getting ready for the baby—you name it."

"If I'd have known you wanted me to save up some dirty work for you, I would have. But as it is, we'll just have to visit. And go to the awards ceremony for the graduating class on Tuesday night, and a potluck baby shower at the church on Wednesday. Think you can handle all that?"

The doorbell rang before Clary had a chance to comment. "I'm not expecting company," Izzy said, as she slid out of the breakfast nook.

As she waited, Clary could hear her cousin say, "I should have known. Coming to check up on me, aren't you?" And then, "It's just Beau, Clary."

Beau Dugan. Like most of the people in Wellsburg, Clary had known Beau all her life. He was the older brother of one of Izzy and Clary's best friends all through school. He was also the town's doctor and the person to whom Clary was about to sell the plot of ground next door.

"Izzy told me you were coming, and when I didn't recognize the car out front I thought you might be here," he greeted Clary as he followed Izzy into the kitchen and set his medical bag on the counter.

"First he and my obstetrician in Greeley make me take maternity leave, instead of finishing the school year. Now he drops in on me all the time, just to try and catch me eating something salty," Izzy complained happily, pouring another glass of iced tea without even asking if he'd like one.

But Clary barely heard what either of them said. Instead, she was taking in the sight of Beau Dugan.

He'd been the quarterback on the football team, student-body president, and nearly oblivious of Clary and Izzy as anything more than friends of his younger sister.

For her part, Clary had only taken note of him as anything other than a friend's big brother when he'd left for UCLA—leaving the place that Clary longed to escape and going to the city she had made her goal. He'd been in medical school by the time she got there, but a request from her grandmother via his father had made him look her up and agree to keep an eye on her.

Through two more years of medical school, one of internship and two of residency, he'd done just that— watched out for her like a brother. And they'd become friends.

Then Beau had come back to Wellsburg to practice and Clary had stayed in L.A.

Was he this attractive then? she wondered. Had he been so tall and lean that even a simple pair of gray slacks and a plain white shirt with the sleeves rolled to his elbows could make him look like a catalogue model? Had his hands always been so big? His shoulders so broad? Had his hair been the color of mink and his eyes as green as kiwi fruit even then? Had his features looked as if one of the great masters had chiseled them out of marble? Had his brow been so well-defined, his jaw so square, his chin so sharp and the dent in the middle of it so pronounced?

Probably, she admitted to herself.

But fifteen years ago she hadn't appreciated what she was looking at now. He'd been a smart, good-looking, personable guy, and it hadn't mattered one wit, because he'd been a smart, good-looking, personable guy from Wellsburg—the kiss of death to young Clary, who'd been so enraptured with being on her own in L.A., so busy trying to carve out a place for herself in the big city, make friends and support herself. Beau Dugan had been okay for friend material. But no comparison to blond-beachboy types for dating.

The foolishness and oversight of youth, she thought now.

"I had a house call up the block," he was saying to Izzy as he sugared his tea. "And I thought I'd stop in to check your blood pressure, since it was a little high when you were in on Friday. Besides, I was just walking by anyway."

"Who do you think you're kidding?" Izzy teased him. "You wanted to be one of the first people to see Clary."

He smiled at that, but didn't deny it, and Clary couldn't help noticing that deep creases rippled out around the corner of his very masculine mouth.

"Jack's not here?" he asked Izzy.

As her cousin explained where her husband and Beau's best friend was, Clary still studied him. She'd known she'd be seeing Beau while she was here, and she'd been looking forward to it—the way she had looked forward to seeing all her old friends in Wellsburg. But faced with him now, a different chord was struck in her. A chord that left her more aware of him as a man than as just an old acquaintance. It seemed very odd to her.

But, then, everything in the past month had been off-kilter, and this reaction was probably less a statement about Beau and more a statement of her own recently haywire existence, Clary decided.

"Clary? I said do you want a brownie to go with your tea?" Izzy must have repeated, because she'd raised her voice as if her cousin hadn't heard her the first time.

Embarrassed to be caught staring, Clary recovered quickly and took a square of the dense chocolate treat the other woman was offering. As she did, she felt Beau's attention turn her way. When she glanced in his direction she caught him oh-so-subtly looking her up and down, the way she'd just done to him.

"It's really good to see you," he told her.

Izzy laughed. "You make that sound as if it surprises you."

His smile turned into a grin, but he didn't address Izzy's comment. And he didn't look away. Instead he said to Clary, "I like your hair long. You always wore it so short that the last time I saw you I had more than you did."

"Adolescent rebellion. My grandmother hated my hair 'cut like a boy's', as she put it, so of course that was just how I wanted to wear it."

"You gave your poor grandmother fits," Izzy put in.

"The job of all teenagers is to give the boundary setters in their life fits," Beau said with a wry laugh.

"And he should know. Beau's daughter, Dori, turns eighteen next Sunday," Izzy informed Clary.

The telephone rang just then and Izzy went into the hallway to answer it, leaving Clary alone with Beau. Feeling the need to make conversation, she said, "You're looking pretty good yourself. Being a country doctor must agree with you."

"I don't have any complaints. And you must not either. Izzy tells me your restaurant—Bermuda's, is it?—is a big success."

"Biminis. And it's doing pretty well, yes." It felt strange to be exchanging formal small talk when the air around them seemed charged with something far more personal. Or maybe she was just imagining it. "I understand you just took over the old bank building and turned it into a medical center."

"Skokie and I bought the place—do you remember Howard Skokes?"

Two years older than Clary, tall, skinny, curly red hair, big ears and charm enough to make up for his funny looks. "Sure, I remember Skokie. But I thought he wanted out of Wellsburg as much as I did."

"Maybe more."

"Not possible."

"Anyway, he's a dentist. He had a practice in Denver up until a few years ago. Then he got fed up with the pace, treating people he never really got to know, dealing with the constant turnover of office help and the whole rat race. He moved back and we decided to go into partnership. When the new bank was built, the old one went up for sale, and Skokie and I realized the building was perfect."

"Izzy said you even do surgery there."

"Only on an outpatient basis. But there's more and more of that being done now. Both Skokie and I wanted this to rival the best medical and dental care any private practice in the city could offer, and I think we've accomplished it."

He was proud of that. It showed in the light in his green eyes and sounded in the enthusiasm of his deep baritone voice. And somehow that pride came without arrogance. It was very attractive. *He* was very attractive.

Izzy came back into the kitchen then, just in the nick of time, because Clary had forgotten where her conversation with Beau had left off.

"That was Jack. He said to say hello to you both and to tell you to stop by the post office when you leave here, Beau. He says he needs to see you right away."

"What if I don't want to leave my present company?" Beau complained good-naturedly, staring straight at Clary the whole time.

"Jack says if you don't come and pay off the bet you lost to him, he's going to spread it all over town that you're a deadbeat."

Beau laughed again, and Clary realized she liked the sound very much—deep and rich, it seemed to originate far down inside his chest.

Then he said, "Well, I can't go anywhere until I check on the patient."

"Is there a problem?" Clary asked, sounding like an alarmed mother.

Izzy rolled her eyes. "Pickles and potato chips and pretzels and bacon and basically everything that tastes good because it's salty."

"She's having some problems with water retention—swollen hands, feet and ankles," Beau explained. "And her blood pressure has a tendency to be slightly elevated, but there's nothing to worry about—all of this can go with the territory of advanced pregnancy, warm weather, over-doing and not watching what she eats." Beau turned from speaking to Clary to frown, with exaggerated ferocity, at Izzy and say pointedly, "She just needs to stay away from pickles, potato chips, pretzels, bacon and basically everything that tastes good because it's salty—like peanuts, which I caught her eating last night."

"You were right to get out of Wellsburg, Clary. I can't even have five nuts at a party without getting caught and reprimanded. Do you know this guy came right up to me and took them away?"

"I also made her sit down and put her feet up like she's supposed to," Beau added, still with a stern expression. Then to Clary he said, "Maybe now that you're here you can play watchdog and keep your cousin down, and out of the salt."

"Absolutely. I'll shove her into a chair every time I see her on her feet, and slap her hand if she reaches for salty foods. Anything else, *mon capitaine?*"

"Believe me, you'll have your hands full with just those two chores," Beau laughed.

"O-o-oh, the cravings are so-o-o bad," Izzy crooned.

Beau slid toward Izzy. "Let me out of here, so I can check you over and go meet your husband before he ruins my reputation."

Izzy made a face. "How depressing—I remember when being checked over had a much more flattering meaning than having my blood pressure taken." She lumbered out of the breakfast nook and then sat back on the end of the bench once Beau was free.

"Talk nice to me and I'll give your ankles an extra squeeze," he said, with a wink, as he brought his medical bag to the table.

"This man is entirely too aware of how gorgeous he is," Izzy said in an aside to Clary.

"Put out your arm," he ordered in mock sternness, narrowing his eyes at her comment.

But he *was* gorgeous, Clary thought.

"Do you know what my assistant principal would give for him to look twice at her?" Izzy went on, as if Beau weren't there.

"I'll bet there's a whole slew of Wellsburg's ladies in love with their doctor," Clary said, joining her cousin in giving him a hard time, though she figured it was probably true.

He put the blood-pressure cuff around Izzy's arm. "I haven't noticed a rash of female hypochondriacs. Sorry to disappoint you comediennes," he said, with a laugh that made it clear he didn't take their teasing or himself seriously.

With the cuff in place, he took his stethoscope from his bag and put it on—first in one ear and then in the other. The way he tilted his head to access that second ear caught Clary's eye. It was an odd thing to find sexy, but she did nevertheless.

"Now keep quiet, so I can see if the fat lady of farm country has high blood pressure," he told the room, in general, when he'd slipped the chest piece under the cuff.

He pulled Izzy's arm forward, bracing it on his hip with the inside of his elbow. Clary's gaze started there and traveled along his forearm, thinking that it seemed too well-developed to belong to a doctor. A weight lifter, maybe, but not a doctor.

His wrist was thick and flat and speckled with dark hair that scattered over the back of his hand where his blunt thumb held the stethoscope in place. He worked the inflation bulb with his other hand, pumping it again and again.

An image came to Clary's mind of that hand squeezing something much more personal than a blood-pressure bulb, and she had a sudden, inexplicable desire to feel it, shocking her.

And then it was her own hand she became aware of— clenched around her iced-tea glass so tightly it was starting to cramp.

She loosened her grip and took a long drink of the frigid liquid in hopes that it would cool her off. Instead, tipping her head back brought Beau's profile into her line of vision as he studied the gauge. Dr. Dashing. One look at him could give her heart palpitations.

"Your pressure is down a little from Friday. Clary must have a good effect," he told Izzy, breaking the silence in the room. Then he unfastened the cuff, took off his stethoscope and turned to put it all back in his bag. But before he did, he held it out toward Clary. "Want to play doctor and I'll take your blood pressure, too?"

Clary had no doubt her own was higher than her cousin's at that moment. She managed a laugh. "I'll pass, thanks. I know I'm perfectly healthy, because I just had a full physical last week."

"Lucky doctor," he said in a suggestive aside.

"She didn't seem to think so," Clary countered.

That made him laugh, and Clary thought she could feel it brush over her skin like sueded silk.

"I suppose that means you're not going to let me poke your ankles for swelling, either, then?"

"Sorry."

His bright green eyes held hers, and it occurred to Clary that the renewal of this relationship was taking on a much different tone than in the past; they'd certainly never flirted before.

Izzy cleared her throat. "You guys want me to leave you alone?" she deadpanned.

Beau smiled at Clary—a small thing that somehow managed to give the illusion they shared a secret. Then he turned back to Izzy. "You know the drill—pull up your pant leg and slip off your shoe."

Izzy shot Clary a look, as she followed Beau's orders. But when her cousin's attention went to Beau, so did Clary's.

He was hunkered down in front of Izzy. His muscular thighs splayed the gray fabric of his slacks, knees spread, hands dangling between while he studied her ankles for a moment before pressing his index finger into the flesh there. "Lookin' good, Iz, my girl."

Izzy drew a circle with her foot. "Not as good as Clary's though, right?" she goaded.

"I don't know, she won't let me look." Beau bobbed back up and snapped his medical bag shut. "Well, I hate to squeeze and run, but I have a bet to settle."

Izzy stood to walk him to the door and Clary did, too.

"So, our closings on the house and lot are set for late tomorrow morning, right?" he asked Clary as they paused at the front door.

"Right," she answered. "Izzy and Jack are anxious, and I imagine you are, too."

His palm was against the screen door, but he didn't open it. "I'll be glad to have the deal done, yes. Dori and I have been talking about plans for the house I'm having built there for a long time."

"Speaking of Dori," Izzy broke in. "She's so anxious to meet Clary that she's been checking in with me three times a day for the last two weeks to find out if Clary was here yet. If the two of you are free for dinner tomorrow night, we could get her over here then."

Beau's gaze slid from her cousin to Clary for what seemed like a long moment before he answered Izzy. "We're free. We'd love to come to dinner—but only if you let your no-good husband stick something simple on the barbecue so you stay off your feet."

"Just what I had in mind," Izzy agreed. "Why don't you come over about seven?"

"Sounds good." Then, still looking at Clary, he said, "It's great to see you again."

"You, too," she answered, surprised by the flirty, feminine timbre to her own voice.

He smiled that secret smile again for a moment, before finally breaking off eye contact and pointing a finger at Izzy. "And you behave yourself."

Then he pushed open the screen and left.

"Well, now, that was something...." Izzy mused.

But Clary didn't answer her cousin. Instead, she just kept watching Beau's straight, broad back as he walked right down the center of the elm-lined street.

Chapter Two

"She's here, isn't she?"

Beau was in the middle of a yawn as he walked into the kitchen the next morning and was greeted with his daughter's question. It was barely seven, and he'd been with an asthma patient in the throes of a serious attack until nearly four. Since he'd missed seeing Dori the whole of Sunday, he'd made sure he got up in time to talk to her before she left for school. But Clary was not the subject he had in mind.

"Who's here?" he responded, as if he didn't know what Dori was talking about, making coffee as he did.

"Clary!" she said, as if referring to her best friend, when if fact they'd never met. "I went by the MacIntires' house on my way home from Danielle's last night and saw a strange car out in front. It has to be Clary's. She's here, isn't she?"

"You don't have to talk so loud, Dori. I'm right here."
Beau sat down across the table from her, wishing she had
this much excitement and enthusiasm for starting college
in the fall.

"Finally, finally, finally!" she said rapturously. "I can't
wait to meet her! Do you think I could miss school today
and go over there?"

"Not a chance. Izzy has invited us to dinner tonight.
You'll have to wait until then."

Dori made a face and shoveled in four quick spoonfuls
of the yogurt she was eating for breakfast.

"It's probably better to wait, anyway," she said after a
moment. "I'll have to come home and wash my Italian
jeans. I *have* to wear them when I meet her, they're the
coolest ones I own. I'll need to wash my hair again—it
turned out so flat today. I wish my ears weren't so big. And
maybe I'll put mud on my face and hope it gets rid of this
huge-mother zit on my chin."

Beau studied her as she spoke, smiling slightly at the
exaggerated tones of horror she used in referring to the way
she looked. The truth was that Dori was an extraordinar-
ily pretty young woman. She was tall, thin, long-legged;
her naturally wavy hair was a rich golden color that fell
straight to her shoulders; she'd inherited her mother's
peaches-and-cream skin tone and perfect oval-shaped face;
and her long-lashed brown eyes were so dark they looked
almost black.

In fact, there had been a number of times in the past
year, when Beau had wished she was a little plainer. Maybe
then, she might have formed other goals for her future.

"We need to talk," he told her, as he went to pour himself a cup of coffee.

"Can it wait? I want to call Danielle and see if I can
borrow her new shirt for tonight."

"No, it can't wait. It's been waiting all weekend."

"But you don't know how important it is that I look good tonight. Clary's from *Los Angeles*."

"So are several million other people. That doesn't have anything to do with you."

"No, it just means everything to me. She's from the place I'm going, as soon as all this graduation junk is over."

Beau didn't miss the challenging tone in his daughter's voice when she said that. Her wanting to go to L.A. was a point that seriously divided them at the moment. "Clary is from a place you would have been going had you followed through with your acceptance to UCLA. But you didn't do that," he pointed out in a level tone.

"College is a waste of time, when I'm only interested in acting."

She'd said that to him more times than he could count lately. It was the gauntlet thrown down. They'd had an agreement—he would pay for her to get her education in California and concede to her trying to get acting jobs as an extracurricular activity. Then, once she had her degree, she'd be free to do as she pleased.

But, instead, Dori had turned down her acceptance at UCLA and decided Beau should contribute the tuition money to support her while she pursued an acting career full-time.

"I talked to the dean at the University of Northern Colorado when I went to Greeley on Friday," he said, as if he hadn't heard her comment. "Because of my seat on the board he's agreed to let you in there in the fall." Beau reached for some papers on the countertop, sliding them in front of Dori. "This is the application. All you have to do is fill it out and get it in the mail to him. I've already stapled the check for the fee to it and even made out the envelope."

She stared daggers at the papers. "I'm going to L.A. as soon as school is out."

Beau took a deep breath, making a conscious effort to hold on to his patience. His sense of responsibility toward Dori had some added elements to it, and he knew those added elements were complicating this tug-of-war between them.

He wasn't Dori's birth father. That man had been killed in a car accident before she was five. Dori was nine when Beau married her mother, Gina, and Beau and the little girl were already crazy about each other by then. Putting the wheels into motion for him to adopt her had just come naturally, not long after the wedding. The process was still underway when Gina died a year later in a blizzard that stranded her in the open countryside surrounding Wellsburg. Beau had seen no reason not to go through with the adoption. Dori had no one else in the world, and he loved her as if she were his own child.

Now, though, he felt a responsibility not only to Dori but to his late wife to keep the teenager from making a mistake that could be disastrous to her future. His stand was that a college education was a foundation to fall back on, no matter what happened in her life.

"We've been over all of this before, Dori."

"Then, let's not waste time going over it again."

"Acting is fine as a hobby—"

"I'm good at it, and it's what I want to do for my life. It isn't a *hobby*."

"Whatever you want to call it, at best it's a risky proposition. You need the safety net a degree offers. We agreed on that."

"I know, but I changed my mind. College would only be a waste of time and money. I'd be ditching classes for auditions, and studying lines and scripts instead of textbooks. It's just silly. Acting is what I'm going to do, and that's all there is to it."

"That isn't all there is to it," he said, his voice a bit louder than it was a moment before.

Dori narrowed her eyes at him. "You're not going to make me give up the one thing I'm good at."

"I'm not trying to make you give it up. I'm just asking that you not put all your eggs in one basket—especially when that basket is full of holes. And acting is not the one thing you're good at. You've been a straight-*A* student all through high school. You could be any damn thing you wanted to be."

"I want to be an actress!" she shouted, throwing her hands up in the air.

"I will never understand how someone as smart as you are in everything else can be so dumb when it comes to your future. Going to UCLA would have killed two birds with one stone—you could have been working on a degree and still trying to do the other. That's the way to go, Dori."

"The way to go is to move to L.A. as soon as school is out and put all my energy into the career I want. I don't know why you have such a problem understanding that. Clary left this burg and didn't go to college, and look at her. She owns her own restaurant. She succeeded. And I will, too."

Damn Izzy for bragging about Clary so much, Beau thought. In Dori's fantasy of making a big splash in L.A., she'd come to idolize Clary as a Wellsburg native to have done that. The fact that Clary's splash was made in the restaurant business instead of acting didn't seem to matter. She was still the closest connection the teenager had to the city and life she dreamed of. So Dori had pumped Izzy for every bit of information she could garner about Clary, Clary's life and L.A., and Izzy's stories had only added fuel to the flames.

Beau took a deep breath and sighed it out to regain some control. "Go the University in Greeley for a semester, reapply to UCLA for the January term, and then go on with what we agreed to."

"That's stupid! It's just plain stupid. I'm not wasting my time. I hate this hole of a town and I'm getting out of it and going to California, just the way Clary did," she shouted, standing up all at once. "Now, I have to get to school," she informed him.

"Dori—"

She acted as if she hadn't heard him and slammed out the kitchen door, once more leaving the argument at an impasse.

"Damn," he said, feeling frustrated beyond belief, as he always did of late when dealing with his daughter.

Beau closed his eyes for a minute until they stopped burning from lack of sleep. Then he opened them and went to the counter to fix himself a bowl of cereal.

Clary's arrival complicated the situation with Dori. There was no doubt about it.

And yet, as much as he knew he should probably be sorry Clary was here, he wasn't. Not at all. In fact, what he felt about her being in Wellsburg was a long way from anything negative.

Before yesterday, the thought of seeing Clary again after so many years had inspired mixed feelings. On the positive side, he'd been happy to see an old friend again and complete the sale on the lot next door to the Mac-Intires' so he could get his new house underway.

But on the other hand, he'd known that the arrival of anyone from L.A. would only stir up Dori's determination to move to that city all the more. And he'd been right about that.

What he hadn't bargained for was finding Clary so attractive.

She looked great. Better than she had the last time he'd seen her—the day he'd left L.A. to come home. She'd been the only thing about that city that he'd missed once he was back in Wellsburg. Her energy, her sense of humor, those golden-flecked topaz eyes. . . .

He'd been attracted to Clary even then, but he'd held it in check. For all her appeal, the six-year age difference had seemed like a much wider gap than that it did now. And their goals had been farther apart still. Like Dori, the teenage Clary had been anxious to leave Wellsburg for city life, while he'd gone to L.A. only for the education and was every bit as anxious to come home again. Plus, she hadn't seemed interested in him. At all. She'd been perfectly content for him to play big brother and leave their relationship at that. He'd had the sense that she viewed him as pretty dull in comparison to what California had to offer in the way of male companionship.

But now here she was, just a few blocks away. And on his mind almost constantly since he'd set eyes on her yesterday.

Very strange.

It wasn't as if he'd been pining for her all this time, he thought, as he rinsed his bowl and cup and put them in the dishwasher before picking up his bag and leaving the house for the day.

Ten years ago he'd come back to Wellsburg and met Gina. She and Dori had just moved into town. Gina had taught third grade and Izzy had introduced them. They'd fallen in love, married within six months and been happy for the short time they'd had together.

And since then, well, he hadn't been a monk.

But through it all, he admitted to himself as he walked toward his office, there were times when something had brought Clary to mind. Usually something that didn't quite fit in around here, something unique and out of the ordinary. Because that was what Clary had always been. That was what she still was—a little outrageous, an original. For Wellsburg, anyway.

Take yesterday. All that long, wild-curly hair flying out untamed, what looked like a man's white undershirt worn beneath a leather vest with a half dozen antique gold broaches pinned to one side of it. Her jeans had been baggy enough to fit someone thirty pounds heavier than her spare frame needed. And she'd been wearing black tennis shoes with sequined half-moons on the toes.

The thought made him smile, as he turned onto Front Street.

Had she been walking this same conservative avenue dressed like that, she'd have stood out like a palm tree in a row of pines. But on her the outfit had looked just right, and he'd felt that she was a breath of fresh air around here.

Not that that was the first time he'd ever thought that about her. He remembered having that same image of her as a kid, too, though he'd never let on about it.

All those years ago—just as now—no one he knew had skin that brought to mind clear lake water, or eyes as wide, or lashes as long, or cheekbones any model would covet. No one had had a laugh as uninhibited or a wit quite as quick. Certainly no one had had her style.

Beau heard the bell ring at the school on the next block, and it brought him out of his daydreams of Clary again. Back to thoughts of Dori.

All the things that he found so appealing about Clary were not going to help matters with his daughter. Dori was going to find her every bit as interesting as he did, and Beau knew it.

But somehow even knowing Clary was going to complicate the trouble between him and Dori didn't change the stirring he was feeling just knowing she was in town. Or the fact that he could hardly wait for the closing on the property he was buying from her today or the dinner tonight at the MacIntires' when he'd get to see her again.

Beau climbed the four front steps of his office building. The door was unlocked, which told him Skokie had beat him in. But no one was in sight as he went through the waiting room they shared, around the common reception desk that stood in the center and on down the long center hallway that ran between his examining rooms to his private office at the rear of the building.

Stashing his medical bag under his desk, Beau went back out into a hallway, this time taking a sharp turn to a second hall that crossed to connect his half of the office to Skokie's. Along the way he stopped at the coffeepot on the cart there to pour himself a steaming cup.

The door to one of the dentist's examining rooms was open and Beau went in. "It's a little early for a nap, isn't it?" he said by way of announcing himself to his partner.

Skokie was in the dental chair, his head back, eyes closed, a coffee mug set on his stomach, both hands around it. He opened his eyes but didn't move another muscle. "It is never too early for a nap," he informed in a voice as slow and lazy as he looked.

As Beau propped himself on the stool Skokie used when he cleaned a patient's teeth, the dentist sat up. "Clary's in town," he said, showing a sudden surge of enthusiasm.

"I know. I saw her yesterday."

"How's she look?"

"Terrific," Beau answered with feeling. "Better even than she did when we were all kids. I was just thinking about that on the way over here."

Skokie made a screwed-up expression that turned his freckled face into a caricature. "I suppose that means you're letting me know you have dibs on her and I better keep away," he said in mock rivalry. "The first new single woman to come into the Burg in two years, you know I'm looking forward to seeing if I can start up what she wouldn't let me start up twenty years ago, and what do you do? Rush over and stake a claim before her engine's even cold."

"Stake a claim?" Beau repeated facetiously.

"Isn't that what you were doing by getting your tail over to Izzy's the minute her cousin got there?"

"I stopped to take Izzy's blood pressure on my way back from a house call." But to be honest, he'd seen the strange car out front and assumed it meant Clary had arrived. And wanting to see her had been a contributing factor to his stopping, there was no doubt about it.

"So, then, you aren't interested in offering her a little male company while she's here, and I can have a go at her?"

"I didn't say that." And he didn't mean it, Beau was surprised to find. He had enough things on his mind, with the situation with Dori. But the image of Skokie with Clary made him feel as if his friend was encroaching on private territory nevertheless.

"I knew it. You're calling dibs, aren't you?"

"You sound like you're twelve, Skokie," Beau laughed.

The red-headed dentist placed his cup ceremoniously on the tray of instruments beside him and said in a phony refined voice, "I will bow to your prior claim on Ms. Clary Parson's company, unless you aren't interested in her."

Beau breathed a small chuckle, more at himself than at his partner. "I, uh, think I'm interested."

"That's as good as you can do? You *think* you're interested? I'm not backing off, if you don't know for sure."

Beau had a sudden vivid image of Clary from the short time he'd spent with her the day before. Of her compact but intriguing body, of her golden-speckled eyes with their brows just unruly enough to give her a slightly wild look, her thin nose, her straight white teeth, lips that looked like velvet . . .

"Okay, okay. I know for sure," he finally said, sounding exasperated, though he wasn't certain if it was exasperation at Skokie for this juvenile conversation or at himself for being as taken with Clary as he was.

"Then you're definitely interested?"

Beau took a deep breath and held it, telling himself he had enough on his hands already without adding anything else, let alone a woman who, he knew, was going to cause him trouble, inadvertently or not. But still, he said, "Definitely."

As she sat watching Wellsburg's only lawyer gather the papers for the closing on the house and property late that morning, Clary couldn't help comparing the fatherly Simon Ortez with Wolf. Her L.A. attorney, good friend and neighbor didn't even wear sweat suits on the weekend, let alone to anything that so much as smacked of business.

And the offices couldn't be more different if one of them were on the moon. Simon's was like a family room furnished from garage sales. Wolf's was all sharp lines in the Plexiglas desk and chairs that outfitted his home away from home.

Still, Clary had to admit, Simon wasn't any less professional as he explained that an emergency had kept Beau away and that he'd made arrangements for the double closing to go on without him. So what did it matter if she, Izzy, and Jack sat on a flowered sofa with half-wagon-wheel ends and signed the papers on a coffee table whose legs were the other half of those wagon wheels?

It didn't, Clary realized, though years ago it would have bothered her a great deal.

When the closing was finished, Jack helped Izzy off the sofa and held her hand as they left the office. Behind them, Clary looked on, appreciating the sight of their affection for one another. The top of Jack's towhead hit about four inches above her cousin's, and no doubt he tipped the scales at 250 pounds without much effort. But for all his bulk he was a handsome man, in a lumberjack sort of way.

"I wish we'd brought the car so you didn't have to walk home," he was saying to Izzy on the sidewalk out front of the office where they paused before he headed back to work.

Hearing his words, Clary glanced at her cousin's hand held between Jack's as he studied the puffy fingers. "Wow," she said. "Did somebody inflate you with a tire pump when I wasn't looking?"

Izzy waved their concern away with that plump hand and then shoved it into the pocket of her maternity smock. "It just happens. I was hot in that office and that's about all it takes these days to turn me into marshmallow mama."

"Get her right home, would you, Clary? And make her sit down," he added when he glanced at his wife's feet where they'd expanded through the straps of her sandals.

"Maybe she should rest inside and I'll run home for my car," Clary suggested, her concern for her cousin sounding in her voice.

"Now see what you've done?" Izzy reprimanded her husband. "You've gotten Clary all worried for no reason. We're two blocks away—less if we cut through the schoolyard. The exercise will do me good, and in the time we've stood here marveling at my bloat, we could have gotten home." She kissed Jack. "Now go on back to work."

He grinned at her, showing the two big, square front teeth that made him look boyish for all his size, said goodbye to Clary and left them.

As Clary and Izzy headed around the corner and toward the old two-story red brick school building, Izzy said, "Wouldn't you know we'd have to have unseasonably warm weather for May the same year I'm a prego?"

"I wish you would have said you were too warm in that office. We could have made Simon open a window or postponed the closing until he could come to the house."

Izzy laughed. "Keep frowning like that, Clary, and you'll get wrinkles. I didn't say anything about it being hot because it wasn't that big a deal. Will you chill out? When did you become such a worrier?"

Not soon enough, Clary thought, but she didn't have to answer her cousin's questions, because as they headed across the playground a young girl broke away from a group of other teenagers to hurry toward them.

"You're her, aren't you?" she gushed to Clary, stopping very close in front of her and staring with round brown eyes as if she couldn't believe what she was seeing.

Slightly taken aback, Clary glanced at her cousin for help.

"This is Dori Dugan—Beau's daughter. To her, you're the embodiment of Los Angeles."

"Ah," Clary said, nodding.

"I *love* your shoes!"

Clary glanced down at the gold lamé loafers she wore. Then she made a face of regret to the teenager and confided, "I got them in Greeley when I passed through on may way to Wellsburg."

"Well, I'll bet they came from L.A. in the first place. It's really rad there, isn't it?"

Clary laughed. Dori's enthusiasm and zest for life were contagious. "You'd love it," she assured, not understanding a frantic shake of Izzy's head from behind the teenager.

"I'm moving there as soon as school is out. I have so many things I want to ask you."

The young girl was strikingly pretty, Clary thought, wondering if Dori's mother—Beau's wife—had been as beautiful.

"I'm hoping that we can talk and you can tell me everything I need to know about L.A.," Dori went on.

Clary caught sight of Izzy behind the teenager again, waving her hands as if to warn her not to say anything. The sight of those puffy fingers reminded Clary of her cousin's condition, a far more important priority for Clary than whatever was going on with Beau's daughter.

"I'm sure we'll have lots of time to talk when you come to dinner tonight," Clary assured Dori, cutting her off at the pass.

"And lunch is over. Your next class starts in two minutes," Izzy added in her best principal voice, pointing at her watch.

"Okay. Tonight, then," Dori conceded, showing her disappointment for a fleeting moment before she patted the air around Clary's hair, and said, "Your hair is so-o-o cool." Then she did a little hop-skip to turn around and ran to catch up with her friends.

"In case you missed it, that was what you call a serious case of hero worship," Izzy informed as they started across the school grounds again.

"What did I do to deserve it?"

"Left Wellsburg and moved to L.A."

"Oh."

"She's obsessed with the idea of going to California and becoming an actress. It's a big bone of contention between her and Beau."

"Let me guess, he wants her to stay here."

"He'd like that, sure. But he hasn't pushed for it. What he is pushing for is college." Izzy explained what was going on between father and daughter. "But Dori has California fever as bad as you ever did, and I don't know what's going to happen."

"Is that why you were doing that little routine behind her?"

"I was afraid you might inadvertently say something that made the situation worse."

"In other words, I'd better walk on eggshells around her?"

"I would."

As they crossed onto their block, Clary said, "She's a gorgeous kid, isn't she? Does she resemble her mother?"

"A lot. But believe it or not, Gina was even prettier. Really a knockout."

"Was she?"

"If Wellsburg had an award for best-looking couple, Beau and Gina would have gotten it. I always thought it was a shame that they didn't have enough time together to have kids of their own. They probably would have been beautiful—his bright eyes and her golden wheat hair. Gina had the most glorious, thick, shiny blond hair I think I've ever seen.''

"How long were they married before she died?"

"Just about a year."

"I suppose he was really heartbroken when he lost her."

"Devastated."

"Of course," Clary murmured, as they climbed the porch steps.

Izzy led the way into the house, heading for the kitchen with a comment about getting them iced tea.

But Clary didn't immediately follow. Instead she paused at the wall mirror in the hallway, thinking that maybe she should have her hair highlighted. It suddenly looked so... brown.

"You'll have to tell me where you shop. I want a denim jumpsuit just like the one you're wearing. And maybe I could get a perm—I'll bet loose, curly hair like yours is what everybody in L.A. wears. Where do you think is the best place to look for an apartment? I'll need to be near a bus stop, so I can get to auditions. Is there, like, a section of town where mostly actors live? Like an artistic community? 'Cause I'd really like to get into something like that.''

"These chicken-divan crepes you made are great, Clary," Beau said before she could answer any of his daughter's questions.

"They really are," Jack added.

"I'm going to try not to eat myself sick," Izzy said. "But I still feel guilty about you cooking. This is your vacation, after all. It won't seem like one, if you're fixing us what you'd be whipping up for your restaurant every night.''

Clary felt torn between the adults in the room, who were obviously trying to steer the conversation away from what Dori was working so hard to talk about. "It was nice to cook on a smaller scale, Izzy. Besides, lately I have had so much of the business side of Biminis to take care of that I've rarely gotten to cook. I miss it."

Then she turned to Dori, "There isn't a concentrated area of starving artists, if that's what you mean. Sometimes I think that the majority of the California population are actors-in-waiting. As for the bus system—"

"I can't believe you actually baked the bread, too." Beau cut in. "I don't remember the last time I had home-made bread. How about you, Jack?"

"Izzy's never made it for me."

"I don't suppose you know any theatrical agents, do you, Clary? Do you think I need one? Or is it better to get some jobs first, and then look for an agent?"

"That I know nothing about," Clary said, without looking at the teenager. Instead, she was distracted by Izzy fidgeting. "Are you okay, Iz?"

Her cousin made an exasperated sound. "I just can't get comfortable tonight. It's nothing."

But Clary was worried enough to miss Dori's next question. She didn't miss Beau's response, though.

"Dori, can we please talk about something else? You're like a broken record tonight."

"These are things I need to know."

"Not if you do what we agreed. You can live in a dorm at UCLA and get into the drama department. There's bound to be information through that about auditions and agents. And then you can learn the ropes of the city from a safe base."

"He's right," Clary put in gently. She liked Dori and didn't mind the teenager's enthusiastic questions. But it was difficult to answer then under the stern scrutiny of Beau, and she didn't want to cause any more friction between father and daughter than obviously already existed.

"I'm not going to college," Dori announced to the room, in general.

The only sound that followed was that of silverware against china.

Clary took a sip of wine and stole a glance at Beau. He had on a snowy white polo shirt that hugged his broad shoulders and well-developed pectorals. The short sleeves were pulled taut around biceps any farmhand would be proud of. His dark hair and swarthy complexion stood out against the starkness of the white shirt, and Clary could see the faintest, sexiest hint of his thick beard. But in spite of how strikingly handsome he was, the tension of the conflict between him and his daughter showed in the downward pull of his brows and in the shadow in his green eyes.

"Wouldn't you rather have me go to California prepared?" Dori said under her breath, then.

"We can talk about this at home," Beau warned.

"But Clary is here now."

"Oh, I'll be around for a while," Clary jumped in. "Plenty of time."

"Who's for more wine?" Jack said a little too loudly.

"And there's still salad left—Clary you're special dressing is wonderful. I wish my slave driver of a doctor here would let me have more of it."

"Too salty for you, Izzy," Beau commented. "But it was great."

"I guess I might as well just leave, then, if you aren't going to let me talk to Clary," Dori said, her tone like the swipe of a knife in the air.

"I guess if that's the attitude you're going to take, maybe you ought to," Beau answered in a firm but level tone.

"You're so stubborn!" the teenager shot out. "Why can't you just accept—"

"That's enough," Beau cut her off, not shouting, but also brooking no further argument.

Dori glared at him, her eyes narrowed, her lips pursed. Then she stood. "Thank you for dinner, Mrs. MacIntire. Good night, everybody."

It wasn't until the sound of the front door closing after her that Beau said, "I'm sorry for that. Things between us are pretty tough right now."

"No big deal," Jack assured.

Everyone seemed to be finished eating, so Clary suggested dessert and coffee. As they enjoyed her lemon tart, the conversation turned toward small talk, draining the tension from the air. But by the time that was finished Izzy was changing position in her chair about every thirty seconds, and Clary was all too aware of it.

"Cleanup duty is mine tonight, so why don't you all go into the living room and get comfortable, while I take care of the mess I made?" she said, with her cousin in mind.

"Good idea," Beau added quickly. "I'm getting antsy just watching you, Izzy. Jack, why don't you go keep your wife company and I'll help Clary?"

It was on the tip of Clary's tongue to say Beau didn't have to help, but the thought of having his company was too tempting to let the words out. Instead, she just stood and piled dishes, as Jack made it a unanimous vote in favor of his wife's condition.

Izzy and Jack headed for the living room, as Clary went in the direction of the swinging door that connected the dining room to the kitchen. Beau beat her to it, pushing it open with his hip, holding it there for her to pass. As she did she caught a wiff of his after-shave, a clean sea scent.

"Thanks." Clary glanced up at him, finding his face more relaxed, his lips quirked in a small smile, and it did strange things to her pulse.

They made two more trips back and forth to clear the table, without saying much of anything to one another. But as they did, Clary took note of the jeans he wore. Time-softened and faded, they rode his thighs snugly and cupped a derriere that was to die for.

"Izzy seems miserable tonight," she commented when they settled in at the sink, Clary rinsing the dishes and Beau taking them from her to place in the dishwasher.

"That's to be expected at this stage." His voice was so low, so rich. There was something reassuring about just the timbre of it.

"Don't take offense at this—but she does have a good obstetrician in Greeley, doesn't she?"

"The best. She goes in to see him once a month and I monitor her here the rest of the time."

"And he'll be delivering the baby?" Clary didn't mean for that to sound as if she was doubting Beau's abilities as a physician, but that's how it had come out.

He only smiled. "Unless there's an emergency. In which case, I think I can handle it. If you'll recall, I graduated first in my class at med school, and I've had a few years of experience since then. Or doesn't it count if I've only been a small-town doctor?" he teased.

"I just don't want any unnecessary risks taken," she hedged, realizing how she'd overreacted to a lot of things lately.

"I don't take unnecessary risks with anyone, let alone with my best friend's wife and baby."

She was being silly, Clary told herself. After all, she knew Beau was a great doctor. There had been any number of prestigious hospitals wooing him when he'd finished his residency. It had been his own choice to come back to Wellsburg. Besides, she thought, she'd had enough experience with other friends' pregnancies to know that water retention and its accompanying discomforts weren't out of the ordinary. And wouldn't every one of her friends have been thrilled to have the kind of special attention Izzy was getting from Beau? Most of them complained that they saw more of the obstetricians' nurses than their doctors.

Still, she just couldn't stop herself from saying, "So you don't think there's anything out of the ordinary going on?"

"I don't think there is. But I'm keeping a close enough eye on things. I should be able to catch it, if something goes wrong."

"I'm probably just being an alarmist."

"Well there's nothing to worry about, so cut it out."

The only exchange of conversation for the few minutes that followed had to do with the dishes she was turning over to him. As she did, Clary became all too aware of his hands and the feel of them when her own brushed his. Warmth was what she was most conscious of, and a sense of power that somehow transmitted itself through just the quick meeting of his flesh with hers.

"I was beginning to think we'd never see you around the old hometown after all this time," he said then. "Especially when even your grandmother's funeral didn't keep you here more than one day."

Clary shrugged slightly. "I've had a change in priorities. Until lately, work has come first. Before everything and everybody. I won't let that be true anymore."

He chuckled. "That sounded very serious."

But Clary didn't address his comment. Instead she said, "I'm sorry I only sent flowers when your wife died. I was going to stop by to see you when I was here that day for my grandmother's service, but I wasn't in great shape."

"I understood that. It was such a coincidence that your grandmother and my wife should die within days of each other. At that point, I was barely aware of the people who did come around. I didn't even send you flowers."

"It must have been especially hard to lose your wife when you'd only been married such a short time."

"It's never easy."

"And you adopted Dori right after that?"

"Mmm. I don't know if I could have gotten through that first year that followed her mother's death without her. She was the reason I got out of bed most mornings."

"Have the two of you been close?"

"Up until the last six months or so, yes. But this L.A. acting obsession she has is driving one hell of a wedge between us."

Clary smiled sympathetically. "I could tell."

"I suppose you could." He paused, as if gauging his words before he went on. "I'd appreciate it if you don't encourage her."

"Shall I tell her horror stories instead?" Clary joked.

"Better that than fueling her fantasies."

"She's right, though, that if she does end up going she'll be better off if I give her a few pointers and steer her away from L.A.'s trouble spots."

"Actually, just encouraging her about UCLA could be the biggest help. That part tonight was good."

"I'll do what I can." The dishwasher was loaded, and Clary had washed off the countertops by then. She put away the dish towel and flipped off the light over the sink. "Well, shall we join Izzy and Jack?"

Beau's bright green eyes caught hers and held them. "Or we could slip out onto the back steps and be alone."

That made her heart do an odd little dance. "Okay."

Beau held the kitchen door open for her and Clary went out to sit on the stoop. The night air was only slightly cool, but when Beau sat beside her she could feel the heat of him as distinctly as if the temperature were frigid.

"So how did you decide to call your restaurant Biminis?" he asked her.

"A friend and I went to the Bahamas on vacation the year before I opened it. We spent a day touring the Bimini islands, hearing all about Ponce de León searching for the Fountain of Youth there, and I just liked the name. It sort of rolled off the tongue in a nice way."

"And where exactly is the place?"

"Remember your friend Biff? That shopping center his father was building just a few miles from Newport Beach? We're in there."

Beau nodded and Clary watched the way the moonlight shot through his hair. It was just the right length, she decided, not too long or too short, but just full enough to look casual and still well-kept.

"I haven't thought about Biff in years. Do you keep in touch with him?"

"He's a bigwig now. His father retired and left him in charge of all the real-estate holdings and the construction company. Occasionally he stops by for lunch, but that's about it."

"Remember when we took his father's sailboat out and got caught in that storm?" Beau laughed.

"It wasn't funny. I was scared to death. Biff lied to us both about knowing what he was doing."

"He wanted to impress you. I went along because he had such a rotten reputation with women and I was afraid for you to be alone with him, but I never thought he'd go so far as to get us all out in the ocean without knowing what the hell he was doing on that boat. Now that I think of it, he was such a jerk I probably shouldn't have introduced you to him at all."

"No, knowing him turned out to be a good thing. For all his arrogance, he did pull some strings with his father and got me a reduced rent when I wanted to open Biminis."

"And what about his sister—Katrina?"

"Ahhh. Katrina," Clary said, her tone full of insinuation. "I'm surprised the two of you didn't keep in touch."

Beau grinned. "She was out of the league of a poor country boy like me."

"Hah! You held your own with her, as I recall. She wanted you *bad.*"

"She wanted me on a leash."

They both laughed at that.

"Puhleeze, Beau-Beau," Clary imitated, propping her forearm on his shoulder and tracing his ear with her little finger. "Won't you stay just a while longer and make Trina a happy woman?"

Beau turned to face Clary. "No, you're not doing it right. She was always up in my face when she did that." He reached around and placed his palm against her back, pulling her toward him. "And you need more of a pout, like you're going to suck on my chin."

Not an altogether unappealing idea, Clary thought.

And then something unexpected happened. Suddenly the teasing tone evaporated and what was left was just Clary and Beau, their faces very close together, their eyes locked in the milky light of the moon.

It occurred to Clary to pull away, to take her arm off his shoulder. But he was still holding her, with his palm so hot against her back it seemed to sear through even the thick denim of her jumpsuit. The scent of his after-shave was more potent up this close and it was heady to her. Not to mention the powerful force of this new attraction she felt for Beau. She didn't really want to move.

His face dipped slightly closer just then, and Clary thought he was about to kiss her. But the moment was brief before his expression turned startled. He drew back and looked up at the moon.

"It must be pretty late," he said. "I'd better get going."

Disappointment settled over Clary like a parachute coming back to earth, nevertheless she stood when he did. Neither of them said anything as Beau opened the screen for her and Clary preceded him into the house.

"There you guys are," Izzy said from the door that led to the dining room.

"Beau's just on his way out," Clary informed her cousin, wondering at the slightly breathy quality to her own voice.

"Jack and I thought you might want to play a game or something."

"Not tonight, Izzy. I have to stop in on Mort Dinty and make sure that broken nose of his isn't bothering him too much. And you should get to bed. I want you well-rested when you come in to see me tomorrow."

"You have an appointment tomorrow?" Clary asked her cousin, hating that she sounded so anxious.

It was Beau who answered her question. "Just a regular checkup."

"Is there such a thing as a doctor being *too* conscientious?" Izzy complained.

"I think I'll give you the job of making sure she shows up, Clary," Beau said. "Somehow she managed to *forget* our last appointment."

"I'll get her there, even if I have to drag her by the hair," Clary assured him, wondering at how excited the thought of seeing him made her feel.

He thanked them all for dinner, then, said good-night, and Jack walked him out.

"I think I will go on to bed." Izzy yawned. "How about you?"

"In just a minute. I may have forgotten something in the kitchen," Clary claimed, though it was a lie.

"Okay. See you in the morning."

Clary watched her cousin walk down the hall to the master bedroom. When she saw the door close she wandered into the dark nursery, where she could watch Beau as he talked to Jack on the front lawn. She studied Wellsburg's doctor as if to memorize him, crossing her arms over her middle in response to the flutter there.

How could she have overlooked how attractive he was all those years ago? she asked herself, thinking that she must have been blind.

But she wasn't overlooking him now. Instead, she felt drawn to him. Powerfully drawn to him. In a way that she couldn't remember ever feeling with another man.

It seemed very strange. Very unsettling. But not unwelcome.

Since arriving in Wellsburg and setting eyes on Beau, he'd been on her mind in place of her friend Lois, and that was a godsend.

"Guess I should take the release where I can get it," she whispered to herself, staying at the window until Beau headed down the street.

Then she made a mad dash to her room before Jack came in and caught her spying, all the while feeling a little tingly inside with the thought that she was going to see Beau again the next day.

Chapter Three

Clary's friend Wolf was not an early riser, and because of the time difference she had to wait until ten the next morning to call him. As it was, his voice was sleepy when he answered.

"Did I wake you?" she asked.

"No, I've been up for—" he paused as if to check the time. "Seven minutes."

"Shall I call back after you've had your coffee?"

"I'm having it right now. If you stay on the phone it'll be like we're having it together."

"Sounds good. I just wanted to check in and see how things are going. Everything all right at Biminis?"

"Of course. You know Marta is on her way to owning her own restaurant. She can handle everything."

"What about the hassle with the liquor distributor?"

"She took care of it. They had overcharged you, the way you thought, and they're crediting you on next month's order."

"Great."

She heard her friend take a sip of his coffee. "Is being in the wilderness helping you sleep, babe?"

Clary laughed. Wolf was a Los Angeles native. Any place with a population of less than a million was a wasteland to him. "Peace and quiet do wonders," she answered, without admitting that the insomnia and nightmares of the past month had followed her to Wellsburg. "How about those buyers for Lois's condo? Have they gone to contract?" she asked to change the subject.

"Not yet, but I'm pretty sure they will. You're selling the place for a song." Wolf seemed to hesitate for a moment. "You know, as executor of Lois's estate, I have to advise you not to sell it for less than the market value."

"I don't care about the money."

"I know. You just want all the loose ends tied up. But really, Clary—"

"We've gone over this a dozen times, Wolf. Consider your advice given, and say I'm just too dumb to take it."

He sighed heavily. Then in a gentle voice, he said, "Ditch the guilt, babe. Please?"

"I'm not selling Lois's place out of guilt, Wolf," she answered honestly.

"I know. You can't face going in there again, you just want it off your hands as soon as possible. But that doesn't mean you have to give it away. The realtor and I will take care of it, no matter how long it's on the market at a reasonable price. You don't need to go near the place."

"Thanks, Wolf, but I feel bad enough that the buyers won't know the whole story beforehand and are likely to hear it later on. At least, if they do and they've gotten a good deal, they might feel better about it—or be able to turn around and sell it right away themselves, if they can't stand the thought of staying there."

"Clary—"

"No, Wolf, I'm firm on this."

After a moment of silence on the line, he said, "Okay. Whatever you say. I was just hoping that being out in the boonies would let you get some rest, and that would make you change your mind."

"So how's *your* life, Wolfgang?" she changed the subject.

"I miss you. Last night I was dying to go out for Mexican food but I didn't have the heart to dine alone. The only person who shares my passion for tamales has run away from her problems, instead of facing them with a little help from her friends."

"I am not running away," Clary said, as if it were the truth.

"We've been pals a long time, babe. I know better. And I don't believe being in Timbuktusville is going to help."

Izzy poked her head into the kitchen just then, pointing at her watch to let Clary know they needed to leave for Izzy's doctor's appointment. Clary nodded to her cousin.

"I have to run, Wolf. You haven't lost the number here, in case you need to get hold of me, have you?"

"Of course not."

"Okay, then. I'll check back with you in a few days."

"Clary?"

"I'm still here."

"Take care of yourself. And like I said before—ditch the guilt."

"Bye, Wolf."

She put the receiver back in the cradle, but didn't take her hand away for a moment. Sometimes it was uncanny how well Wolf knew her.

Beau's office was in the middle of Front Street. It had been a bank through all the years Clary had grown up in Wellsburg. A one-story plain brick structure with black shutters around the windows and a heavy carved door, it looked just the same on the outside as it always had. But the inside had been changed considerably, from the open space with a counter on one side, a few desks on the other and the vault in the rear. Now Clary and Izzy walked into a small waiting room with a receptionist's island straight ahead.

Clary didn't recognize the receptionist until Izzy introduced her as the minister's daughter.

"Oh, that makes me feel so *old*. You were only about seven or eight when I left here," Clary exclaimed.

"I'll make it worse," Izzy put in. "She's getting married in two months."

Clary groaned.

The young woman stood, then, to show Izzy to an examining room.

"Want to come in and listen to the heartbeat?" Izzy invited Clary.

"Can I? Is that okay?"

"Sure, come on."

The receptionist led them through a door directly behind her desk, into a T-shaped hallway with more doors opening off either side of it and a coffee cart at the far end. To the immediate right was a bathroom, and the receptionist stopped there.

"Why don't you go in and leave us a little something, Mrs. MacIntire?" Then, to Clary, she said, "You can wait for her next door."

Clary gave Izzy a fluttering-fingered wave and they followed the young woman's instructions.

Alone in the examining room, Clary put her hands in her jean pockets and looked around. The walls were a pale blue, and the linoleum dove gray. The examining table and the countertop around the single sink, the chair and rolling stool, were all in various coordinating shades of the two—standard doctor's decor.

On the back of the door, was a clothes hook and under that a long, thin mirror, apparently to allow patients to make sure they hadn't tucked their skirts into their panty hose before leaving.

Clary caught sight of herself there and brushed a speck of lint from her bright orange camp shirt. Then she pulled at a curl at her temple that was too short to catch in the elastic ruffle that held the rest of her hair in a low ponytail in the middle of her back.

The sound of Beau's voice in the hallway outside caused her to make a fast dash away from the mirror so he wouldn't catch her primping.

"Oh. Hi," he said, stopping short as he came through the door and spotted her instead of her cousin.

Clary pointed with her thumb over her shoulder. "Izzy will be right here. She said I could listen to the baby's heartbeat—if that's okay."

He smiled, making the dent in his chin deepen. "Sure, it's okay with me, if it's okay with Izzy."

He came the rest of the way into the room then, closing the door behind him. He had on a stark white lab coat that hung open to reveal tan slacks, a cream-colored dress shirt and a brown knit tie.

He looked morning-fresh and alert, and Clary had the sense that the kiwi green of his eyes lit up the whole room as he stopped at the end of the examining table and propped the side of one thigh up on it. Then he leaned forward enough to cross his arms over his leg, leaving him not far away from her. "Have any health problems you'd like me to take care of while we wait?" he asked with a devilish smile that said health problems were not what he was referring to.

"No, I'm feeling fine, thanks. How about you?"

"Better every minute."

His eyes seemed to bore into her with a message of their own. The titter of excitement it stirred in her felt out of place in a doctor's office. Trying to ignore it, Clary said the first thing that came to mind. "Isn't it awkward to have all your patients be people you know personally?"

He shrugged one broad shoulder. "Occasionally. For folks who are particularly uncomfortable, I try to be conscious of it and do what I can to preserve their modesty and put them at ease. Not all, but a lot of women opt for some of the more personal exams to be done by doctors in Greeley, which is okay, too. Izzy, for instance. I listen to the baby's heartbeat, take her blood pressure and do some lab tests to monitor things, but her OB/GYN does the other exams."

"Are there some women who come to you for... everything?" Clary asked, thinking that she, for one, would not want to meet her gynecologist in the grocery store, thank you very much.

"Sure. There are a lot of people who realize that they aren't going to like what'll happen to them, no matter who does it, and for the most part we all seem to separate what I do as their doctor with who I am outside of the office. That's all part of life in a small town."

Part of what Clary was glad she didn't have to deal with.

"I'm not interrupting anything, am I?" Izzy said as she came in right then.

"We were just waiting for you, Mom," Beau told her. He moved away from the examining table and took her arm to help her climb the single step attached to the end, so she could get up on the padded top.

"What do you want to do first?" Beau asked her once she was settled. "I'll need to take some blood and check your BP, along with listening to the heartbeat. You choose."

"Let's do the heartbeat first and then Clary can go back out into the waiting room while we do the rest. She isn't good with blood."

Beau smiled at Clary, as if he found that very amusing. "No?"

"The sight of it makes her hyperventilate."

"Izzy you're a blabbermouth," Clary accused, narrowing her eyes at her cousin.

"Happens to a lot of people," Beau reassured her, but he still seemed to find it funny. "Okay, then, Mom, lie down and we'll grease you up."

"Doesn't he say the sweetest things?" Izzy joked to Clary as she followed doctor's orders, pulling up her smock and stretching the elastic panel on her maternity pants down so that her belly stuck up in the air all by its lonesome.

Clary watched as Beau squeezed a tube of clear jelly-like ointment in a mountain just above what was left of her cousin's navel. She'd seen pregnant stomaches before, but never so close. It struck her as incredible that skin could be pulled so taut and not split wide open.

"Is it as hard as it looks?" she asked, without thinking about it.

"Want to feel?" her cousin offered, taking her hand and placing it on her side as Beau checked for the position of the baby before putting the ends of a special stethoscope in his ears. Then he plunged the amplifying end of the stethoscope into the jelly, and ran it around Izzy's stomach as if it were the planchette on a Ouija board.

The baby gave a kick just under Clary's hand and seemed to dart away, as if to escape what Beau was doing.

"Amazing," Clary nearly whispered as Izzy guided her palm to follow.

"Here, listen," Beau said then, taking the stethoscope from his ears and gently placing it on hers. "You'll hear a sound like rushing water and the heartbeat muffled through it—strong and fast."

It only took a moment for Clary to recognize just what he'd described. She'd never heard anything sound quite so vibrant and alive and wonderful. And yet, when, along with the sound, she felt the baby roll against her palm again, a thought other than of Izzy's baby popped into her mind and brought with it a flood of unwanted emotions, filling her eyes instantly with tears.

Blinking them back, she pulled her hand away and took the stethoscope out of her ears as if she'd heard something she didn't want to, thrusting the instrument back at Beau.

Only then did she realize that Izzy and Beau were watching her intently, both with very serious expressions on their faces as she fought a hard battle not to cry.

"Clary?" Izzy said.

"Are you okay?" Beau asked.

"Sure," she answered too brightly, too loudly. "But I think I need some air." She sounded desperate, even to herself, but that was the best she could do before she rushed out of the room.

The hallway was deserted, and Clary had never been so grateful for anything in her life. She stayed there a moment, swallowing emotions she didn't want to feel, fighting images she didn't want to see, thoughts she didn't want to have, trying to make her hands stop shaking.

Then, when she finally managed to gain some control, she made a beeline for the front of the building.

"Clary!" Beau's daughter was standing on the other side of the reception counter, the only person in the waiting room when Clary opened the door to it.

Clary forced as much of a smile as she could manage. "Dori. How come you're not in school?"

"This is my study hour. I needed some money, so I came over. I didn't know you were here," the teenager said, as if it were the best surprise she'd ever had.

Clary nodded over her shoulder at the door she was just closing. "Izzy...Mrs. MacIntire...had an appointment with your dad. I came with her."

"Is everything all right? You look really weird," Dori said, squinting at Clary's face as Clary rounded the desk to where the teenager stood.

"Everything's fine. Great."

Dori smiled again, apparently satisfied. "I'm really glad I ran into you. I'm in this play—*The Rainmaker*—I have the lead. Anyway, Friday night is the last performance and I wondered if maybe you'd come to see it?"

"Sure, I'd love to," Clary answered, her thoughts still not completely on the present or what the girl was saying.

"Terrific! It's in Greeley—we're doing it in an introductory drama class I got to take with special permission."

The door that led to the examining rooms opened just then and Beau came out, his well-defined brow pulled down to shadow his eyes. He looked straight at Clary and opened his mouth to say something, but before he got the words out he noticed his daughter.

"Dori, what are you doing here?"

"A bunch of us want to get pizza for lunch and I didn't have any money. I thought you might spot me. But listen—I have the best news. Clary just said she'd come to the play Friday night! Isn't that great?"

Beau turned back to Clary. "That is great," he answered.

"Maybe you guys could come together," Dori suggested enthusiastically.

The appearance of Beau helped bring Clary back to her senses, and she smiled at him. "You're going that night, too?"

"Dori didn't want me to see the play until the last performance. She said I would make her too nervous before that."

"You wouldn't mind riding with him, would you, Clary?" Dori asked as if it would be a chore for anyone to put up with her father's company.

Clary had to laugh at the absurdity of that. Any chance to see Beau was proving to feel like a stroke of good fortune. "I think I could handle it," she understated.

"Thanks," Beau deadpanned. "The only problem is that I have to leave just after noon and make a few stops to see some patients between here and there. But if you'll play nurse for me, I'll buy you dinner when we get to Greeley."

This was getting better and better—a whole afternoon and evening. "Will there be blood involved?" Clary joked.

"When we make the house calls or at dinner?" he countered.

"Both."

"I don't think so. But if you pass out, I promise to catch you."

The tone of innuendo in his voice was a little unnerving in front of his daughter. But it gave Clary a thrill anyway. "Deal."

"Oh, totally cool! Then it's all settled," Dori said.

But rather than looking at the teenager, Beau's eyes stayed on Clary's for a moment before his daughter reminded him she needed money.

As he complied Izzy came out along with the receptionist, at the same time another patient arrived through the front door, and suddenly the room was full of other people. And yet Clary's strongest awareness was still of Beau, and she couldn't help regretting that the few brief moments before Izzy had joined them in the examining room were the only ones she was going to have alone with him today.

Then before she knew what was going on, Izzy was steering her out the front door and goodbyes were being said. "We'll see you tonight at the awards ceremony, Dugans," her cousin called to Beau and Dori.

"The awards ceremony," Clary repeated, just remembering it herself.

Maybe she'd have another chance to see Beau after all.

Beau walked his daughter out the front door of the office not five minutes after Clary and Izzy had left. Watching Dori leave, he caught sight of them as they went up the street toward the park square. His gaze stayed on Clary, even though all he could see was her back—wild hair tied loosely halfway to her waist, bright shirt, great rear end....

"Is that our Clary?" Skokie asked, as he came up the steps from the other direction.

The dentist's plural possessive made Beau bristle, but he hid it. "That's her," he confirmed without moving his eyes.

"She looks better than I remembered. Not like anyone around here, that's for sure. We must seem like small potatoes to her."

Beau wished he didn't think the same thing. But he didn't say anything about it. Instead, he changed the subject. "No appointments this morning?"

"None until about fifteen minutes from now. I got to sleep in—eat your heart out."

He nodded back toward the door. "If May Bentz is your first patient she's already here. Has been for a while."

"Oh, wonderful. I'll catch it for keeping her waiting, even though she was the one who was early." Skokie slapped Beau on the back as he passed him. "Better go in and get to work."

Beau raised one hand in a little wave as the dentist passed him on the steps. But his eyes were still trained on Clary as she and Izzy stopped several doors down to look in a shop window. Skokie's words seemed to echo in his mind. Clary was definitely different than anyone in Wellsburg. And Wellsburg certainly must seem like small potatoes to her.

And yet even knowing that sooner or later she would go back to L.A. couldn't keep Beau from becoming obsessed with her.

Yes, obsessed, he admitted reluctantly. That was the only word for thinking about her all the time and plotting how to see her next; for wondering why he'd left only friendship between them all those years ago, and what it would have been like if he'd have gone through with the urge to kiss her the night before.

But obsession or not, he couldn't help it.

He wished he could. Especially since it seemed as if she was giving him some second looks, too, and if she was . . . well, that could lead to something Beau wasn't too sure he wanted to get into.

She'd have let him kiss her if he'd tried last night. He'd known that, sensed it, seen it. In fact, he'd almost thought she might kiss him first. But, then, if she was feeling half as attracted to him as he was to her, it was understandable.

But whatever was brewing between them didn't change the old issues that still existed. She hadn't come back to Wellsburg to make it her home again. She probably felt the same about the town that she always had and couldn't wait to return to L.A.

And he still loved the old burg. He still didn't want to live anywhere else.

Which only meant one thing—a relationship between them was the same as turning up a dead-end street; things could only go so far before they had to stop cold.

So why start anything at all? he asked himself.

Because maybe he didn't really have a choice. Maybe something was starting all by itself.

Vines of ivy grew up the red brick walls of the school into which half of Wellsburg's population streamed for the awards ceremony that night. It was a big event for the small town, with grandparents, aunts, uncles, cousins and even godparents turning out.

As principal, Izzy had a lot of mingling to do, but Clary and Jack stood off to one side of the clean white lobby. Clary was enjoying the sight of so many people she hadn't been in touch with in such a long time. It was fun to see who had married whom and had what kids, who had gained weight and lost hair, or lost weight and gained hair.

But there was really only one person Clary kept an eye out for, and that was Beau.

She'd been hoping that, as Jack's best friend, the single doctor might choose to keep Izzy's husband company while Izzy made the rounds. But that didn't happen. Instead, Clary didn't even spot Beau in the crowd until it was nearly time to go into the auditorium.

But when she did, it was worth the wait.

He looked like a debonair playboy in a Monte Carlo casino, she thought. He wore an impeccably tailored white suit that fit his every masculine angle like river water running down rocks. Beneath it was a lime green shirt and matching tie that brought out the color of his eyes.

Beau seemed to catch sight of her then, and she watched him take a long, slow look that started at her black shoes and white spats and worked slowly up her black silk crepe pants and the jacket that covered the white V-necked vest she wore underneath. Then he reached her pinned up hair for a moment, before settling on her face and realizing she was watching him assess her. His expression erupted into an unabashed grin as he raised one eyebrow, as though giving her his approval and something else a little lascivious along with it.

Clary smiled her own appreciation and waited for him to approach her, now that they'd made eye contact. But it didn't happen. Instead his attention was snagged by the bank president at about the same time Izzy brought her assistant principal over to meet Clary.

Tall, blond, attractive, Clary was barely aware of the other woman as she lost sight of Beau and tried to find him again.

When the introduction was complete, Izzy suggested Jack and Clary lead the way in so they could get this show on the road, while she and Eve went around to the back-stage entrance.

Clary wished for a way to stall in hopes that Beau still might join them, but when Jack took her elbow and moved toward the auditorium doors she didn't have much choice but to go along.

Once inside and seated, it took Clary several minutes to locate Beau again. He was two rows ahead of them and about four seats to Clary's right—something she thought of as compensation. If he wasn't going to sit with them, at least she could look at him.

And look she did. All through the ceremony. His broad shoulders spanned out wider than the old wooden seats, and he sat a head taller than the men on either side of him.

His dark mink hair looked all the more rich where it barely waved against his neck a scant inch above his collar. And in profile his face was even more strikingly good-looking, as the stage lights threw the angle of his strong jawline and the hollow of his cheek into relief.

All in all, he cut a pretty dashing figure for a Wellsburg native. Or for a native of anywhere, she realized, as she watched him watching his daughter on the stage, his pride in Dori evident in the curve of his lips.

Coffee and cake were served by the PTA in the gymnasium afterward and again Clary waited anxiously for Beau to say hello. But when he still kept his distance she began to think he was purposely avoiding her. She caught him watching her a time or two, but not even when Dori left him to speak to Clary did he come, too.

Well, if that's how you want to be, Clary thought, feeling as unreasonably miffed as if a divine upperclassman had overlooked her every attempt to get his attention, when, in fact, she hadn't made any attempt to approach Beau, either.

She could, though, she offered herself.

But she didn't. There was pride involved by then.

As the evening wore on, not having contact with Beau took the fun out of it for Clary. Besides, she'd talked to just about everyone she knew and been introduced to everyone she didn't, and the others all had settled into locally flavored conversation that she couldn't participate in. Feeling like a wallflower at a dance, she decided to take a private tour of the school she'd attended herself from kindergarten through graduation.

She slipped out through the double swinging doors of the gym, leaving behind the hum of voices for the quiet of the deserted hallways. And the farther she went, the quieter it got, until the only sound was the click of her own heels on the polished linoleum floors.

Strange how little the school had changed, she thought. Like all of Wellsburg. The classrooms were designated for the same grades they had been when she was there, and as she peeked through the high window in each door she found that most of the desks were in the same places. She could even pick out which ones had been hers.

Walking down the halls, her strongest memory was of how different from the other kids she'd felt. In a family-based close-knit community, it wasn't easy to be a kid whose unmarried parents had both run off and left her to her grandmother. True, her mother had surfaced every now and again, in between boyfriends—usually when she was short on money—but she wasn't part of Clary's life in any real sense. Of course, this scenario had set Clary apart from the very beginning. Made her feel as if she were outside the circle.

And it hadn't helped that she'd had different taste in clothes and shoes, that she'd wanted to take wood shop instead of home-ec, that she'd never found an understanding or appreciation for football or basketball, or a desire to baby-sit the way most of the girls she went to high school with had. She'd read horror novels when everyone else was reading romances, couldn't sew a straight line with or without a machine, and—worst of all—had hated gossiping, probably because she'd been the brunt of so much of it herself.

From her feeling of not fitting in had grown her dream of leaving Wellsburg and going to L.A. Where the sun shone most of the time and she would never have to shovel snow. Where there were beaches like in her magazines, instead of field after field of cornstalks. Where there would always be noise and excitement and something to do and interesting people to do it with, rather than endless quiet, a pace so slow she wanted to scream, and the same people doing the same things in the same places day after day. Where she might not be so different. Where she could have some privacy.

Clary trailed her hand along the cool tile wall of one of the junior-high hallways. Dreams never quite came out the way it seemed they would, she reflected.

Not that she didn't love her life in L.A., because she did. But a person could get sick of sunshine all the time and long for the sparkle of white snow. And sometimes all the noise drove her crazy. And she always had too much to do. As for just being one of the crowd—well, sometimes people got lost in crowds. Sometimes even friends. So lost that a person might not even realize what was going on with them or how really deep their feelings might be. And that wasn't good at all.

"Now that's a melancholy expression, if ever I've seen one. Don't tell me you were wishing you were back in these hallowed halls again?"

Clary recognized Beau's deep, resonant voice even before she looked up to find him coming her way. "Poor diagnosis, Doc. I wouldn't relive those years for all the tea in China," she told him with a laugh, wondering at how just the sight of him could chase away dark feelings. She waited for him to catch up and then they both sauntered farther down the hall toward the high-school wing.

"I'm surprised to see you," she told him. "It seemed like maybe you were steering clear of me tonight. I thought I might look as if I had a communicable disease or something." She glanced at him out of the corner of her eye and found him doing the same.

"You look incredible. But I'm afraid I *was* steering clear of you."

"Oh. How come?"

"I've been arguing with myself."

"About me?"

"Mmm."

They went on walking through the dimly lit halls without him expounding, until Clary realized he had no intention of being more forthcoming. Finally she said, "Does your being here now mean you won or lost the argument."

"It means I just couldn't stay away," he said simply enough. "So what were you thinking about out here all alone?"

"I was remembering school, but not wishing for those days back again." They came to a dead end and Clary stopped to peer into the window of the auto shop room.

"I wouldn't want to do it over again, either," Beau agreed with a laugh.

"You wouldn't?" she repeated, surprised. "But you were so popular—I thought that was the secret to happiness."

"Sorry to disillusion you," he said with one of those quirky half smiles as he came to stand close beside her and look into the classroom window himself. "In there, for instance. I had one of my more mortifying experiences."

"When you got your hand stuck in the engine of that car," Clary guessed, only partially suppressing a grin.

"Having a date the next Friday night did nothing for me, as I had my hand greased and my arm nearly pulled out of the socket trying to get free while the whole damn class stood around and made jokes about it. And being on the football team didn't keep me from being the laughingstock for a week afterward. In fact, the rest of the guys were brutal every day as we suited up."

"Okay, being a kid isn't easy for anybody," she conceded.

The entrance to the shop room was recessed, so they were standing close together in the small doorway. Clary could smell Beau's after-shave and she couldn't resist taking a deep breath. If she'd ever been more attracted to another man, she didn't know who or when.

"Being a kid wasn't all bad, though," Beau said, leaving her to cross the hall as he seemed to spot something near the row of windows there.

As he did, he slipped his coat off and her gaze slid down to his rear end in those white pants, realizing they were every bit as well-tailored as the rest of the suit.

With the jacket hooked over one finger he motioned to a small cubicle between the windows and a brick pillar. "This spot, for instance. I spent some pretty good times here."

"The kissing cubbyhole," Clary recalled the infamous locale as she stepped back out into the hall after him.

"It was everybody's favorite place when I was in high school."

"It was when my class got up here, too. It probably still is."

"As I recall, the trick was to wedge yourselves in just right so that the only way a teacher could see you was if they went out of the chemistry lab across the courtyard."

"I never knew there was a technique."

"Handed down from man to man in the locker room after gym. Here, I'll show you."

He slung his coat over the radiator beneath the windows. Turning to Clary, he took her by the shoulders and guided her into a corner of the small space. Then he squeezed in in front of her.

He was so close, and her heart was beating so fast and hard, that Clary wondered if he could feel it against his chest. She hadn't had many opportunities to experience the comforts of the kissing cubbyhole as a teenager, and never with a partner quite as big as Beau. His body ran the whole length of hers without a hair's breadth between them, his shoulders were curved around her, and his forearms rested against the wall at her back on either side of her head. And she liked it.

Then she glanced up into his face, so near above hers, and was surprised to see him frowning.

"What? Are we stuck? Don't tell me we're going to have to call somebody to grease our way out of here."

That made him smile, but only with his mouth while his brows were still pulled together. "No, we're not stuck. We could get out right now. If we wanted to."

Clary had the sense that he was reminding himself of that, more than reassuring her. She was just about to ask him if he wanted to escape their close quarters when his extraordinary green eyes caught hers and the intensity of them made her forget the question.

And then he lowered his mouth to hers in a slow, soft, tentative kiss.

His lips were warm and parted only slightly, and Clary thought that it was probably a good thing that the cubbyhole was too small for her to raise her arms or she might have grabbed Beau and hung on for dear life. As it was, all she could do was keep her head tilted and savor the tenderness of his kiss while her hands ached to touch him and her body cried out for the feel of his arms around her.

Then, as quickly as it had begun, it was over and he'd raised away from her. "I guess there are a few things worth coming back for."

"Yeah," she said, sounding as breathless as she might have had he done this so many years ago when he was a senior and she a mere seventh-grader.

Then all of a sudden he stepped out of the cubicle, pulling her with him. "How about if I walk you home, so you don't have to wait for Izzy and Jack?"

Clary wondered if he'd left her knees too weak for it, but accepted his offer anyway. She longed for him to take her hand, but instead he seemed to be keeping his distance again as he picked up his suit coat, slung it over his shoulder and led the way to the nearest door, holding it open for her to precede him out into the cooler night air.

They didn't say much until they were away from the school parking lot. Then, in a dark, smoky voice, Beau said, "I guess you'll be leaving, now that you've sold your grandmother's house and property."

"Actually, I thought I'd stay a while. Maybe until the baby is born." She could feel him stare at her and she knew she'd surprised him.

"Has life in L.A. paled?"

She laughed at his tone. "If I said, yes, I think I'd get an I-told-you-so, wouldn't I? Well, hang on to it, because, no, life in L.A. hasn't paled. I just needed a little time away. A vacation. Some peace and quiet. I'm happy there."

"So it's everything you thought it would be," he said, as if she'd disappointed him.

"Well, it isn't perfect," she allowed.

"How so?"

She shrugged. "For one thing, it's easy to lose track of important people in a place that big and busy. To lose sight of who in your life deserves your attention."

"Like Izzy?"

"Like Izzy, for one."

"So you came back to spend some time with her."

"Right."

"Sounds nice. And purely pleasurable. But if that's true, how come I keep catching you looking sad instead? Like a few minutes ago, and earlier today when you heard her baby's heartbeat?"

Clary dropped her head all the way back and looked up at the stars through the web of tree branches. She valued her privacy more than anything and considered how much of it to offer up. After a moment she said, "I haven't been sleeping too well lately. I think it's left me not quite myself."

A car passed them on the street at that moment, honking a greeting. Beau waved and then took Clary's arm as they stepped off the curb to cross to Izzy's house. "What's disturbing your sleep?"

Clary laughed and tried not to like the feel of his touch as much as she did. "That sounded very doctorish of you. Do I suddenly look like a patient?"

"This morning in my office you looked like a lady in some pain—emotional, not physical."

"Come on," she said as if he was imagining things. "Do you mean you've never seen anyone get teary-eyed over the wondrous sound of a fetal heartbeat?"

"Many times. That's not what I saw this morning."

Clary led the way up the walk and onto the front porch, where the light cast a bright glow like a candle in a pumpkin. "I thought doctors knew better than to make mountains out of molehills?"

"So this morning was a molehill?"

"Yep." She could feel his gaze on her, but Clary couldn't bring herself to meet it. Instead, she opened the front door. "Want to come in for coffee? A nightcap?"

He didn't answer her right away. He just stood very nearby, watching her still. "No, thanks. I'd better get home."

She nodded, suddenly feeling like a young girl at the end of her first date—all jittery inside with wondering if he was going to kiss her again, and wanting him to.

"I guess this is good-night, then," she said, hoping he'd take it as a cue.

"I guess it is."

He didn't turn to leave, but he didn't come any closer either and when she finally glanced up at him, she found that the same frown that had wrinkled his brows just before he'd kissed her in the school cubicle was back again.

"Thanks for walking me home."

"My pleasure." He took a deep breath that raised his chest, and then sighed it out. "Well, good night, Clary. Sleep tight," he said with a finality that made her think he'd come to some sort of decision.

He turned away then.

As Clary watched him go, she deflated a little. Her gaze stayed with that broad expanse of very straight shoulders, trying to will him to come back and kiss her after all. But on he went, across the yard, down the street, until distance and darkness came between them and she couldn't see him anymore.

Clary made a face and sighed out a breath of her own—frustrated at being left standing there, unkissed—damn him. And she couldn't help wondering why he hadn't given her a second taste of what he'd allowed her at the school, when she knew, as surely as she knew she was standing there, that he'd wanted to. As much as she'd wanted him to.

"Well, okay for you," she muttered, as she turned into the house.

It was just too bad that it wasn't okay for her.

Chapter Four

"You're sure about this now?" Clary asked, scissors poised above Izzy's head.

Izzy made a face that suggested she wasn't sure at all, but said, "Yes, do it. I feel so big and fat and ugly, I wanted *something* done. I used to like the way my hair came out whenever you fiddled with it."

"We could always just curl it."

Izzy worried her bottom lip. But then she heaved a big breath and said, "No, go ahead. Short hair is easy to take care of, and when the baby gets here I'll need that."

"You're sure?"

"No, but do it anyway."

Izzy closed her eyes as if she couldn't bear to watch. "Beau called and offered to drive us all in his car to-night."

There was a potluck co-ed baby shower being given for Izzy and Jack in the church basement. Clary had assumed

Beau would be there, but hearing it for sure set off a little flutter of anticipation in her stomach.

Izzy went on, "He made a good point—he drives one of those big, all-terrain four-by-fours so it can substitute for an ambulance if need be. It'll work a lot better for carting home the gifts than our little compact car. But somehow I had the feeling he was thinking more about you than the inconvenience of Jack having to make a lot of trips back and forth."

"Do you want bangs?" Clary asked rather than saying anything about her cousin's comment.

"Yes! I can always feather them," Izzy said. Then, "Whatever it is you're cooking for the dinner tonight smells terrific."

"It's olive, mushroom and artichoke heart marinara."

"I can tell it's going to be worth the heartburn all that tomato will give me." Izzy felt the side of her hair that Clary had finished, judging the length. "You know, Sylvia retired last year and no one has reopened The Kitchen."

"I noticed that it was closed when we went by the other day."

"That whole place is just sitting there collecting dust. Why don't you move back here and open it? I've always hated that you're so far away. You could let your manager at Biminis run it and open a Wellsburg branch so you could go back to doing some of the cooking, the way you said you'd like to."

Clary took a sip of iced tea and went to work on the crown of her cousin's head. "Sylvia served six different varieties of meat and potatoes," Clary pointed out with a laugh at Izzy's idea. "Plain, old, home-style meat and potatoes—that's what kept her open around here for forty-plus years. Somehow I don't think Wellsburg would support a place that serves three Italian dishes, four Mexican, puts bordelaise and capers over the only steak on the menu and doesn't serve hamburgers or chicken-fried steak at all."

"You might be surprised. In fact you might find that people would come in from all around just to eat those things. And then you could settle down here and have a family of your own, instead of working like a crazy person and crying over my baby's heartbeat."

Clary wondered if she was ever going to live down that moment in Beau's examining room. "People settle down and have babies in L.A., too, Iz."

"But they don't settle down and have *Beau's* babies there."

"Oh, I see where this is headed."

"And I see what's happening between you and Beau. Was there something going on with the two of you all those years ago when you were both in L.A. that you didn't tell me about?"

"We just became friends."

"You didn't even date?"

"Not each other. There were a couple of double dates when each of us was with some else, but that's it."

"And now here you are, all these years later, with the hots for each other."

"Who says we have the hots for each other?" Clary exclaimed. If she had to be absolutely honest, she'd admit that it was true of her, but was it true of Beau? Sometimes it seemed like it and other times she wasn't so sure.

"This is a small town, Clary," Izzy reminded her, as if she should know better than to ask who knew anything. "The Stewarts behind us saw the two of you sitting together on the back stoop the other night. Ben Beard was over at the market across the street from Beau's office yesterday morning, and he said Beau came all the way out to stand on the sidewalk watching us after we left—and I don't think it was my big behind he was interested in. And *everybody* saw the two of you watching each other and pretending you weren't last night, not to mention that both of you disappearing at the same time livened up the conversation pretty well afterward with speculations about where you'd gone and what you were doing."

"Oh, good. I'm so happy to know that I'm giving everybody around her something to talk about."

"Just like old times," Izzy countered. "So, what *is* going on between you and Beau?"

Clary laughed. "You sounded just like you did when we were kids and you wanted me to confide a secret to you. You even almost whispered it."

"Come on, tell me."

"I don't know what's going on, to tell you the truth."

"But something is."

"I've definitely discovered things about him I didn't pay any attention to fifteen years ago. Or before that, either."

"And what about Beau?"

Clary shrugged. "I don't know. He moves in and then he backs off again."

"I'll have Jack talk to him."

"No!" Clary shrieked, making a horrified face. "We aren't kids, for crying out loud. I *do not* want Jack asking if Beau might like me, as if we were in grade school."

"Well, I think he does," Izzy said authoritatively. "I think that's why he offered to drive tonight. And I also think he'd be good for you."

"You think too much."

"You could come back here, the two of you could get married, build a nice house right next door, have kids, and yours and mine could all grow up together just the way we did,'' Izzy daydreamed out loud.

Clary declined to make a comment, and seized upon a handy change of subject. "All finished! Go look in the mirror and see what you think."

Izzy brushed hairs off her nose. "It *feels* good."

Clary watched her cousin disappear into the bathroom down the hall. She had to admit to herself that the idea of having Beau's babies was sort of titillating.

If only it didn't have to be in Wellsburg.

Beau left the office right after his four-thirty appointment that afternoon and went to the barbershop for a haircut. Then he stopped by the dry cleaner's for the new shirt he'd left off there at noon to be pressed. He could have ironed it himself, but his shirts always looked so much better when Bernie over at the cleaner's did them. And tonight he wanted to look his best.

His new gray slacks were finished being hemmed by that time so he picked them up at Rose's house—her payment to him for his house calls the past month when her migraines had laid her low. By the time he got home it was nearly six.

As usual, he went in through the kitchen, dropping his medical bag on the table as he passed it. He wasn't trying to be particularly quiet, but apparently he had been, because when he went into the living room he startled Dori standing at the mantel looking at one of the photographs of her mother.

"Oh, hi," she said, replacing the picture in a hurry, as if she were doing something wrong.

"Sorry. I didn't mean to scare you. I thought you'd be gone by now."

"Derrick is late. As always."

Derrick was Dori's age and had also won a part in the play at the college. He had a car and drove them both to Greeley for rehearsals and performances.

Beau nodded in the direction of the picture on the mantel. "Thinking about your mom?"

"A lot lately."

"Any special reason?"

Dori shrugged. "Do you suppose she'd be proud of me?"

"Very. There's a lot to be proud of." He clamped a hand around the teenager's nape and pulled her against his shoulder for just a moment.

"I think she would have liked that I have some acting abilities. The artistic part of me came from her, you know. Even though I don't paint the way she did, it's still sort of the same."

"I'm sure it is."

"I think she would have been all for my skipping college and trying to make a go of my acting."

Since this argument began, there had been any number of ploys Dori had used to try winning Beau over to her side. But now he didn't think that was what she was attempting to do, so he didn't get up in arms over her remark. But he also couldn't let it slide. "I think you're wrong," he said calmly.

"I was reading her diary last night. She always wanted to paint as more than a hobby. She would have understood my wanting to act as more than that, too."

"She would have understood your wanting to, but I don't believe she would have supported your not getting a degree first. She didn't pursue her art as a career, because it was too unstable. She didn't even become an art teacher, because there were fewer of those jobs available. And there were several times she told me how grateful she was to have her education to fall back on when your father was killed.''

But even as Beau said this and believed it, there was a part of him that wondered if Gina would have chosen the same practical path for Dori that she'd chosen for herself. He knew Dori was right, her mother had wanted to paint as more than a hobby. In fact, had she not died when she did, that year would have been her last at teaching. Beau's income was enough to allow her not to work and they had planned for her to stay at home, paint and have a couple more kids.

''I guess I do remember her saying it was a good thing she could teach, otherwise she didn't know how she would have supported me,'' the teenager conceded.

''You know I don't want you to just give up on your acting, Dor. It isn't that. It's only that I want you to keep it in perspective with the real world. If you have a degree and you become a big movie star there's no harm done. But if you don't make it as an actor and then don't have an education either, that makes for a lot rougher road. I don't want that to happen to you.''

''I could always go to school later, after I try acting for a while, if it doesn't work out.''

''I know, but the odds are against it. By then life will have intruded to complicate things—you might be married or have kids. And the books are harder to go back to when you've been away from them. Right now you can do both, go to school and pursue acting, without a problem.'' Beau was careful to keep his tone conversational. This was the first time they'd been able to discuss this subject calmly since she'd turned down UCLA.

''I don't think you understand that I don't even know what I'd major in in college. There isn't anything in the world I can imagine wanting to do other that act.''

"A lot of people go to college without knowing exactly what they want to do right off the bat. That's why you don't have to declare a major at first. You pick a general direction—which for you would be the arts—and go from there. Maybe you should think about doing what your mom did, and get a teaching degree. You could teach drama, help to put on plays, keep your hand in it, that way, if you don't make it yourself."

She shook her head. "I couldn't stand to just sit on the sidelines. I'd want to be out there on the stage or nothing."

"I know you feel that way now, Dori, but that could change. You can't control whether or not you make it as an actor. If you don't, you may find that teaching and directing plays for schools and maybe getting into small local productions, is still better than nothing."

"Oh, that's so depressing!" she said with teenage horror.

Beau had to laugh. "No, that's life."

A horn honked outside and Dori swung around to the front door. "Finally," she said. Then she grabbed her oversized carryall bag and stood on tiptoe to kiss Beau's cheek.

Kissing him or him kissing her had become "uncool" long ago, and Beau was so surprised by the buss that she was gone before he could respond.

Was this a new tactic—trying to catch flies with honey instead of vinegar—he wondered.

But he rejected the idea, trusting his instinct that her impromptu show of affection was genuine. He felt good about their exchange. Maybe he would get through to her yet.

On his way into the bedroom he took his shirt off, shedding the rest of his clothes in short order before getting into the shower in the adjoining bathroom. The past few pleasant moments with Dori had buoyed his already good mood. He was looking forward to the potluck tonight. He had been all day long. In fact, it had been the first thing he'd thought about when his alarm went off this morning.

Not that he was wild for baby showers in the church basement. But Clary would be at this one, and that made a difference. A big difference. Hell, he was nearly itchy with wanting to see her.

He'd tried to resist the draw. Through most of the evening the night before, he'd forced himself to stay away from her. But it hadn't been easy. She'd stood out in the crowd and his gaze had followed her like a magnet. And all he'd wanted to do was go to her, talk to her—do more than talk to her.

It had helped his willpower to realize that any exchange with her meant drawing the stares and curiosity of everyone else in the room. And polite chitchat hadn't been what he was craving, anyway.

Then he'd seen her slip out of the gym by herself and he was a goner. She might as well have had a string attached to him, because when she went he'd had to follow.

He turned off the shower and yanked the towel from over the glass door, and as he did he could see her again the way he'd found her—on her toes, peeking into the classrooms. She'd looked good. Great. Wonderful.

And like a lost soul.

Why was that? he wondered suddenly, thinking of those tears in her eyes at his office the day before, too, and the fact that she'd said herself that she wasn't sleeping.

Something was wrong. And that something was what had brought her back to Wellsburg for an extended visit when even her grandmother's death couldn't keep her here

more than a single day in all the years she'd been gone—
he'd bet on it. But what was happening with her?

Did she come to heal a wound? And if so, did that mean
some part of her might actually still consider Wellsburg the
place to retreat to? Maybe even home?

"Whoa," he said out loud, stopping short as he recognized what had welled up inside of him when he wasn't on
guard against it—it was hope that there might actually be
a chance of her staying. And that wasn't good.

The odds were against it and he knew it. She'd told him
she was happy in L.A., and Beau had seen it with his own
eyes all those years ago. She'd loved the place. She'd
thrived on everything that he'd hated about it. Her ambi-
tion had blossomed, she'd loved working nonstop, had
been fueled by the pace.

No, it was a bad idea to pin any hopes on her staying in
Wellsburg. A really bad idea. Whatever her reasons for
being here and for staying awhile, he knew they wouldn't
last. The day would come—probably before too long—
when she'd be over whatever it was she'd come here to deal
with and then she'd go back.

"And in the meantime?" he asked his reflection in the
mirror as he combed his hair.

He wished he could say that in the meantime he'd just
see her when their paths crossed, pay her no more attention than any acquaintance, not give her a second thought.
But he knew better. He knew it because he hadn't been so
hot and bothered over any woman in his life the way he
had been walking home last night after one measly kiss. He
knew it because he couldn't stop thinking about her or
picturing how she looked. He knew it because there was
literally an ache inside of him to hold her, to kiss her again,
to know what it would feel like to be inside her.

And he knew he couldn't treat her being here casually, because even though there wasn't a doubt in his mind that her time in Wellsburg would be brief before she disappeared back to L.A.—maybe forever—he was still counting the minutes until he could see her again.

As Clary sat in the front seat of Beau's large four-by-four, with Izzy and Jack in the back, she felt as if she were on a double date. And no matter how many times she reminded herself that that was not the case, that the four of them just happened to be going to the baby shower together, she couldn't shake the feeling. Maybe because she didn't really want to shake the feeling.

"I like your new hairdo, Iz," Beau said over his shoulder as he pulled out of the driveway.

"Clary did it," Izzy answered with a little toss of her newly shorn tresses. "She didn't do a bad job, did she? Even Jack likes it and he hates change."

"I don't hate change," Jack put in, affronted.

But there wasn't time to argue the point as they arrived at the church.

Two small boys sat on the curb in front of the steepled white frame structure. When they spotted Beau's car they jumped to their feet, waving wildly for him to park in the space nearest the door.

"Looks like the guests of honor get special privileges," Beau said over his shoulder as he pulled in.

While Jack helped Izzy out of the car, Beau rounded the front end and opened Clary's door. "Let me take that," he said as he reached for the covered bowl she held in her lap.

Clary handed it over, getting her fill of how he looked while she did. He was dressed in a crisp white shirt, the long sleeves rolled to his elbows, and dove gray slacks with razor-sharp creases down the legs. She could tell Izzy wasn't the only one who'd had a haircut today. His hair looked neat and clean and shiny, but not too short. And he smelled wonderful.

As they headed up the brick walk, she had the urge to take his arm. But of course she fought it and instead kept her distance at his side.

"This looks more like a town meeting than a baby shower," Clary said as they descended the steps into the church basement.

Rather than formal invitations sent out to a guest list, signs had been posted announcing the shower. Clearly, Izzy was popular in Wellsburg.

"Looks like the food is supposed to go over on that table in the corner," Beau said to Clary, as Izzy and Jack were drawn into the party.

He led the way through the crowd, holding the bowl up over heads as they went. Behind him, Clary couldn't resist a peek at his derriere, in spite of the fact that if anyone saw her it would likely be reported throughout all of Wellsburg and its surrounding area. It was worth the risk. Great buns. Tight and narrow, without being too slim. Just the way Clary liked them.

"Clary Parsons!"

Clary had just made a space for Beau to set down her contribution to the potluck when she heard her name called from close behind. She turned to find Howard Skokes headed her way.

Two years older than Clary, he didn't look much different than he had in high school, with his curly red hair and oversized ears.

Clary's first impulse as she watched him nearing, was to glance down at what she was wearing. In the old days, anything short of a turtleneck had always ended up having a quarter dropped down the front by Skokie. For a moment she regretted having worn what she had. The long-sleeved black knit off-the-shoulder top edged with stretch lace was an easy target. And should Skokie pull one of his old tricks, the tight belt at her waist would keep a coin from falling all the way through to the bright patchwork-and-black-lace skirt she wore below, leaving her with the embarrassing option of having to fish it out.

"It's okay. Skokie doesn't drop change down women's shirts anymore," Beau whispered in her ear.

Clary laughed. "You're a mind reader?"

He shook his head, pulling her hand away from holding her shirt to her chest.

Skokie reached them then. He stood directly in front of Clary and unabashedly looked her up and down. "Wow! You grew up good," he enthused with intentionally bad grammar.

"Thanks," she said with a laugh.

"No wonder Beau's tried to keep you all to himself."

"He has?" she asked, with a sidelong glance up at Beau who was suddenly standing so close that his arm was against her back.

"Don't pay any attention to him," Beau advised, this time near enough to her ear that she could feel the heat of his breath against her cheek.

Skokie went on, "I was all set to whisk you off your feet when I heard you were coming home, and what did Beau do? He beat my time." The dentist stared at her for another moment. "So how've you been?"

Clary answered him and they fell into small talk. But even as she asked Skokie about himself, her mind was more on Beau. Standing the way he was, his shirt was against the bare skin of her shoulder. For some reason she didn't understand, it felt incredibly intimate to her. And that didn't help her composure.

"I promised Clary a glass of wine, Skokie, so you'll have to excuse us," Beau said after a few minutes, taking her elbow and steering her away from the other man.

"Funny, I don't remember that promise," she couldn't resist goading when they were out of the dentist's hearing range.

"I just thought that a little of Skokie goes a long way."

"For you or for me?" she teased, trying to ignore the little shots of electricity that emanated from his touch.

Beau smiled slyly and nodded in the direction from which they'd come. "Want to go back and spend more time with him? I'll just mingle, if you do."

There was nothing she had found wrong with the dentist, but given the option of Skokie or Beau, there was no way she was going to take Beau's challenge and lose his company. "Wine sounds nice," she said instead, making his smile turn into a knowing grin.

Clary's sense that she was on a date with Beau only increased as the night wore on. He never left her side or went to talk to anyone without taking her with him.

His attentions made things go smoothly for Clary, who had been a little concerned that the whole evening might be a reenactment of the end of the awards ceremony, with all these people who shared so much leaving her out of the conversations. Instead, Beau made sure she was included and helped her to feel a part of everything.

Her pasta and marinara sauce was a huge hit, prompting Izzy to poke her in the ribs and say "I told you so," as they retrieved the dish at the end of the shower and headed out to the car.

Beau and Jack had preceded them, leading a parade of men bearing the gifts. By the time Clary and Izzy got to the curb, there was barely enough room for the four of them to ride home.

"You'll have to get in on my side and sit in the middle," Beau told Clary, though she would have figured it out for herself, since there was a stack of baby things on the other end of the bench seat.

Not that she minded. Oh, no. She was more than happy for the excuse, as he joined her in the small space that was left. His thigh ran the length of hers, something she was uncommonly aware of. It was so thick it stretched the dove gray twill taut, and she thought she could feel the hardness of it against the softness of her own leg. Somehow it was very sexy.

Beau started the motor and then stretched his right arm along the top of the seat behind her to ask if Izzy and Jack were all set. And there it stayed as he eased out of the parking place and onto the street, leaving Clary feeling as if he almost had his arm around her. Her side rested against his, strong and steady, and she didn't remember ever having been so conscious of such a thing.

"Get on up to bed," Beau ordered Izzy when they pulled into the driveway. "We'll unload all this stuff. You haven't been off your feet all evening and it's late—doctor's orders."

Izzy was apparently tired, because she didn't argue. She just said good-night and disappeared inside.

It took the three of them nearly half an hour to get everything into the house, but the time flew for Clary. Trip after trip allowed her to watch Beau without seeming to, and she reveled in the sight of his broad back, his narrow waist, and oddly, she thought, of the muscles in his forearms and his big hands as he carted in boxes and delicate baby things.

Then all the gifts were in the nursery and Jack yawned broadly. "I don't know about you two, but I'm beat. I'm going to bed."

Clary and Beau said good-night at the same time, neither of them adding any encouragement to the idea of ending the evening.

"You know Wellsburg doesn't have much to offer in the way of nightlife, but the convenience store is open for about another..." he consulted his watch "... five minutes. If we cut across the Thorns' yard, I think we can make it. I'll treat you to anything in the place, if you're game."

She was, but only because she didn't want him to leave yet. "An offer I can't refuse."

He took her hand, but there was nothing romantic about it. He was just helping her keep up, as they made a last minute dash to the brand-new building that housed the kind of store that could be found open all night long on half the streets in L.A.

The clerk was just closing up, but he conceded to giving them a few minutes inside first. Beau and Clary both chose frozen-lemonade fruit bars without much deliberation. Then the clerk took Beau's money and locked the door after them, leaving them alone in the stillness of the night.

There wasn't a cloud in the sky and the air was cool. Without a word, they crossed the street to the park square, meandering through the trees until they reached a bench.

Clary sat down first, curious about how close or faraway Beau would sit when he joined her. Given her druthers, she'd have had him as close as they'd been on the way home from the shower. But she wasn't given her druthers as he sat down—not all the way to the other end of the bench, but with about six inches between them.

Those six inches seemed like a mile to Clary.

For a while they ate their fruit bars in silence, surrounded by the scents of freshly mowed grass, pine trees and the perfume of the flower bed they faced. Pale yellow light bathed them and the only sounds were of a dog barking somewhere off in the distance and the low-grade hum of the convenience store's neon sign.

"Do you think we're the last two people awake in the whole town?" Clary asked Beau with a laugh, keeping her voice low, as if she might wake everyone else by speaking any louder.

"I'll bet that reminds you of why you wanted out of here, doesn't it?"

"Actually I was thinking that it was peaceful and kind of nice, to be able to have a park all to ourselves late at night without worrying about getting mugged." She glanced at him then, finding him staring at her with those kiwi green eyes of his, their color dimmed by the light from the street lamp, but still striking nonetheless.

He glanced away, staring at the flower bed where red and purple pansies had been transplanted from the greenhouse. "Do you miss L.A., Clary?"

"No more than anyone misses home when they're on vacation."

He didn't say anything to that, and in the silence that fell once again Clary stared at his profile. His nose came to a sharper point than it seemed to from the front, but it went well with the other angles of his face—his square brow, his defined cheekbones and strong dented chin.

Her gaze caught and stayed on his lips for a moment. Pale and somewhat thin, but very masculine. And Clary had never wanted any man to kiss her as badly as she wanted him to.

"I keep having the feeling that something isn't quite right with you," he said then. He turned those eyes of his on her again, like an interrogator's spotlight daring her not to tell him the truth.

"I'm fine," she insisted.

But he didn't seem to believe her. "You wouldn't be here nursing a broken heart, would you?"

"Is this some sneaky way of finding out if I'm involved in a serious relationship?" she teased.

He smiled as if she'd seen through him. "Partly. But it's also because I'm worried about you."

"Thanks, but there's nothing to worry about," she said, inordinately aware of the way his leg was crossed ankle-over-knee beside her.

"And the serious relationship?" he prompted.

Grateful that he'd taken the hint, she said, "Good men are hard to find. I'm still looking. How about you?"

"I never started looking for a good man."

She gave his glib remark a sly grin. "How about a good woman? Have you found one of those?"

"I know a lot of good women."

"Are you trying to avoid answering this question?"

He looked up at the stars. "There's a nurse I see when I'm at the hospital in Greeley, but it's nothing serious."

"Does she feel the same way?" Clary asked, over-whelmed with a sudden sense of jealousy.

"Yes, she does. She just went through a messy divorce and she's in the process of relearning to be her own person. We're both happy with things between us being pretty casual. I don't think you could even call it dating. We get together when we can both arrange it, and if we can't— well, it's no big deal."

But the image of him with another woman, even casu-ally, still bothered Clary. To hide it, she tilted her head back and took a deep breath. "I forgot how good clean air can smell."

"Careful. That comment could be construed as a compliment to Wellsburg."

He took their Popsicle sticks to the trash receptacle not far away. When he came back he sat closer than he had been before, stretching his arm along the bench just behind her. She could tell just where his sleeve left off and exposed his forearm because it was warm against her bare shoulders. It was silly, she told herself, but the contact of his skin against hers sent a warm tingling all through her.

"For your information, I *was* complimenting Wellsburg," she admitted.

"I find that hard to believe."

"Maybe I'm just older and wiser now. Enough to realize that the Burg isn't *all* bad."

"Have you realized that?"

He posed his question so seriously that Clary thought about it for a moment. She wasn't sure if she'd realized that Wellsburg wasn't all bad or just that it didn't seem that way anymore because of Beau. But she certainly couldn't tell him that, so instead of answering him, she said. "You still really like it here, don't you?"

He shrugged and her gaze rode his broad shoulders before sliding down to his bicep and then on to this thick, flat wrist. His hand rested on his thigh and Clary couldn't help wishing it was on hers instead.

"I've always loved Wellsburg, that hasn't changed," he said. "It just feels right for me to be here, like it's the one spot on earth where I'm meant to be. It's home."

Clary felt slightly envious of the contentment in his tone. L.A. was home to her, but she couldn't say she felt as if it were the one spot on earth she was meant to be. Not that she'd ever experienced that feeling anywhere, but still it sounded so appealing.

Or maybe it was just Beau who was so appealing.

She could feel his gaze on her again. She glanced up to find his expression thoughtful and intense at once. "You know, this is the third time I've caught you staring at me as if I'm some very serious proposition. Are you sure *you're* okay?" she asked.

His smile was slow and one-sided. "Actually, I'm trying to figure out just how serious a proposition you are."

"Serious for whom?"

"Me."

Clary's gaze got lost in the cleft of his chin for a moment before she said, "Why would I be a serious proposition for you?"

"I'm incredibly attracted to you."

"That sounded very formal." And standoffish. "Being attracted to me isn't a bad thing, is it? I mean, I'm incredibly attracted to you, and it feels pretty good to me."

That made him laugh. "I always did like the way you blurted things out."

Somehow his arm had moved from the bench back to curve around her. His hand was on her shoulder and he was kneading it just slightly, sensuously. Clary knew she should say something to his comment, but her mind went suddenly blank. All she could think about was the feel of his hand against her skin; his palm was the texture of Italian leather, warm, smooth, soft but tough, and it set her stomach aflutter; her breasts felt very sensitive, and she didn't know what to do with all these feelings when Beau seemed so reticent.

But then his reserve seemed to change. Slowly he pulled her toward him, pressing the palm of his other hand against the side of her face to draw her nearer. He lowered his mouth to hers, taking her lips between his parted ones. At first the kiss was light, tender, but before long he deepened it, opening his mouth wider, teasing her with his tongue. Deeper, deeper, he kissed her, with an urgency that ignited the same in Clary.

She wrapped her arms around him, reveling in the roll of his muscular back beneath her hands. Opening her mouth to him, she met his tongue with her own, boldened, enlivened by this, which she'd been craving since he'd kissed her at the school the night before.

Lord, but the man could kiss! Clary melted against him, lost in the bliss of his body, his mouth, his arms, wanting it to go on forever, not caring that they were out in the open, that anyone might happen by, see them and bandy the tale around town.

And then, just when she'd have had more of him and given him more of her, he stopped, leaving her breathless.

"Something's happening here, Clary," he said in a deep, passion-raspy voice.

"I know. It must be this country air," she joked, trying to hide just how much he'd swept her off her feet.

But he didn't say anything else. Instead, he took her hand and pulled her with him to head home.

The porch light was still on at the house, and he led her up into its glow before ever turning to look at her again.

"I must be out of my mind," he said to himself just before he took both of her shoulders in his hands and pulled her into another kiss, as intense as the first.

Hungry for more of what he'd started in the park, Clary was all too willing to give in to his arms, so tightly wrapped around her. One hand cupped the back of her head, holding her to a kiss she had no desire to escape from.

She clung to him, one arm around him, one hand on the hard mound of his bicep under his sleeve. Her head was light, her body was alive, and for one fleeting moment she wondered how anyone could have such an instantaneous, powerful effect on her.

But all too soon he ended that kiss, as well.

Slowly he raised his head, taking a deep breath as if his willpower was being fortified by the cool night air. Then he let her go and stepped away from her. "Are you still planning on coming with me to Dori's play, the day after tomorrow?"

"Do you want me to?" she asked, feeling a little bewildered that he had ended both kisses just when they seemed to be gaining momentum, and that he now stood more than an arm's length away.

He gave a wry laugh, tilting his head to glance over his shoulder. "Oh, yeah," he answered, as if there were no question about his wanting her to go along.

"I'd like to, then."

"I'll pick you up around one." He took a step toward her as if it were involuntary. But then stopped short and just waved a little halfheartedly, as if it kept him from taking her into his arms again, backing off the porch as he did. "Good night, Clary," he said in a gravelly voice. "I hope you sleep tonight." And then he was gone.

Desire and passion were still pumping through her. She could feel his lips against hers as surely as if they were there yet, and she wished with all her being that they were. She took a deep breath and held it, as if to smother the flames inside her.

He hoped she slept tonight, she thought as she watched him drive off.

Fat chance.

Chapter Five

When the phone rang at nine the next morning, Clary was surprised to have Izzy hold out the receiver to her and say, "It's for you."

"Is it Beau?" she asked, the words slipping out on a wave of unfounded hope.

Izzy laughed. "Beau? Why would it be Beau?"

"It wouldn't be. I don't know why I said that." But of course she did. It was because he was on her mind. All the time. And because she'd gotten up this morning hating the fact that she didn't have any reason to see him again until tomorrow. The unfounded hope was that for some reason—any reason—he would call her and ask her to dinner or to take a walk or anything that would let her spend even a small amount of time with him today.

Her next thought was that the caller was Wolf and something was wrong at Biminis. She took the phone in a hurry then.

"Hello?"

"Hi!"

Wrong again. It was Beau's daughter on the other end of the line. "Dori. This is a surprise."

"I know. Is it okay for me to call you?"

"Sure."

"Oh, good. I want to ask a favor. Can I do that, too?"

"You can ask. That doesn't necessarily mean I can do it."

"*Everybody's* told me about your outfit last night. My friend Danielle said it was totally awesome. But, then, I love everything you wear and when I go to L.A. I don't want to be out of style. So what I was wondering is—if you aren't busy this morning, would you come over and look at my clothes and give me some advice?"

"It just occurred to me, are you calling from school?" Clary asked.

"No, I don't have to be there until eleven today—my earlier classes are doing makeup tests, and I don't have to take any. Are you busy? Is this morning a bad time? Because we could do it, like, after school or something, if that's better. It's just that I got all excited hearing about what you wore to the potluck and I had this idea and—"

Clary laughed. "It's okay, it's okay. But I'm not sure what I can tell you, hon. There isn't a uniform for residents of L.A. You just need to wear whatever you're comfortable in and what works for you."

"I know, but I don't want to look like some hick from a small town." She paused. "Well, I suppose that's what I am, but I don't want to announce it. And I *love* the way you look, so if you could just give me some advice, it'd be really cool."

Clary thought about it for a moment. She didn't mind doing this for the teenager, but she wondered what Beau would think of it. Would he see it as encouraging his daughter in what he was trying to discourage?

"Please?" Dori said.

It was only fashion advice, Clary decided. And if the subject came up of Dori foregoing college to move to L.A., she could always put in a few good words for getting an education. "Just let me check with Izzy a minute and see if she has anything planned. Hang on."

Clary put her palm over the mouthpiece and explained to her cousin what Beau's daughter wanted.

"My assistant principal is coming over to work on some scheduling for next year. You'd probably have a better time with Dori than sitting in on that," Izzy said.

Clary spoke into the phone again. "Looks like I'm free. Do you want me to come over right this minute?"

"Oh, totally cool! Now is perfect."

Clary suppressed a laugh at the teenager's enthusiasm. "I'll be right over."

Beau's house was at the opposite end of Wellsburg, but it was a glorious spring day, so Clary opted for walking. Stores and businesses were already open or just opening, by then, and as she walked down Front Street she took in what had stayed the same and what had changed—though there wasn't much of the latter.

The combination beauty salon/barbershop was still owned by Mr. and Mrs. Samson. Split right down the middle, Mr. Samson cut men's hair on one half in brown leather chairs, while Mrs. Samson's side of the shop was done up in pink-and-lavender for the ladies.

The bakery was now Lucy McCutcheon's, where before it had been run by Lucy's father, Fred. But other than the change in names in the corner of the display window, the place was the same.

There was a gift shop where there used to be an insurance office. Beside it remained the hardware-and-paint store, and next to that the lumberyard. The liquor store was in the same spot, sitting between a pizza place that previously had been an auto-parts store, before the auto-parts store expanded into two storefronts on the west side of Front Street. And there was the coffee-and-doughnut shop where Clary and Izzy and their friends had hung out when they were in high school, before the pizza place opened and began to draw that contingent.

In the middle of the block was the family-owned grocery, which also sold some items of clothing, housewares and dry goods. It had begun along with Wellsburg, as a general store, for a time had been called the Variety Store, and was now The Emporium. But through all its evolution, it had been owned and run by various generations of the Whitmore family.

Even though it was The Emporium's side of the street down which Clary walked, her gaze drifted across it as she passed the grocery. Not much over there caught her attention before, but directly across from here was the medical office Beau and Skokie shared.

What did she expect to see? she asked herself as she stared into the plate-glass window that exposed the empty waiting room.

It wasn't that she *expected* to see anything, she thought in answer to her own self-reproach. It was what she *hoped* she'd see—Beau.

But she couldn't just stand around on the sidewalk, so she moved on past, not looking ahead again until it became impossible to watch the waiting room without walking backward.

She was only one door down, in front of the bank, when she bumped into a woman who had been a friend of her grandmother. Courtesy dictated that she stop to talk to her, and if that meant she could look over at Beau's office a little more, well, Clary considered it compensation for listening to the eighty-eight-year-old woman's complete medical history.

She must have stood there for a full fifteen minutes, but not once did she catch so much as a sight of Beau. Finally resigning herself to that, Clary managed to excuse herself and went the rest of the way to Beau's house.

The homes at this end of town were more modern, though for Wellsburg modern meant anything dating from the late fifties or very early sixties. For the most part, they were larger, constructed of brick and lacking the big porches and the charm of the older houses.

Beau's, in particular, was a peach-colored, L-shaped bi-level. It was trimmed in tan and brown, with a double-car garage. Dori was waiting anxiously on the small stoop out front.

"Sorry if it took me longer than you expected. I was waylaid by old Miss Crown."

Dori held the screen open for Clary and rolled her eyes. "I'll bet she had to tell you all about her cataract operations last year."

Clary laughed. "Yep. Every gory detail."

Stepping into the living room ahead of the teenager, Clary's first impression was of a cozy, lived-in family home. The furniture was in nondescript rust and cream colors, the lamps slightly outdated, the coffee and end tables handsome oak. And over it all was a slight clutter—a newspaper here, schoolbooks there, a jean purse hung over a doorknob, a coffee cup stenciled with "Dr. Dad" on top of a videotape on top of the TV, a remote-control unit on the couch, a compact disc on the floor in front of the stereo. And the shirt Beau had worn the night before over the back of an easy chair.

"My room's upstairs," Dori said as she headed in that direction. "You can sit down here and I'll bring the stuff out so you can tell me what you think."

"Okay," Clary agreed.

Left alone in the living room, she headed for the couch. But on the way she had to pass the easy chair where Beau's shirt was.

It was crazy, she knew, but she couldn't resist fingering the collar. In her mind's eye, she could see it against the back of his neck where his hair came just short of reaching it. He'd worn the two buttons unfastened, and every now and then, when he'd moved a certain way, she'd caught glimpses of dark, curly chest hair a few inches below his throat.

Clary cast a guilty glance at the stairs. She couldn't believe what she wanted to do, but when she found no sign of Dori, she bent low enough to breathe in the lingering scent of Beau's after-shave on the shirt. The memories that erupted in response were instant and vivid—of him pulling her near, of the feel of his back beneath the shirt, of his kiss. . . .

"Look out below," Dori called from the landing.

Clary snapped up straight and took a quick step away from the easy chair.

"Don't you want to sit down?" the teenager asked as she came downstairs, her arms full of clothes, as if they'd been in a pile and she'd just grabbed them up in a big bear hug.

"If I sit down, where will you put all that stuff?" Clary asked with a laugh.

"I can just dump it on the floor."

"No, put it on the couch and we'll go through it from there," Clary suggested instead.

Dori dropped the armload unceremoniously and it tumbled across the whole sofa, pieces of it threatening to fall to the floor anyway.

"Now I'll go get my shoes," the teenager said, dashing out of the room and coming back again moments later. "Okay. This is everything."

"Wouldn't it have been easier for me to have gone up to your room?"

"Oh, no, you couldn't do that. It's a mess."

Clary didn't doubt it.

The telephone rang just then and Dori excused herself to answer it, half skipping around the table in the connecting dining room to disappear through a swinging door that revealed a portion of the kitchen beyond.

Clary didn't feel right delving into the girl's things without her, so she refrained. But she didn't want to go back to being silly over the shirt on the easy chair, either. Instead, she glanced around the room for something else to take her attention while Dori was gone.

That was when she spotted the photographs on the mantel.

There were more than a dozen of them, most of Dori through the years. There were pictures of her as a young child at field days with ribbons pinned to her T-shirt; in costume, for school plays; in fancy dresses, with dates, for homecomings and proms. And there was her graduation portrait, in which she leaned against the trunk of a tree, dressed in a dark sweater that set off her golden good looks.

But there were other photographs, too.

There was Beau and his bride, with Dori standing in front of the couple as their flower girl. It was easy to place

the wedding at Christmastime because the altar behind
them was adorned with matching trees, poinsettias were at
their feet and Dori's dress was red-and-green tartan plaid.

The second picture of Beau and his bride—in street
clothes rather than wedding garb—had them in an embrace under a sprig of Christmas mistletoe in this very
house. The third photograph Clary looked at was again of
all three of them, apparently at Disneyland in the summer.

It was that picture Clary took off the mantel, studying
it.

They made a nice family, she thought, imagining how
difficult it must have been to have all the happiness these
pictures showed shattered so soon by Dori's mother's
death.

Dori's mother.

Gina, Clary remembered her cousin saying the woman's name had been. Izzy had been right—she had had the
most glorious blond hair Clary had ever seen. Thick, wavy,
shining as if sunlight emanated from within it. And she
was even more beautiful than Dori, just the way Izzy had
said. Her features were delicate and perfect enough to be
a fashion model's.

Strange, Clary thought, how much a picture told.

Dori was obviously a part of their union from the start,
looking for all the world as if she were just happily posing
for a picture with her parents. She even seemed to be leaning into Beau's hand on her shoulder.

As for Gina and Beau—Gina's eyes held adoration for
her new husband as she gazed up at him. Her expression
seemed to shout how happy she was, and Clary couldn't
help but notice the possessive hand the woman had on
Beau's chest, her wedding ring in plain view.

But the affection wasn't one-sided. Beau's love for Gina was clear in the protective way he had his arm around her, holding her as close as if he really had taken her to be a part of him.

"Sorry about that," Dori said as she came back into the living room, referring to the interruption of the phone call. She joined Clary at the mantel. "That's my mom."

"I guessed," Clary answered affectionately.

"That was our vacation the summer after they got married," the teenager said. Then she pointed to the other two pictures still on the mantel. "And that was their wedding, and that was Christmas Eve, when they came home from their honeymoon."

"You all look so happy."

"We were. Too bad it could only be for such a little while," Dori said wistfully.

"Your dad told me how upset he was when your mom died. It must have been awful for you, too."

The teenager nodded. "It was really frightening," she confided, without seeming to have a problem discussing the subject. "I mean, I was an orphan—both my real parents were dead. I didn't know what would happen to me, if Beau—I called him Beau, then—if he'd still want me or where I'd go if he didn't. It seems strange to say this, but when he realized what I was thinking and told me he loved me and wanted to adopt me no matter what, well, I was so happy and relieved that I remember that, more than feeling bad about my mom's death. The grief stuff came a little later."

"I don't think that's strange at all. I think it's pretty normal."

"Mrs. MacIntire says you were raised without your parents, too."

"By my grandmother."

"I'm glad I had my dad. Once I knew he was going through with the adoption, I didn't feel all that different from my friends. But I know a girl who had to live with her grandparents the whole time she was growing up, and she felt really weird about it."

"It's a little strange. You aren't dealing with someone just twenty or thirty years removed from what you're going through, you have to convince someone fifty years away from being a kid that what you want to do is just what everybody else is doing. My grandmother and I had a hard time agreeing on a lot of things, and I felt pretty smothered."

"I'll bet she *really* hated it when you went off to L.A."

"Oh, she hated it, all right. She said no decent girl left home until she was leaving it to get married."

"Wow, that is old-fashioned. What happened when you went away?"

"Things were never the same between us," Clary answered honestly, hoping that it might make Dori think twice before doing the same damage to her relationship with her father. "I never came back here while my grandmother was alive, and she only visited me once. We talked on the telephone on holidays and birthdays, but not much more." Clary looked the teenager in the eye. "I always regretted that we ended up that way."

"But what else could you have done? She'd have only been happy if you did what she wanted you to do, and that would have meant staying in Wellsburg and getting married, right?"

Clary shrugged. "I only know that I've always wondered if there might have been a better way," she said pointedly.

"So. Dad says that you guys went all the way to L.A. to become friends," the girl said, obviously changing the subject.

Clary didn't push it. "I was just his younger sister's friend before we met up in California again—no one to pay attention to." She replaced the photograph on the mantel and they both turned to the pile of clothes on the couch.

"Well, he's sure paying attention now."

"I don't think you could call it that, really. Wellsburg is just such a small town that it's impossible for us not to bump into each other."

"Oh, no, there's more to it than that," Dori said slyly as she began to hold up clothes in front of her for Clary's consideration. "I've never seen him daydream before, and he's doing lots of it now. And he must be thinking about you when he's at it, because he mentions your name at the weirdest times. Yesterday, he called me Clary twice."

Clary pulled a bright striped scarf out of the pile and showed Dori how to use it as a belt on the T-shirt dress the teenager held up, blousing the dress over it to make a peplum tunic out of it.

"Anyway," Dori went on, after exclaiming over the look, "I think it's great that he's having fantasies about you, because that means he's thinking about something besides me and college."

"Don't kid yourself," Clary demurred, hoping it hid how pleased she was to hear she was on Beau's mind. "Unless I miss my guess, your dad thinks a lot about you and college."

"Couldn't you do something about that?"

Clary laughed. "Like what?"

"I mean, couldn't you, like, talk to him about how college isn't important, and how great L.A. is, and how good it's been for you to be there even without a degree?"

Clary shook her head. "Sorry. In the first place, it isn't my business or my place to talk to him about any of that. And in the second place, college is important. I've always been sorry that I didn't go."

Again, Clary saw a wall drop over the teenager's expression that said Dori didn't want to hear what she was saying.

For a few minutes they only talked about clothes, shoes and accessories. Then Dori said, "My dad really does like you," as if she were playing matchmaker between two of her friends. "How do you feel about him? I mean, are you, like, interested?"

Interested enough to keep watching the door and hoping Beau would make an impromptu appearance. Interested enough to be awake all night reliving his every word, his touch, his kisses. Interested enough to fondle his shirt and breath in the leftover scent of his after-shave.

But none of that was anything Clary wanted to say to Beau's daughter. She settled on, "I like your dad."

"Rad. You know, he's going to need somebody else in his life, now that I'm leaving."

And Clary might like to be that somebody else in his life. Just not in Wellsburg. "I'm sure he'll miss you, but I'll bet he can take care of himself pretty well," she said. Then she pulled a pair of stirrup pants out of the pile. "But if we don't get down to brass tacks here, we'll never get through all these clothes."

Clary and Dori finished their fashion conclave by ten-thirty and since the teenager had a class at eleven, they left Beau's house together. But Clary only went as far as the corner of Front Street, where Dori was going to turn to go over the block to the school.

"I think I'll do some window-shopping before I go home," she informed the teenager then.

"Okay. Thanks again for your help."

"Anytime."

For a moment Clary watched the girl go on without her, seeing the glow of the sun reflected in her hair. But more than Dori, what Clary saw was the image of the girl's mother from the pictures. For some reason, it made her long all the more to see Beau. Or was she longing to stake a claim on him? She wasn't sure.

What she was sure of, was what she was window-shopping for—a sight of him that was discreet enough so that no one would realize she was playing Peeping Tom. And the grocery store directly across the street from his office seemed like the most opportune location.

Okay, so it was sophomoric, she told herself as she headed down Front Street. But being in his house, where there was such a pervasive sense of him, had only intensified her yearning to see him today, if only from a distance.

There was an old bell above the door to the grocery store, which announced all entrances and exits. As she went in, Clary felt as if it announced her intentions, too.

The store had been modernized considerably since the last time she was in Wellsburg. Before, there had only been shelves around the walls and two down the center that stood not higher than shoulder level. But the Whitmores had taken over shops on both sides, broken through the walls and expanded, so that now there were several rows of shelves, all of them as high as Clary's head.

She was glad to see the improvements—it meant she could spy without being easily observed at it.

As if she were actually shopping, she wandered slowly up and down each row trying to find something on the ascending trip to buy to legitimize this visit and free her on the descending trip to watch Beau's office through the big window at the front of the store.

She saw two patients in the waiting room, and the receptionist as she filed charts in the cabinets against the facing wall. She even saw Skokie come out and lean against the desk, idly chatting with one of the waiting patients, a man Clary thought she recognized as the town plumber. But she didn't see Beau.

She'd gathered apples, a bag of peanuts and a package of cookies by the time she discovered candy bars on the end of one aisle. She picked up two and then headed the rest of the way around, keeping her eyes on the medical office. Walking in one direction and looking in another, she misjudged the turn and ran smack dab into the sharp corner of a shelf.

For a moment she saw stars and wobbled backward, feeling something warm and wet on her forehead.

"Oh, my gosh!" a woman said from not far away.

Clary regained enough of her senses and equilibrium then, to realize she was bleeding like a stuck pig, one eye already obscured with the stuff.

"Sam Whitmore, you'd better come over here! This girl is hurt!" the same woman called to the store owner.

He rushed over as Clary managed to set down her groceries and fumble in her pocket, hoping for a tissue.

"Look at all that blood!" the woman said, her distaste for the sight in her tone.

Clary was only vaguely aware of the man, as her search of her own pockets located only the coin purse she'd taken with her when she'd left Izzy's house.

"I think I need a tissue," she told the grocer.

"You need more than that," he answered. "Let's get you across the street to the doctor."

"No! I'm sure that's not necessary," she said in a hurry.

The disclaimer sounded feeble, when there seemed to be blood everywhere—running down the side of her face and neck, all over her white camp shirt and down one leg of her jeans. There were even spots on her white leather oxford shoes and splatters on the floor. But the grocer paused, as if uncertain whether or not to believe her.

The woman who had alerted the whole store thrust a tissue at Clary. Muttering thanks, she took it. But the tissue was soaked in a split second, with no effect whatsoever on staunching the flow.

Seeing that, the grocer said, "We have to get you across the street!" Only this time he put his arm around her shoulders in insistence.

The last thing in the world Clary wanted was to meet up with Beau at that moment or under those circumstances. But her head was bleeding so fast and furiously that it was oozing out between the fingers of the hand she'd placed to the wound, and before she knew it she was climbing the two steps to his front door.

"We need some help here!" the grocer said, as he steered Clary inside.

She could feel both patients turn to stare at her, while the receptionist and Skokie rushed to her at once.

There was very little pain and Clary knew this wasn't as serious as it must look to everyone. She kept trying to tell them all that, but no one seemed to hear her. Skokie took over from the grocer, clamping his arm around her as the receptionist orchestrated getting her back into one of the examining rooms.

"I'm really okay," Clary said for what seemed like the hundredth time. "I can walk fine. I'm not even shaky. I just need something to mop up with."

But still Skokie and the receptionist ignored her words.

"Beau!" the dentist called. "We need you in here now!"

"No, really! I'm fine!"

The nurse joined them, and between her and Skokie they half lifted, half forced her onto the examining table.

"Lie back," the nurse ordered.

"I just need a bunch of tissues. Or a towel, maybe?"

Beau came in then and everyone stepped away from the table. "Clary? Is that you?"

She wished to God it wasn't. "Yeah, it's me."

"What happened?" he demanded as he parted her hair in search of the wound.

"I walked into the corner of a shelf at the store," she said simply, feeling as if even in that brief statement she was confessing what she'd really been up to. "It's not a big deal. I'm not even hurt. I'm just a mess."

"You sure are," he agreed with a laugh. Then, to the room in general, he said, "She's right, this isn't as bad as it looks. If you'll all clear out of here I'll get her taken care of."

There was marginal relief in the crowd dispersement and the sound of the door closing her and Beau in alone. But Clary still felt ridiculous. It was bad enough to walk into a shelf, but to do it because she was behaving like a schoolgirl with a crush on a football player only made it worse. Especially when she ended up under the care and scrutiny of the football player.

Beau came back with a cold, wet towel, which he held to her head, applying slight pressure to the wound. "Let's get the bleeding slowed down first, so I can see if you need stitches. How are you feeling? Dizzy? Light-headed? Sick to your stomach?"

Stupid. But that wasn't on the list. "No, none of that. Just a slight headache." Which was probably more from tension.

He took the towel away and leaned very near so that Clary was staring into his shirt front with her clear eye. "That's the shape of the corner of a shelf, all right. But it doesn't look like it needs to be stitched."

"Great. I'll just get out of here, then." She started to sit up.

"Hold on," he said, pressing her back down. "Don't be in such a hurry. It needs to be washed out and I want you to lie still for a while and let that bleeding really stop."

Since he wasn't giving her any choice, Clary relented, watching him as he gathered what he needed to scrub the wound. "I'm not going to like this part, am I?"

"If you did, you'd be the first. But I'll be gentle."

That last had been said with a devilish wink that almost made the pain that followed worth it. Clary endured it with her eyes closed much of the time, appreciating that he was being as careful as he possibly could.

When he was finished, he returned the soap, swabs, cotton balls and pan he'd used to the counter, rinsed the towel from before and came back with it.

"Head wounds always bleed a lot," he informed her, as he began to wash the blood out from around her eye. When he'd managed that he said, "How's your vision?"

"Fine." Good enough to enjoy the sight of him. Why did the man have to be so terrific-looking? He wore a white shirt under his lab coat and his tie had small green swirls on it that made his eyes seem all the more vivid.

"You're not seeing double are you?" he asked.

"No." And it was a good thing, because one of him was enough to make her heart race.

From cleaning her eye, he went to work on the rest of her face. He had a tender touch that was very soothing. And very arousing, though Clary was sure she'd gone crazy to think so.

"Were you just not watching where you were going?" he said, interrupting her thoughts.

She nodded. "Guess I'm a klutz."

He'd cleaned most of her face by then. Setting the towel beside her, he went over to the counter to get an ophthalmoscope, using it to peer into her eyes, each in turn. "Is there any chance you blacked out and fell into the shelf?"

"None at all."

He straightened away from her again. "Well, you look okay," he said finally, taking the towel and the scope back to the counter, where he again rinsed the towel.

As he stood there Clary glanced over at him, hoping for a glimpse of his great rear end. But the lab coat obscured it, and instead she had to satisfy herself with a look at his broad shoulders.

Hopeless, Clary, you're hopeless, she told herself. Trying to get a peek at him was what had gotten her into this predicament in the first place. And here she was, lying on an examining table with a head wound to show for it, full of blood and still trying to ogle him.

He turned and came back with the towel once more, beginning to work at the blood on her neck.

"You must have more important things to do," she said. "If you want to go I can just lie here a minute and then leave."

Those kiwi green eyes of his looked into hers and he smiled devilishly. "I don't have anything I'd rather do."

The blood had run down the front of her shirt and he followed it with the towel, reaching just inside the open top to wash her collarbone and the area of her chest just above her breasts.

Clary's heart was pounding even harder than before, and apparently he could feel it because his ministrations slowed there.

"Are you sure you're feeling all right?" he asked.

She tried to control her body's response to his touch. "Fine," she said, her voice a deep, more sensual sound.

Very slowly he pulled his hand and the towel with it from the neckline of her shirt, trailing back up to her throat. Was she only imagining that the action was no longer that of washing, but more of a caress?

Then he took the towel away completely and pressed his hand to the side of her neck, finding her pulse. "Your heart is beating pretty fast."

She swallowed hard. "It doesn't have anything to do with colliding with that shelf," she managed, embarrassed to admit it, but worried that she might be more embarrassed if he decided there was cause for further physical examination.

He grinned down at her. "Are you telling me I'm turning you on, Parsons?"

She closed her eyes and made a mortified face. "Give me a break, will you?"

He laughed, a low chuckle from deep in his chest. "I'd like to give you a lot more than a break."

She tipped her head up far enough to glance at her bloody clothes. "I know, I'm just sexy as hell at the moment."

"You're sexy as hell all the time," he said in a way that left her unsure of whether or not he was teasing her. "Now lie back until I tell you to move," he finished in a mock menacing tone.

He gently parted her hair to study the wound again. "I think we can put a Band-Aid on it to get you home." When he'd done that, he took her hand and helped her sit up. "How do you feel now?"

"Ready to take on the world."

He motioned toward her clothes. "You look like you already have."

"Can I clean up a little here before I go?"

"Sure. I'd like to see how you do on your feet for a few minutes before you leave, anyway."

He kept hold of her arm as she got down, only letting go when he knew she was steady. Then he propped one hip on the corner of the table while Clary went to the sink to assess the damage.

No wonder they'd rushed her to a doctor, she thought at the first sight of herself in the mirror above the sink.

"There are towels in the cupboard to the right," Beau said.

It didn't help her embarrassment any to have him sit there and watch as she finished what he'd started, washing her face, neck and hands completely clean. There was nothing she could do with her bloodstained clothes, and after a few futile attempts to mop at them, she gave up.

Then she turned back to Beau. "Shall I pay out front?"

He smiled again. "For what? The Band-Aid? We give them out free around here." Then he shoved away from the edge of the table and walked over to her. "And for my services, I want the payment in person."

Clary took a step back and shot a glance down at herself. "You don't really want to come too close, do you?"

"A little closer, yeah," he said as he did just that.

She made a face and waved him off, stepping backward another pace. "I'll get blood on you."

"The part I'll settle for today is clean," he said, staring pointedly at her mouth.

He had her backed into a corner, by then, and his hands came up to the wall on either side of her head. "You're sure you feel all right?" he asked, as if he just wanted to make sure one last time before dropping all medical pretense.

Clary gave up trying to warn him away from her messy state and smiled slyly instead. "I'm sure. But isn't it unethical for a doctor to exact this kind of payment from a patient?"

"Absolutely," he agreed without remorse. He kissed her temple just below her wound and then dropped another on the tip of her nose. "But you want to compensate me, don't you?"

"Well, I do always pay my debts." She let her eyes drift closed and breathed in the scent of his after-shave, enjoying it far more on the man than she had on his shirt earlier.

His mouth came down over hers then, once, twice, softly, sweetly. He tasted faintly of mint, and his lips were warm and smooth. Clary reached a now-clean hand to the side of his face, reveling in the texture of his clean-shaven cheek as he coaxed her lips to part for him. He traced the tip of her teeth with his tongue for a moment before plunging inside and deepening the kiss.

One hand came away from the wall and he placed it along the side of her neck, much the way he had when he'd checked her pulse. But there was something different in this touch, something intimate. Like warm honey, he slid his hand lower, inside the collar of her shirt, until it curved around the spot where her neck dipped into her shoulder. His thumb made small circles in the hollow of her throat and then swung down lower to that part of her chest where he'd touched her before, but with the towel separating his hand from her skin. This was infinitely better, and streaks of lightning shot through her in response.

Maybe she was feeling a little light-headed, after all, Clary thought. But her health had nothing to do with it.

She let her head fall farther back and opened her own mouth to his, hungry for his kiss, for him.

It seemed like agony to have any distance at all between them, but with her clothes in the state they were in, she could hardly expect Beau to pull her up against him. And the only immediate solution wasn't an option. But, oh, to have him hold her close, to feel his skin against hers! She craved it more than she'd ever craved anything in her life!

She raised her other hand to the opposite side of his face, as if that might bring him nearer, her back arching instinctively, as if her breasts were reaching out to him. In fact, she'd have given just about anything to feel his hand slip inside her shirt....

And then suddenly the voices of his nurse and receptionist in the hallway just outside the door reminded Clary where she was.

Beau must have had the same realization because, with a deep, quiet groan, he ended the kiss, lightly pressing his forehead to hers. "Maybe I need *my* head examined," he muttered more to himself than to her. Then he pushed away from her. "I didn't bring my car in today, but I think my nurse might have hers. I'll get her to drive you home."

"It's okay. I can walk."

He shook he head. "No, you can't. And if your headache gets worse or your vision blurs or anything seems out of the ordinary I want to know about it."

"I think I liked the part where I wasn't a patient better than the parts where I am."

He grinned and kissed her once more, fleetingly. "Me, too." Then he opened the door a crack, stopped and looked at her again. "We're still on for Dori's play in Greeley tomorrow, aren't we?"

"I wouldn't miss it," she assured him, thinking that seeing him now only made the time until she would be with him again seem all the longer.

He stared at her for a moment, as if he were considering closing the door and coming back for a second round of what they'd been doing before to tide him over until the next day. Or maybe that was just how Clary read it, because it was what she wished he'd do.

But then he swung the door all the way open with determination and bellowed for his nurse instead, disappearing down the hallway.

Chapter Six

When Beau arrived at Izzy's house the next day, Clary wasn't quite ready. And not only because he was ten minutes early. It wasn't easy to know what outfit would take her from visiting his patients on the outlying farms that afternoon into the play that evening.

Of course the choice wasn't made any easier by the fact that she was dressing for Beau. Not just any old thing would do.

After much deliberation, she settled on a black jumpsuit she'd brought with her. The armholes were cut at a sharp angle to a simple crewneck, and at the waist she wore a plain matching belt.

But with the evening in mind, she packed her purse with a bright scarf to tie around her neck, a dozen bracelets and a second belt, this one a hip-hugger with a polished gold buckle.

Lastly, she french-braided her hair so that it would stay looking neat through all the hours ahead of her, careful to camouflage the cut on her head. Then she dusted a little blush across her cheekbones and applied just a hint of pale lipstick.

"That's not good, Iz. Let's take it again in your other arm to see if the reading is right," Beau was saying to Izzy when Clary finally found them in the kitchen. He had his stethoscope in his ears and the blood-pressure cuff on her cousin's arm.

"Is everything okay?" Clary asked, immediately concerned by what she'd overheard and the frown on Beau's face.

But the minute he glanced up at her his expression eased and he smiled. "Our mom-to-be is spiking a higher BP than usual today." He transferred the cuff and took another reading.

"It's those french fries I had before bed last night," Izzy whispered. "I thought it was okay as long as I didn't salt them, but Beau says the preservatives in some frozen foods will do the same thing." She shrugged. "How was I supposed to know? I've never had this problem before."

"Well, you have it now," he said when he'd finished and was replacing his instruments in his bag.

"Is it dangerously high?" Clary asked.

"Not dangerously, no. Don't get alarmed. It's just higher than it was the last time I took it." He checked Izzy's puffy hands and ankles.

"Maybe she should come to Greeley with us today and see her obstetrician."

"No way," Izzy said. "I have class schedules to do."

"Then I'll stay home so you won't be here alone."

"That's nuts," her cousin proclaimed. "Tell her that's nuts, Beau."

"That's nuts, Clary," he repeated by rote. Finished with his exam, he turned to Clary and clasped the back of her neck. "This is not a big deal. Now sit down and play patient number two."

"I'm fine. Just take care of Izzy."

"I'm finished with Izzy. But you're not fine until I say you are. So that makes it your turn," he insisted.

Clary didn't have much choice as he maneuvered her into sitting on the edge of the breakfast nook's bench seat. "I just combed my hair," she complained and warned at the same time.

"I'll be careful," he said, as if it were a ridiculous request.

She was left staring at his leather belt as he explored her wound. It was hooked through the loops of a pair of khaki slacks with crisp creases down each long leg.

"Ouch!" she said, when he touched the gumball-sized lump on her head.

"Sorry."

She'd glanced up when he'd hurt her and now her gaze settled on his shirt. It was pale yellow, the long sleeves rolled to his elbows.

He patted her hair back in place and stepped away. "It looks pretty good."

So did he, she decided, noticing how the light shade of the shirt set off his dark coloring. She wondered if he'd come straight from a morning at the office, thinking that he must not have because he seemed so fresh. But one way or the other, he was very appealing.

Clary checked her hair in the side of the toaster as Beau closed his bag and gave Izzy instructions to stay off her feet and watch what she ate today. Then he turned to Clary. "Ready?"

Ready, willing and anxious. But still concern for her cousin made her hesitate. "You're sure I shouldn't stay here with Iz?"

Beau looked at Izzy and rolled his eyes. "Why do you suppose she refuses to believe your condition is not dire and immediately dangerous?"

"Beats me," Izzy answered with a shrug. "But she fusses over me like I'm on the verge of death, no matter what you or I tell her."

Beau stared straight into Clary's eyes and spoke firmly. "Once and for all—Izzy will be fine."

"Okay. So, let's go," Clary said, as if they'd both read too much into her concern. Then, just to show them, she grabbed her purse, breezily told her cousin to have a nice day and went out to Beau's waiting four-by-four.

"All set?" he asked her as he joined her.

"If you're sure it's okay to leave Izzy," she couldn't help saying, in spite of her display to make him think she was taking her cousin's high blood pressure lightly.

"I'm absolutely positive," he answered, as he started the engine and backed out of the driveway.

The weather couldn't have been more ideal if they'd ordered it direct. Spring was alive in the bright greens of budding crops, the sky was a cloudless canopy of crystal-clear blue, and the air was sun-warmed to perfection and spiced with the fresh smell of clover.

With very few exceptions, they had the ribbon of road to themselves. Beau popped a tape into the car stereo, sending low notes of soft jazz music to waft around them. Then he settled into his driving, his left elbow resting on the top of the door to poke out the open window, his big right hand holding the steering wheel at one o'clock.

"How many patients do you have to see this afternoon?" Clary asked, wishing there were a reason for her to sit in the center of the four-by-four's bench seat the way she had on the drive home from the shower the other night.

"Depending on how long the visits take, I may stop in on seven or eight. I have a diabetic and a hypertensive out here who don't really need me at the moment—to my knowledge, anyway—but I'll check on them, if we have the time."

The fact was, Clary realized as the afternoon wore on, that Beau made the time to see all his patients and to spend as long with each of them as they needed.

Seeing him in action, he was pretty impressive. Not only was he a good doctor, but she thought that his bedside manner alone could have cured a number of ailments.

No one could have asked for a more compassionate and caring physician. Or friend, for that matter. He was welcomed into every home like a visiting son or brother, which was just how he responded. He teased, cajoled, coaxed and kindly reprimanded. He also spent as much or more time asking questions about crops, the farmers' market, family members and goings on, as he did about everyone's health.

Clary couldn't help comparing him with her own doctor at home. She'd been going to her for years, and the woman still had to check her chart in order to recall her name, let alone anything else about her. And when Clary talked to her, she always had the feeling she wasn't really listening, and was only in a hurry to get her out to the desk where she could pay.

As for the matter of Beau's fee—some of his patients wrote him a check on the spot, but for those who couldn't, he put them at ease by saying they could catch up to him later. And in one instance he refused payment, when it was offered by a woman who clearly couldn't afford it. Instead, he insisted that he would far rather have a jar of her

NO RISK, NO OBLIGATION TO BUY ... NOW OR EVER!

CASINO JUBILEE
"Scratch'n Match" Game

Here's how to play:

1. Peel off label from front cover. Place it in space provided at right. With a coin, carefully scratch off the silver box. This makes you eligible to receive two or more free books, and possibly other gifts, depending upon what is revealed beneath the scratch-off area.

2. You'll receive brand-new Silhouette Special Edition® novels. When you return this card, we'll rush you the books and gifts you qualify for ABSOLUTELY FREE!

3. If we don't hear from you, every month we'll send you 6 additional novels to read and enjoy months before they are available in bookstores. You can return them and owe nothing but if you decide to keep them, you'll pay only $2.96* per book, a saving of 43¢ each off the cover price. There is **no** extra charge for postage and handling. There are **no** hidden extras.

4. When you join the Silhouette Reader Service™, you'll get our subscribers-only newsletter, as well as additional free gifts from time to time just for being a subscriber!

5. You must be completely satisfied. You may cancel at any time simply by sending us a note or a shipping statement marked ''cancel'' or by returning any shipment to us at our cost.

YOURS FREE!

This lovely heart-shaped box is richly detailed with cut-glass decorations, perfect for holding a precious memento or keepsake—and it's yours absolutely free when you accept our no-risk offer.

CASINO JUBILEE
"Scratch'n Match" Game

SCRATCH HERE

PLACE LABEL HERE

?

CHECK CLAIM CHART BELOW FOR YOUR FREE GIFTS!

YES! I have placed my label from the front cover in the space provided above and scratched off the silver box. Please send me all the gifts for which I qualify. I understand I am under no obligation to purchase any books, as explained on the opposite page.

(U-SIL-SE-11/92) 235 CIS AGNF

Name _____

Address _____ Apt. _____

City _____ State _____ Zip _____

CASINO JUBILEE CLAIM CHART	
🍒🍒🍒	WORTH 4 FREE BOOKS, FREE HEART-SHAPED CURIO BOX PLUS MYSTERY BONUS GIFT
🍒🔔🍒	WORTH 3 FREE BOOKS PLUS MYSTERY GIFT
🔔🔔🍒	WORTH 2 FREE BOOKS

CLAIM N° **1528**

▼ DETACH AND MAIL CARD TODAY! ▼

SILHOUETTE ''NO RISK'' GUARANTEE

- You're not required to buy a single book—ever!
- You must be completely satisfied or you may cancel at any time simply by sending us a note or a shipping statement marked ''cancel'' or by returning any shipment to us at our cost. Either way, you will receive no more books; you'll have no obligation to buy.
- The free books and gift(s) you claimed on the ''Casino Jubilee'' offer remain yours to keep no matter what you decide.

If offer card is missing, please write to: Silhouette Reader Service™ P.O. Box 1867, Buffalo, N.Y. 14269-1867

▼ DETACH AND MAIL CARD TODAY! ▼

BUSINESS REPLY MAIL
FIRST CLASS MAIL   PERMIT NO. 717   BUFFALO, NY

POSTAGE WILL BE PAID BY ADDRESSEE

SILHOUETTE READER SERVICE
3010 WALDEN AVE
PO BOX 1867
BUFFALO NY 14240-9952

NO POSTAGE
NECESSARY
IF MAILED
IN THE
UNITED STATES

pickles, taking them in exchange for an ample supply of the medicine he wanted her to take, as well.

And all through the afternoon of watching him at work, Clary not only gained a greater respect for him, she found herself feeling as proud of him as if she had a right to, discovering in that that she was coming to care for this man a great deal. Over and above her attraction to him.

It was after seven that evening by the time Beau pulled away from the last farmhouse. He and Clary had arrived right at mealtime and of course they'd been asked to eat. Mindful of the fact that he'd promised to buy Clary dinner, he declined, intent on quickly removing the cast from the arm of the ten-year-old boy who was his patient and leaving. But the boy's parents had insisted and in the end Clary had been a good sport and agreed that they should stay.

And now, on the last stretch of quiet highway to Greeley, Clary had dozed off against the door to the passenger side of his car, making Beau wonder if she was sleeping any better at night. Probably not, he decided, if she needed a nap.

He took his eyes from the road long enough to glance at her. She looked so peaceful. So beautiful. Even with her mouth slightly open. And he felt a tug on his heart.

There was no denying his feelings for her. Feelings that were gaining strength at an incredible rate.

Never before had he had it this bad for any other woman, he realized. Not even Gina, though he felt a twinge of guilt to admit that even to himself.

He'd loved Gina, it wasn't that he hadn't. And he'd desired her. But what was happening inside him over Clary was more intense. Hotter. Beyond all reason or rationale.

Beyond his control.

With Gina, there had been love tempered with practicality. Wellsburg didn't offer a wide choice of available women, and not just any woman wanted to live in a small town or could acclimate herself to it.

And there had been Dori, too.

Beau had been especially fond of the little girl, right from the start. He and the child had just clicked.

Together, Gina and Dori had been a package he wanted. And not once had he been sorry for inviting them into his life. Not even when his marriage had ended so soon and he'd been left alone to raise a child who wasn't his own. Not even now, when he and the teenager were so at odds.

A truck hauling a horse trailer passed him just then, honking and waving.

Beau waved back through the open window, then he looked over at Clary to see if the horn had disturbed her. Her brow wrinkled up for a moment, but her eyes remained closed, and she wiggled a little, snuggling deeper into the seat. Lord, how he wished she was snuggling deeper into his arms, into his side. In bed with him.

He cleared his throat and forced his eyes back to the road.

There had been other women since Gina. Women he'd cared about. But none of those feelings had been so overwhelming. None had the power of a speeding train. And not one of those women had monopolized his thoughts the way Clary had since her arrival. They hadn't distracted him all day long and then tormented him in his dreams at night, as Clary had. Certainly there hadn't been anyone he'd wanted so much that he woke up in a sweat over it.

And there she was, next to him, within arm's reach.

He only glanced from the corner of his eye this time, thinking about the two occasions when he'd actually had her in his arms. Agony and bliss. Bliss to have her there, to have her kissing him back with abandon, holding on to him in a way that let him know she wanted him as much as he wanted her. But agony not to let it go any further, to know that having her within arm's reach was short-lived.

He couldn't do anything to control his feelings—they were snowballing, no matter how hard he tried to stop them. But his actions were another story. So far, anyway. Those he could leash. And he had. Maybe not as successfully as he had fifteen years ago, but he sure as hell hadn't taken the physical part of their relationship as far as he wanted to.

Because the fact was that he couldn't forget that they led two completely different lives in two different states, and that the time would come when she went back to that city where she'd made her home, where no matter how much he wanted her or needed her, he couldn't have her, where she wouldn't be within arm's reach.

The trouble was, he thought, that his attraction to her now was so different than the passing thoughts he'd had about her all that time ago.

And keeping his distance was getting tougher and tougher.

In fact, it was getting just about impossible.

Instead of the nightmare that had been tormenting Clary over the past month and keeping her from getting much sleep, she was dreaming she was on a sailboat. The sun was warm on her face, the boat glided through the water, she was lounging on a deck that was somehow cushioned so her body could sink into softness, and she was so comfortable. So relaxed. So carefree.

She heard her name called by a deep baritone voice. Beau. She hadn't known he was on board, but it was a wonderful realization, and her first thought was that maybe he'd come and lie with her. Hold her. Kiss her. Make love to her.

Oh, yes, that would be perfect. Maybe he would finally feed this craving she had for him....

Then he called to her a second time and she woke up.

"I was sleeping," she said, as if it came as a surprise.

"For the past half hour. I hated to wake you, but we'll be at the theater in five minutes."

"No, I'm glad you did," she assured him. "I want to spruce up a little."

She used those next five minutes to transform her outfit, exchanging belts, slipping bracelets over her left wrist, wrapping the scarf around her neck twice and then tying a knot at the hollow of her throat.

By the time Beau pulled into the theater lot she had smoothed her hair, blotted the shine on her face and reapplied blush and lipstick.

Beau parked, stopped the engine and turned to look at her. His face erupted into a smile. "Very nice. You even look rested—quite a trick to accomplish with only a short nap."

"I didn't mean to fall asleep on you."

"I wish you had fallen asleep *on* me," he said with a lascivious half grin. "You must have needed the rest. Are you still having insomnia?"

She shrugged. "It's no big deal."

His expression seemed to say that he didn't believe that. But he let it drop. Instead, he pointed at the glove compartment directly in front of her. "Would you hand me the comb, shaver and smelly stuff out of there? My turn to spruce up."

He'd flipped down his visor by the time she set all he asked for on the seat between them. Tucked neatly behind two straps on the backside of the visor was a tie that he slipped out and laid with everything else on the seat. Then he picked up the shaver and applied it to the shadow of his beard.

Clary watched without compunction, enjoying the sight too much to care that she was staring. It struck her as very intimate somehow. And very sexy.

When he was finished he poured just a little after-shave into his palm, rubbed his hands together and then patted it onto his cheeks. As he did the clean scent filled the car and went right to Clary's head.

Next he slid the comb through his hair with four careless swipes and tossed it into the still-open glove compartment. Clary watched again as he pointed his chin to the visor mirror and fastened to top button of his shirt. Then he raised the collar to brush the sharp angle of his jawbone and reached for his tie.

She was no good at knotting them, and yet Clary had an inordinate urge to do so. She didn't understand it, but she itched to perform the service for him. Barring that, when he'd finished and folded down his collar over it, she reached to straighten the back even though there was no need, just to have the contact and a little of the proprietary pleasure.

One last glance in his mirror and he snapped the visor back into place. "Ready?" he asked, smiling at her.

Clary discovered she could only return his smile and nod, because she was too aroused by the simple sight of his grooming to trust her own voice not to give her away. She took the opportunity of his coming around to open her door to clear her throat.

The fact that Beau held her elbow as they crossed the parking lot didn't help her composure any. His warm hand on her bare skin was suddenly an erotic sensation that enlivened her every nerve.

Get a grip, Parsons, she told herself. But it wasn't a simple task with the all-over tingling sensation he was imparting through her.

The auditorium theater was nearly full, but Dori had had front-row seats held for them. The lights were dimming just as an usher led the way in.

Beau's broad shoulders were a slightly wider span than the seat back, edging over onto Clary's side. She didn't mind. In fact, she had to fight to just leave the contact casual, when she really wanted to lean into him.

"Looks like we just made it," Beau whispered as the curtain rose. His breath was warm against her ear and it set off a chain reaction inside her. She crossed her legs to try dousing the sparks at the end of the chain, and forced herself to concentrate on the play.

That was only difficult until Dori came on stage.

As Clary watched the first half of *The Rainmaker* she found herself in awe of the teenager.

The girl had a certain something that made her stand out from the other players, making them all look like rank amateurs.

Clary had wondered about the strikingly pretty Dori in the role of the plain Lizzie, and while the lack of stage makeup and the severe bun into which her hair was pulled aided the cause, the impression of her as unattractive came through in her acting. She made the audience feel the emotions of a woman who saw herself as ugly and that left little awareness of her actual fine features.

By the time the curtain fell for intermission and the houselights were lit, Clary had a fuller understanding of the girl's desire to put all her energies into her acting. But she picked her words carefully as Beau angled in his seat and asked her what she thought of his daughter's performance.

"She's very talented. She makes it hard to remember that offstage she's just a kid."

Beau nodded. In his expression there seemed to be a mixture of pride and something else that made him look troubled underneath. "She's even better than the last time I saw her perform. And you're right—offstage she's just a normal, energetic teenager, an adult one minute and an unreasonable two-year-old the next. But up there—" he looked at the stage as if it were an island of temptation, "she's in complete command, isn't she? She's in her element. There are no doubts, no insecurities."

Clary had the feeling that he was coming closer to a realization, or maybe an acceptance, of his daughter's talents. But she could tell it wasn't easy for him. "Are you wondering if you've made the right stand in insisting on college?"

He drew his glance from the stage back to her, smiling. "It'd be pretty hard to watch her tonight and not wonder, wouldn't it?"

"Does that mean you're changing your mind?"

"No, it doesn't." And he didn't even need to think about it before he answered.

"You still want her to forego acting for school, then?"

"I never wanted that. All I ask is that she get her education along with pursuing the acting. I don't think that's unreasonable."

"It isn't," Clary said, without hesitation herself, because she agreed with him. "I know you just want what's best for her all the way around, that you're only looking out for her future. I think Dori must realize that, too, deep down."

He let out a wry chuckle. "Not that my wanting what's best for her or her realizing it has any effect on her."

"She isn't looking at the future. She's looking at the here and now. She's a kid with a dream."

"That's why I have to take the stand I have."

"But she'll be eighteen soon—"

"On Sunday."

"And what happens when she's legally of an age to make her own decision?"

Beau took a deep breath and dropped his head back, before blowing it out in a way that let her see his frustrations and worry. "I don't know. I honestly don't know," he said just as the lights dimmed and the curtain rose again.

When the play was over, Clary and Beau went backstage. It was hard for Clary to believe the same person who had had such presence onstage could be found giggling with her girlfriends in the dressing room not ten minutes later. But there she was.

One of the other girls spotted Clary and Beau standing in the doorway and alerted Dori. She half skipped to meet them, her face beaming.

"Well, how was I?" she asked.

"You were great, baby," he said, taking her by the arms and pulling her close to kiss her forehead.

Dori came away looking surprised. Sudden tears glistened on the very cusp of her lids. She clasped her father's arm as if to keep him close a moment more, and Clary saw a suspicious shimmer in Beau's eyes, too.

It touched her to see what was between them in spite of their disagreement over the teenager's future. She didn't offer any words of praise because she didn't want to intrude. And, in truth, she couldn't have anyway, because seeing them had put a lump in her own throat.

But then Dori blinked back her tears and seemed to latch onto Clary to bridge the rising tide of emotions. "What did you think, Clary?"

"I thought you were wonderful," she said very quietly.

"Good enough to turn pro?"

"Better than anyone else on that stage," Clary hedged because she knew she was in dangerous territory. She was grateful when Beau stepped in before his daughter could pursue the subject any further.

"You're riding back to town with Danielle and the other girls?"

Dori's excitement apparently left her immune to the fact her direct question to Clary had only garnered an indirect answer, because she turned excited eyes back to Beau. "Yeah, and then there's a party at the Fitzwaters' house."

Beau gave some fatherly warnings to be careful, agreed with one of Dori's friends who joined them to marvel at Dori's acting, and then Clary and Beau said good-night and headed for the car.

By the time they got there, Beau had pulled his tie off and loosened the collar of his shirt. It was an appealing sight—and not just because his open top button showed off more of his oh-so-masculine throat. He looked more comfortable and Clary wanted some of that for herself. She removed the scarf from around her neck as he got behind the wheel and started the engine.

They passed even fewer cars on the way back to Wellsburg, driving miles and miles through nothing but sleeping fields, an occasional dark house and the indigo sky.

Clary and Beau rode along in companionable silence for a while. The windows were down to let in the clean, sweet-smelling air with just the slightest hint of coolness to it. The quiet hum of the car barely disturbed the peaceful stillness of the night—even the radio was off as if it might wake someone.

Clary had a new awareness of the flat ground that seemed to be met just up ahead by the star-flecked sky, appreciating the sight as she never had before.

"What are you smiling about?" Beau asked.

She hadn't realized she was, or that he'd looked over and caught her at it. "I was just thinking about the nights Izzy and I would come out here to get away from the Burg. We'd sneak two bottles of beer from her parents' refrigerator and drive until we couldn't see the lights from town anymore. Then we'd pull into a cleared field, sit on the hood of the car and talk and talk."

"That sounds a lot nicer than the male version."

Clary glanced at him, thinking that he seemed so far away at the other end of the bench seat and wishing he were closer. "What was the male version?"

"A group of us would all pile into the back of some-body's truck, come out here and drink enough beer to float a tanker, lie about female conquests, hoot and holler and behave like wildmen trying to outdo each other, being rude and crude to prove what tough guys we were, along with participating in some competitions I wouldn't want to give graphic details of."

The wheat fields on either side of the road gave way to a fallow stretch of land just then, and Beau slowed the car to turn off onto it, driving far away from the road.

"Let's try your version," he suggested as he stopped the engine and turned off the headlights.

Clary had no complaint with that. She got out of the four-by-four without waiting for Beau to come around and open her door, meeting him at the front of the car.

He held his hand out to take hers, helping her climb from the bumper onto the hood.

Clary sat with her back against the windshield, watching as Beau joined her, ending up very close beside her.

"This is nice, all right," he said, resting his head on the glass to look up at the sky.

They were far enough from the highway that the streetlights there were nothing more than a faint glow in the distance. That left only the moonlight to cast a blue white haze over everything.

Clary glanced at Beau, studying his profile. Deep shadows made him look all the more handsome, the angles of his face seeming sharper.

"So what did you and Izzy talk about when you came out here?" he asked.

Not wanting to be caught staring at him, Clary, too, rested her head back and looked up at the sky. "The usual things. Hair, clothes, boys, the hideous injustice of having to take out the trash or fold laundry or meet a curfew. Sex."

"No! You sweet young things came out here and talked about *sex?*" he teased. "What could you have possibly found to discuss?"

Clary played along. "Who'd done the deed, who was doing it, who was thinking about doing it, who was pregnant because they had done it—"

Beau laughed. "What about you?"

"You mean was I doing it then?"

"Mmm," he confirmed.

"Not on your life. There was no way I was going to risk getting pregnant, having my grandmother force me to get married and ending up spending my life in *Wellsburg,*" she said, purposely sounding like the teenager she'd been when she'd made that decision.

Silence fell between them again. Wondering about it, Clary glanced at Beau. She found him frowning slightly.

But then he seemed to recover the lighter mood that had been between them. He looked at her from the corner of his eye and said, "So you lost your virginity in L.A. But I know it wasn't to good old Biff."

"How do you know?"

"Because I threatened him with his life if he touched you."

That made Clary smile. "No, it wasn't Biff. But it will ruin my image as the Los Angeles woman of the world if I tell you more than that."

"Do it anyhow," he coaxed, grinning at her in a way that caused her heart to skip a beat.

"I didn't lose my virginity until I was twenty-five and not before I was engaged to the guy," she said as if admitting to a crime.

"I didn't know you were engaged."

"For seven years. Actually, though, I think it was more like going steady grown-up style."

"How come you never made it to the altar?"

She shrugged. "We always put it off by mutual agreement—he was too busy, I was too busy, one of us wasn't sure, then the other wasn't. Then he was offered a big-deal job in Chicago. He wanted us to finally get married and me to move with him. But I wasn't willing to leave L.A. and all I'd built there, so we called it quits, instead. That was two years ago."

"And how's your love life been since then?"

She made a face. "Nonexistent. I realized, after getting cold feet on a couple of romantic evenings, that I'm carrying around a lot more small-town sensibilities than I thought I was—I just haven't been able to have casual sex."

"So there's only been one lover in your life?"

"I told you this would blow my image."

He took her hand, holding it between both of his and studying it. "I'm glad to hear there's still some small town in you."

For a moment Clary was lost in the feel of his big, powerful hands around hers. He ran his thumb across her knuckles in a slow, sensual way. She tried to ignore it and concentrate on making conversation instead.

"Okay, your turn. I don't want to be the only one here sharing secrets. Did you lose your virginity to a girl in Wellsburg?"

"Nope. I misplaced it on a trip to Greeley in my sophomore year of high school with an older woman—she was the seventeen-year-old cousin of a guy I knew there. And after that, well . . ."

"You managed to accumulate a few notches on your belt?"

"A few. Enough to teach me a long time ago that I'm strictly a one-woman man."

And Clary realized that she'd give just about anything to be that one woman.

He brought her hand to his mouth then, placing a feathery kiss there, a kiss so light it had no business setting fire to those sparks from before. Then he pulled her nearer, angling toward her as he did.

"You're doing some pretty incredible things to my insides, city girl," he said in a raspy tone.

"Then we're even," she answered, her own voice barely above a whisper.

He let go of her hand then, cupping the side of her neck instead, just as he leaned forward to kiss her.

Unlike before, there was nothing slow or tentative about this kiss. Instead it was instantly intense, demanding, hungry. His mouth was open wide, taking hers with a forcefulness that was heady all in itself, urging her lips to part so that his tongue could invade and conquer.

Clary lost herself in that kiss, anxious for it to go on forever. There was no doubt in it, no hesitation, no inhibition, unleashing desire in her like a brush fire.

She reached around to the nape of his neck, plunging her hand into the silkiness of his hair, feasting like a glutton on what he offered her as her body cried out for more—more of his touch, more than the feel of his thigh along hers or of his massive chest pressing her back into the windshield, their bodies separated by what suddenly seemed like so many clothes.

He still held her to the kiss with one hand at her jawbone, but his other was splayed against her back, and as if in answer to what Clary willed him to do, he slid it from there to her side, the heel just reaching the beginning mound of her breast.

Her back arched with a will of its own, urging him on, silently pleading for more, as her engorged flesh yearned to be taken into that expert hand all the while his mouth worked magic over hers.

And then he granted her wish, slowly, slowly coming to cup her breast in his big palm. Kneading, learning the contours, finding the hardened crest. But still her craving was only intensified by the barrier of her clothes until he finally, finally, reached into the angled arm opening of her jumpsuit to her naked breast.

She couldn't help the tiny groan that escaped her throat at the first feel of his hand on her bare flesh, her nipple kerneling into his palm not in retreat but in divine pleasure and a demand for still more.

And more was what she got as he nudged the fabric of her jumpsuit out of the way, freeing her breast to his seeking, powerful hand and then to his mouth as he drew her up onto his lap.

He circled her nipple with his tongue, teasing, gloriously tormenting, nibbling, sucking, pulling it far into his mouth and then deserting it to chill-dry in the cool night air while he nibbled his way around the sensitive-aureola.

Clary tugged his shirttail free and slid her hands under to his back, broad and hard and muscular. His skin was warm and silky enough for her hands to slip around his sides to find the curly hair on his chest and hardened nibs of his own.

But still she didn't feel as if she were getting enough of him.

"Beau—" she said in a breathy whisper. But she couldn't go on and instead only arched her back even farther, coming up against the long, hard shaft at her side that let her know he wanted her as much as she wanted him.

While his mouth went on tormenting her breast, he clasped her hip and pulled her more tightly against him, flexing there.

Clary grew bold enough to trail his side with her own hand, but only as far as his thigh, unable to reach for what she really wanted to hold.

And then, all of a sudden, he stopped.

He laid his cheek against the side of her bare breast and let out a soft, agonized groan before he drew away from her completely, staring off in the distance while he eased her top into place again.

"Why do you keep pulling back?" she blurted out in frustration, before she'd even thought of it.

But instead of answering her, Clary saw his Adam's apple rise and fall as he swallowed hard. His jaw clenched, and she had the feeling she was watching him fight a battle for control of what she didn't want him to control at all.

"You are frustrating me to death," she said, as the fires of desire still singed her from the inside.

He collapsed back against the windshield and breathed as if he'd been holding his breath a long time. "I'm doing a pretty good number on myself, too," he admitted in a voice that was rough around the edges.

"Why?"

She watched him shake his head, marveling at his oh-so-masculine beauty in the luminous glow of the moon. "I'm fighting hard not to lose my heart to you, Clary. I don't know how I'll be be able to live without it, if I let you take it back with you to L.A."

She didn't know what to say to that. She had come to Wellsburg for some time out. To escape. And she honestly hadn't thought beyond the moment since she'd arrived. She hadn't considered the fact that she would be going back to California and Beau would be staying here. Or that anything they started up would have to end.

It was a sobering consideration.

Beau slid off the hood of the car then. He reached for her hand and pulled her to the side, lifting her down with his hands around her waist. But the minute her feet touched the soil he let go.

Silently, he held open the passenger door for her. Then he rounded the four-by-four and got behind the wheel.

As he drove the rest of the way home, Clary felt heartsick herself. She cared for Beau. She was coming to care for him more and more by the minute. And there was no denying that she wanted him with a greater intensity than any man she'd ever known.

But that didn't change the fact that when the time came she'd be going back to L.A., and if it was possible that she'd be taking Beau's heart with her, there was an equal likelihood that she'd be leaving her own here with him.

They still hadn't exchanged a word as Beau pulled into the driveway at Izzy and Jack's house. Glancing up at Beau when he opened her door, she found his brow furrowed, his expression troubled, and she had the sense that he was debating with himself.

Then, as they walked up onto the porch, he sighed as if in surrender. "How about if you come to my place for dinner tomorrow night?"

That surprised her, and coming along with her own newly risen concerns about what was happening between them, Clary hesitated. "Is that wise? For either of us?"

"Probably not." He faced her under the porch light, taking her by the shoulders, his thumbs slipping just inside the arm openings of her jumpsuit to massage gently. "But I need to see you anyway."

She understood that need because she shared it. It overruled all else. "I'd like to have dinner with you tomorrow night," she said softly.

He nodded solemnly, as if they'd just entered into a very serious agreement. Then he kissed her, sweetly, chastely, lingering over her lips as if he were tempted to do more again.

But suddenly he ended it, taking a deep breath and sighing it out. "Seven?"

"I'll be there."

He stared at her, his bright green eyes delving into hers for a long moment before he finally said, "Good night, Clary."

Watching him leave, her body still cried out for him to soothe the yearning he'd provoked in her. She should be guarding against losing her heart to him, she knew.

But if it meant denying herself even a moment with him, she couldn't do it.

And then, again, maybe it was already too late.

Chapter Seven

It was late when Clary got up the next morning. The frustrating end of the previous evening had done nothing to help her insomnia and she hadn't fallen asleep until nearly four in the morning, only to be awakened at five by the nightmare that was tormenting her. After that, it had taken her another half hour or better to fall asleep again.

As she lay in bed trying to figure out just how late it was by the angle of the sun coming in through the crack in the curtains, she realized the house was still and quiet, like her condo at home every day. It gave her an unpleasant pang.

She hadn't realized how much she'd been enjoying getting up these past few mornings to the sounds of Izzy and Jack's chatter and Izzy clattering around the kitchen. And it was really nice to have someone to talk to rather than turning on the television for company. She'd never thought of herself as lonely, as Lois had, but now she realized in the contrast that there was an element of that to her life.

But rather than dwelling on it, Clary swung out of bed, threw on her sweat suit and went out to pour herself a cup of the coffee that scented the house with its fresh-brewed aromatic temptation. The back door was open, and through it she could see Izzy working in the garden.

For a moment she watched her cousin, flooded with old memories of good times shared. Funny how she'd taken them for granted when they were happening. Did all teenagers overlook those moments as they strove for the future and what they perceived as the freedom of adulthood?

Dori did, she suspected. Certainly Clary had. She'd been so intent on getting out of Wellsburg that she hadn't ever really stopped to appreciate the advantages and fun of adolescence.

Clary breathed in an ironic laugh at herself.

Who was she kidding? Striving for the future wasn't just what she'd wrapped herself up in as a kid, it had become a chronic condition with her.

Sure, she'd strived to leave Wellsburg. But once she was out of it, she'd strived to take care of herself in L.A. Then to open Biminis. Then to make it a success. Now to keep it a success.

Striving was what got her out of bed every morning, what propelled her through her day, what took up nearly every waking hour. To the exclusion of everything and everyone else.

But she wasn't going to do that anymore. She'd sworn it to herself. And to prove it, she was here, enjoying Izzy, appreciating Izzy, the way she should have all along, the way she intended to do from now on. The way she intended to appreciate and enjoy all the people in her life from now on.

Including Beau? a little voice in the back of her mind asked.

She was certainly enjoying and appreciating him.

But what about the other part of that vow to herself? The part that said she was going to nurture her relationships, rather than letting them die on the vine? The part where she was going to make her relationships top priority?

When she left here she'd make absolutely sure she called Izzy and wrote and kept in closer touch than she had in the past fifteen years.

But phone calls and letters wouldn't maintain what was growing between her and Beau, and knowing that put a knot in the pit of her stomach.

With her living in L.A. and Beau in Wellsburg there couldn't be much nurturing of their relationship, and she knew it wouldn't have a high place on any list of priorities—no long-distance romance did. Absence did not make the heart grow fonder, it just made people go on with their lives without the absentee. And when it came to romance that usually meant finding someone else.

So if she couldn't accept a relationship in her life that she knew she wouldn't end up nurturing or making a priority, she shouldn't pursue it, should she?

Probably not. Not when she'd seen what kind of damage the neglect could wreak.

And yet, her feelings for Beau were making him a priority whether she liked it or not. Whether she fought it or not.

Because no matter how illogical or ill-advised it was, she was afraid she might be falling in love with him.

Izzy glanced up just then and caught sight of her. "Oh, hi. You're awake," she called from outside.

"I didn't mean to sleep so late," Clary answered, as she took her coffee and joined her cousin.

"You must have needed the rest." Izzy sat back on her heels and slapped dirt off her hands. "There's nothing quite like mucking around in soil on a spring morning. Want to try it?"

Clary laughed and made a face. "Yuck." She pointed with her chin. "What are you planting?"

"Lettuce and radishes—probably what I'll have to live on after the baby is born, to get this weight off." She nodded toward the house. "You looked awfully deep in thought in there. Something on your mind?"

Clary shrugged. "You." And Beau. But she didn't add that. "I was thinking how much I've missed you."

Izzy laughed. "I've missed you, too. That's why I write so much. I'm always talking to you in my head, and then I just get the urge to put it down on paper—it makes me feel almost as if we're visiting."

Guilt stabbed Clary. "I'm sorry that I don't keep up with your letters more, and that I've let so much time go between calls. It doesn't mean I'm not thinking about you because I am—every day. I mean to write you every time I get a letter, but before I know it I have a stack of yours waiting to be answered and I still haven't done it."

Izzy laughed. "Do you think I'm keeping count?"

"I hope not. But it isn't going to happen anymore."

Her cousin frowned and looked at her as if she thought Clary was crazy. "Clary, I love you like a sister and I couldn't care less if I write two or three…or ten…letters to your one. It doesn't change anything between us."

"That means a lot to me," Clary said, thinking that she wished she had been the kind of friend to Lois that Izzy was to her, feeling very selfish that she hadn't. "I've let myself get too wrapped up in Biminis and lost sight of the people who are important to me. I'm glad to know that you haven't given up on me because of it."

"You lead a different life than we do here," Izzy allowed. "There isn't all that much to do in good old Wellsburg, you know. And believe me, there are times when I envy your busy life and the variety of people you must meet every day. Me, I've been in the same place with the same people since I was born."

"Izzy, I'm surprised at you," Clary said, as if she were scandalized. "Are you telling me you're not happy as a townie?"

"I'm happy. I wouldn't leave here for anything in the world. But sometimes I'd like a little more privacy. Surely you remember what it's like to have everybody in town know everything about everything. Sometimes it gets old."

"Mmm. If you'll recall, that's one of the many things about Wellsburg that drove me crazy as a kid. It seemed like I couldn't sneeze without there being four reports of it to my grandmother."

"It's still that way. And it can be stifling sometimes. For instance, when Jack and I finish a bottle of wine we have to make sure it's buried in a bag in the trash because it looks bad for the principal of the school to have an empty liquor container going out. If I don't hide it and someone sees it, as sure as I'm sitting here, I'll get a couple of calls complaining that I'm a bad example for the kids, and wanting to know how I can tell the high-schoolers not to drink when I do. I'll bet you don't have to worry about that, do you?"

"No, that wouldn't be a problem," Clary admitted with a laugh.

"I remember when we were kids and you found out what claustrophobia meant—you said it was another word for Wellsburg. Then, I thought you were nuts, but there are times now when I understand what you meant, when the walls close in around me and I wish for things you talk about in your letters—movies, theaters, lots of restaurants, a shopping mall . . ." Izzy laughed at herself.

"But on the other hand," Clary put in, "I've never been to a baby shower that could bring in almost a whole town, like yours the other night, either." Nor had she ever thought about the town as a supportive, protective extended family, which was what she was discovering it was. For Izzy, anyway. And for Beau.

"Am I imagining it, or are you saying something positive about Wellsburg?" Izzy asked with mock amazement.

"There are a few good things about it, I guess."

Izzy laughed again. "Now there's a concession, coming from you. Or are you referring to Beau and not to the town, at all."

Clary had to smile. "He's definitely one of the best things about Wellsburg."

"Have you slept with him yet?"

"Izzy!"

"I'm hoping he's going to make you his love slave so you'll stay," she said matter-of-factly.

"His love slave? Now that would be grist for the mill, wouldn't it?"

Izzy held out a hand for help getting to her feet and Clary gave it. "Beau might be worth getting talked about, who knows?"

Clary knew. He was definitely worth it. But she didn't say that. "I wouldn't want to cause a big scandal for the town doctor," she joked as they went into the house. "How would that look? Old Miss Crown would be afraid to go to him for her rheumatism, for fear he might seduce her."

"Then, again, there are a few women in town who would willingly give their gall bladder for that chance."

And that was not something Clary was happy to hear.

Beau accepted a refill on his coffee, but not a second doughnut, as Jack gave in to having his third of Sophie's special cinnamon twists.

"Don't say it," Jack warned, as Beau eyed the eight-inch concoction. "I'm eating for two."

Beau just nodded, responding to the "'Morning, Doc," of the hardware store's clerk as he came into the coffee shop.

"Izzy heard Clary come in last night. Pretty late," Jack said then.

"The play wasn't over until about ten-thirty. Then we had to drive all the way back. I didn't know she had a curfew."

"I'm supposed to ask what your intentions are."

Beau gave a short burst of laughter. "Izzy's nesting instincts at work?"

"Nah, I think she's just being nosy."

"Well, tell her my intentions are honorable. Not that it matters. I'm pretty low on the competition scale for the lure of the big city—with my daughter and no doubt with Clary, too."

"Did you and Clary have a fight?" Jack asked, clearly referring to Beau's disgusted tone of voice.

Beau took a drink of his coffee and waved in answer to yet another greeting. "No, we didn't fight. I'm just aggravated."

"With Clary?"

"With myself. I'm a grown man, for God's sake. I should be able to control what's happening with her. And instead, I'm crazy about her."

"What are you going to do about it?" Jack asked.

"Suffer," Beau said derisively. He raised his chin to the mayor's goodbye nod. When he went on, it was with resignation. "As far as I can tell, there's not a lot I can do about what's going on with Clary. Like I said, I'm no match for the lure of L.A. But on the other hand, I've tried to keep from having feelings for her, I've told myself to stay away from her, and I can't. Maybe I'm just a glutton for punishment." Beau finished his coffee. "Hell, I've just gone crazy. What else can I tell you?"

"Love'll do that to you."

Beau stopped a little short at that. Love? Was he in love with Clary? Lord, that was even worse. He was getting himself in big-time trouble. But he couldn't deny it, so instead he tossed two dollars on the table and stood. "I have to take off. I invited Clary to dinner tonight."

Jack laughed. "Oh, yeah, you're doing a really good job of staying away from her."

Beau shrugged. "Hey, I told you I was hopeless."

"You were right," Jack called after him as he left.

On his way home, Beau went by the grocery store to pick up two steaks, potatoes and a head of lettuce—what he considered a reasonably safe dinner to fix for a woman who made her living with food. Then he checked on a throat culture at the office, found it was positive and called the child's parent and the pharmacy for a prescription before he went home.

Dori was on the phone in the kitchen, the same place she'd been when he'd left to have breakfast with Jack this morning. Only in the meantime she'd fixed herself a bowl of cereal, leaving milk and raisins spotting the table, with shampoo, conditioner and a flood of water beside the sink and a school folder open on the counter.

"Dammit, Dori, clean your messes," he said, as he began to do it himself.

That was when he saw the college application in the pocket of the folder. The check for the application fee was still stapled to the corner, but rather than being filled in, there were doodles of palm trees and ocean waves all over the form.

Dori hung up just then, opened the refrigerator door and took out a stem of grapes. "I did some laundry because I needed my pink shirt clean, but there wasn't enough for a load, so I took the sheets off both of our beds and did those, too."

Beau just looked at her for a moment before picking up the application. "You were suppose to get this in to the dean."

This time it was Dori who didn't immediately answer. Instead, she poured herself a glass of orange juice and drank it as if she were dying of thirst.

"Dori—"

She put the glass down, but avoided looking at him. "Why would I send in the application when I'm not going to college? I'm going to L.A. The fee will buy my first week's groceries once I get there—you'll just have to write me another check."

He shook his head. "You have it all figured out, don't you?"

She shrugged. "You saw my performance last night. You said yourself how good I am. And so did Clary. Acting is what I'm suppose to do."

"I'm not going to argue this again, Dori."

"Good. Neither am I."

Beau took a deep breath and held it for a moment, debating with himself. He had one last card to play. He didn't want to use it. He hated to use it. Money as a weapon had never appealed to him. But that was all he had left.

"So your mind is made up? You won't go to college at all? Not even in Greeley for a semester, until you can transfer to UCLA and go on the way we planned?"

"I know this upsets you and I'm sorry. But it's my life."

He nodded very slowly. "You're right, this does upset me. I believe wholeheartedly that it's a mistake and that in the long run you'll regret it. But I guess you're also right that it's your life."

He saw her expression brighten with the assumption of victory.

There was a part of him—that same part that had always made sure she got everything she wanted for Christmas and birthdays and just about everything else that had ever come up—that wanted to simply give in. To accept defeat, pave the way for her, and be there to pick up the pieces if and when the need arose.

But there was another part of him. The part that had meted out punishment even when it hurt him more than it ever hurt her—the part that wouldn't let him take the easy way out.

"So you're going to let me go?" she asked hopefully, when he didn't finish what he'd started to say.

"I can't stop you after your turn eighteen tomorrow." Still he paused, storing up the strength to finish. Then he sighed and plunged in. "But I also won't help you."

Dori's brows pulled together suspiciously, instantly hostile. "What does that mean?"

"It means that if you do this," he said in a calm, quiet, deadly serious tone of voice, "if you refuse to go to college and just head for L.A. to be an actress—you're on your own. The money I would have used to pay for your education and your room-and-board isn't available to bankroll you while you try to get acting jobs."

"Oh, that's low!" she shouted, and it didn't help Beau at all to agree with her.

Still, he held his ground. "I'm sorry, Dori. But if this is what you're determined to do, you'll have to support yourself."

"Fine!" She threw her arms up in the air. "I'll just do that. If you think you can keep me from acting that way, you're wrong. I'll make it without your money. Keep it."

She slammed out the swinging door so hard it flip-flopped back and forth another half dozen times before it slowed and then stopped.

Beau stood there watching it, wishing to God he knew if he was doing the right thing.

Clary was late in leaving for Beau's house that evening because she couldn't decide on the position of the zipper that ran from her navel to her chin on the gray jumpsuit she'd chosen to wear.

Zipped all the way up it looked pretty forbidding— Hands off! it seemed to say.

And that was probably the message she should give, she told herself. It was one thing to enjoy Beau's company while she was in Wellsburg. But it was something else again to take that enjoyment to a physical level—no matter how much her body was craving it—when she knew this was only a temporary encounter.

But her body *was* craving it.

She pulled the zipper down to the beginning of her cleavage. But that looked like an open invitation she wasn't sure she wanted to make.

Instead she settled on zipping up to the base of her throat. Half mast. Half decided. Before she finally left.

Fifteen minutes later, Clary was just coming up the walk to Beau's house when Dori slammed out the front door. The teenager stopped short when she saw her.

"Oh, hi," Dori said, trying a smile that didn't quite work.

"Hi," Clary answered, the inflection of a question in the single word.

Dori seemed suddenly frozen in her tracks.

"Is everything okay with you?" Clary ventured.

"No! Everything is horrible! *He's* trying to ruin my life!" she said with an angry nod back at the house.

"Your dad?" Clary asked, as if she were walking through a mine field.

"He was going to pay for all of my college, plus room-and-board, anyway, so I planned on using that money for an apartment in L.A. and to keep myself going until I got acting jobs. But oh, no. Now he says he pays for college or nothing. If I don't go to school, I'm on my own. Have you ever heard anything so unfair?"

"I don't know that I'd say it was unfair—"

Dori didn't seem to hear her, charging on as if Clary hadn't said a word. "I can't believe he'd do this. He's trying to run my life! Will you talk to him, Clary? Please? Make him see that he's just being stupid. He was going to spend the money anyway, so what difference does it make if it's for college or not?"

Clary shook her head and held up her hands, palms outward. "Sorry, but it's not my place to get into this, Dori."

"Come on, please? Make him see he's being unreasonable. Maybe he'll listen to you."

"This is between you and your dad, kiddo."

Dori threw another disgusted look over her shoulder at the house. "He's so stubborn!" she shrieked, before storming off down the walk.

Clary went the rest of the way to the front door and found Beau standing behind the screen. If the troubled expression on his face was any indication, he'd heard his daughter's tirade.

"Seems like I've come at a bad time," Clary observed as he let her in.

"The last eight hours have been a bad time—we've been fighting since this morning."

"If you'd rather skip dinner tonight . . ."

Beau shook his head. "No, you being here is the only bright spot in this miserable day. And believe me, I need a bright spot." He drew a deep breath and blew it out, jamming both hands through his hair as he did. "Unless, of course, you think I'm a monster, too, and don't want to fraternize with me."

Clary took in the tight jeans that smoothed their way down his thighs, and the neon-white polo shirt that stretched across his broad chest, and she wanted to do a lot more than fraternize. "Some of my best friends are monsters," she said, fiddling with her zipper.

He smiled a little and for the first time Clary had the sense that he was focusing exclusively on her. "Lord, but it's good to see you."

She pointed a thumb over her shoulder at the front door. "You're sure you don't want to go after Dori and have this out?"

He shook his head. "Wouldn't do any good. Besides, she went to the all-night seniors' bash at the school and I think we both need some time-out."

Beau came to stand in front of Clary, resting his arms on her shoulders and bending to kiss her nose. "And I am definitely in need of some adult company. How about a glass of wine while I throw our steaks on the barbecue?"

"Sounds great."

He slid one arm around her waist and guided her through the living room into the connecting dining room, and then through a swinging door into a nondescript, functional kitchen done in oak and almond.

While Beau poured wine, Clary wandered to the open back door where the smell of hot charcoal wafted in. Outside, there was a large porch, with a bricked-in barbecue on one side. In the center were a table and chairs, with a huge umbrella over them.

"Your yard is gorgeous," she said, glancing out at the manicured lawn and the profusion of flowers already growing around the patio, bordering the redwood fence and in a tiered arrangement with a waterfall in the corner.

"Thanks, but I can't take credit. I pay to have it done," he explained as he handed her a wineglass. Then, from the refrigerator, he took a plate that held two steaks and pushed the screen open with his hip, holding it there for Clary to go through. "We can enjoy it while the steaks cook, though."

There was something very inviting about that lush green grass, and since she'd noticed that Beau was barefoot, Clary gave in to the urge to kick off her shoes before she traipsed over to the waterfall. Curling her toes into the lawn, she enjoyed the sight of crystal-clear water running down tiered moss rock. Then she heard the meat sizzle on the grill and turned back to Beau. He was rolling up blueprints that were spread out on the table.

"I'll bet those are plans for the house you're going to build on the lot next to Izzy and Jack," she guessed, as she went to sit on one of the big, padded chairs.

"Would you like to see them?" he offered, stopping in mid-roll.

"Sure."

"I came out here this afternoon to take a look at them and escape hearing Dori tell her tale of outraged woe to all of her friends on the telephone," he said, as he opened the architectural drawings again. "Take a look, while I get us set up for dinner."

He disappeared back into the house, while Clary did just that. When he returned he carried a tray, balancing plates, silverware, napkins, a salad and what looked like two steaming potatoes wrapped in foil. Clary helped him, and then went back to studying the blueprints.

"This looks like a pretty big place," she said.

"Three thousand square feet all together."

"Wow. Won't you sort of rattle around in it? I mean, one way or another, Dori won't be living with you for most of the time from here on."

He flipped the steaks and added the potatoes to the outer edge of the grill to keep them warm. "I don't plan to live in it alone forever."

"You're going to take in boarders?" she joked.

"I'd like to get married again, have a couple more kids. I deliver a fair share of babies, and more and more I have the urge to keep them. I think I'd like to raise one or two from the get-go—I missed that with Dori."

He joined her at the table, pulling his chair out to angle it toward her, propping his bare feet on the edge of her seat.

Clary didn't glance down directly, but she did peripherally as she sipped her wine. His toes were blunt, his feet long and square. And she found them unbelievably sexy.

"Don't you ever want kids, Clary?"

She shrugged and tried to forget about his naked feet so near her thigh. "Someday."

"The clock's ticking, you know."

She laughed. "Are you proposing something?"

One of his eyebrows arched charmingly, while his green eyes seemed to sparkle. "What if I was?"

She decided to assume he was teasing. "Then you'd better be careful, because I might take you up on it," she said glibly, standing suddenly to go to the barbecue to check on the steaks. "I think these are done."

Beau answered her a little belatedly, she thought. "Go ahead and bring them over, then—I'll get rid of these plans."

She did as he'd instructed, serving him the larger of the two steaks before sitting down again.

"So you made a decision about Dori today," Clary said, just to get things rolling again.

"Mmm. I've made a lot of decisions in the past twenty-four hours, actually."

"More than about Dori's college money?" she asked, as she took a bite of meat.

"I've made a few about you, too."

Her mouth was full, so she could only raise her eyebrows in question.

"I've decided that my feelings for you are too overpowering to deny."

Gulp. Clary took a sip of wine to wash down the steak, while goose bumps erupted on her bare arms.

"I also decided," he went on, "that sometimes a person has to live for the moment and not pass up what's here now because it might not be here tomorrow."

"*It?*"

"You."

How could he expect her to eat and have this conversation at the same time? She couldn't. But, then, she noticed that he wasn't eating much either.

"It scares the hell out of me, but I'm falling in love with you, Parsons," he said then.

A little skitter of delight danced up her spine and she didn't know what to say. Before she could think of anything, she heard herself flirt, "Yeah? What are you going to do about it?"

His eyes captured hers and held them. "That's the second time I've been asked that today. But I think I'll save the answer for later."

Dessert always was her favorite part of the meal. And yet, when she realized she was fiddling with her zipper again, she also realized she'd moved it up a couple of notches.

Small talk took them through the remainder of dinner and on into cleaning up the mess. Then the phone rang and while Beau took a call that was medical in nature, Clary wandered outside again.

She should probably go back to Izzy's she thought. Beau had invited her to dinner—well, here she was, they'd eaten, spent a pleasant evening, and now it was nearing ten o'clock—a respectable enough time to leave. Before anything else got started. If it was going to.

And suddenly L.A. was on her mind. Would it really be any easier to go back, if this relationship between them stayed where it was? If it didn't get any more physical than it already had? she asked herself.

Maybe.

Or maybe not.

What was it Beau had said earlier? That he'd decided sometimes a person had to live for the moment and not pass up what was here now, because it might not be here tomorrow. Because *she* might not be here tomorrow.

Was he right? Or did she just want him so much it seemed right?

Clary couldn't be sure. But what she was certain of, was that she didn't want to go back to Izzy's right then. That for that moment all she could do was let nature take its course.

The sun had set and a clear night sky took its place. She sat down at the table again, slipping far enough in the seat so she could rest her head against the back of the fluffy cushion. Closing her eyes, she tuned out Beau's questions about how long someone's gout attack had been going on and listened to the soft sound of the water running down the rocks of the falls in the corner of the yard.

"You didn't nod off on me, did you?" Beau's voice came to her a few minutes later, deep and quiet, as if he didn't want to wake her if she was asleep.

Clary opened her eyes and looked at him where he stood in the doorway, silhouetted against the golden light of the kitchen. "No, I'm awake."

He stepped out onto the patio then, and came to stand behind her chair, placing both his hands on her shoulders and kneading gently. "Sorry about the interruption."

But Clary didn't answer. She was too enraptured by the feel of his big thumbs firmly pressing the back of her neck. Instead, she rolled her head into his motions.

"Want another glass of wine?" he asked.

"I think I've had enough." Enough to make her feel warm, and so relaxed she could have been floating.

Beau bent over the back of the chair and kissed her head. Then his massage stopped, he reached for her hand and pulled her to her feet and into his arms at once.

"I'm in big trouble over you," he said in a raspy voice, drawing her close and resting his chin atop her head while his arms rode her hips.

"I'd say I'm sorry, but I'm in the same trouble over you, and right at this moment it feels too good to apologize for."

He raised his hands into the free fall of her hair, running his fingers through it. "What would you say to my taking you upstairs now and making love to you?"

His hands were splayed against her back by then, working magic there. Clary looked up at him, drinking in the sight of the angular planes of his handsome face awash in moonlight and shadow. "I'd say I don't have any objections," she whispered.

He smiled down at her and then stepped away, much as he had earlier, keeping one arm around the small of her back to guide her into the house. As he passed the light switch he flicked it off, leaving them in complete darkness. But he maneuvered them through the house without a hitch, up the stairs and down the hall to the doorway at the end.

The bedroom was large and very masculine, done all in brown-and-navy-blue plaid. But more than furniture, Clary noticed the glass-domed skylight in the ceiling. And as she looked up at it, Beau kissed the arch of her throat and on down into the open collar of her jumpsuit.

"I've been dying to unzip this zipper all night," he told her, as he took hold of the pull and inched it down just slightly, following it with feathery kisses.

With his jeans in mind, she understood the urge, but she didn't admit it. Instead, she indulged herself in reaching for his biceps, pressing her palms against the rising mounds of muscles there.

He took her mouth with his, then, in a kiss that was instantly urgent and unleashed an equally instant and urgent passion in Clary, as if what he'd begun the night before and left unfinished had been waiting just under the surface to come back to life.

His tongue came searching and she opened the way for it, meeting him, matching him circle for circle, thrust for thrust. Oh, how hungry she was for this man, for his touch.

His hands were at her back, kneading, holding her tightly to his kiss. And then they coursed around to her zipper again, sliding it all the way to its end at her navel.

He deserted her mouth and Clary felt the heat of his breath against her skin as he dropped lower, ending at the sensitive valley between her breasts to kiss her again.

Her back arched of its own volition, straining against the confinement of her clothes.

The message conveyed itself to Beau because he slid his hands into the open ends of the jumpsuit and smoothed it off her shoulders, freeing her breasts to the cooler air and his powerful grasp at once.

She couldn't have stopped the tiny groan that escaped her throat if she'd tried, as he kneaded her flesh, turning a nipple hard, teasing it with his thumb and forefinger. He took her mouth with his yet again, wide open and seeking.

Craving the feel of his skin, she pulled his shirt free of his jeans and slipped her hands up inside. Warm, silky, hard . . . it made her yearn for other parts of his body that would fit that bill as well.

He eased her jumpsuit down over her hips, letting it drop to the floor along with her panties, and then he swept her up into his arms, swinging her onto the bed.

From there Clary watched as he crossed his arms over his middle, grabbing his shirttails to pull off his shirt in one smooth movement. His jeans joined her jumpsuit, and then he joined her, naked and magnificent.

Beside her, partly covering her body with the long length of his, he took her in his arms again, kissing her, one of his massive thighs crossed over hers, the hard proof of his desire for her introducing itself to her hip while his hand found her breast again, and glorious sensations ran through her body in a symphony.

She wanted this man. She loved this man.

The very size and power of him were daunting and arousing at once. Her hands traveled his body, learning the strong and soft spots, the smooth and the coarse. She discovered the smattering of curly hair on his chest and the fact that she could make his nipples go hard, too. She trailed her palm down the flatness of his belly, but lost her courage to keep going and instead circled his waist and found his derriere felt as good as it looked. Better, even.

And, oh, what he was doing to her with his hands, with his mouth, with his tongue!

He kissed her, he caressed her, he worshiped and cherished her. And when he'd driven her to the brink of insanity with wanting him, he rose above her and found a home in that spot that was crying out for him with a desperation Clary had never known before.

He filled her deeply, completely, embedding himself inside her body as surely as he'd imbedded himself in her heart.

Slowly he moved at first. Carefully, cautiously, gently. Until she couldn't stand it any longer and arched her hips up to urge him on to what they both needed—the deep, forceful, powerful thrusts that brought them to the peak of passion, letting them soar together from there in a climax like nothing Clary had ever experienced before.

And then, little by little, everything stopped and Clary sank into the mattress beneath the wonderful weight of Beau, feeling complete in a way she didn't know was possible.

"I think I'm falling in love with you, too," she whispered into the heat of his neck nearby.

"Good, then you won't mind if I keep you right where you are for the rest of your life?" he answered in a husky voice.

"Not a chance," she joked. "Before it gets too late tonight, I'm walking home down the middle of Front Street so there's no way Wellsburg will know we slept together to talk about it."

"You'll ruin everyone's fun," he warned her, slipping from her and pulling her to lie against his side. He smoothed her hair back and then rubbed light strokes on her upper arm. "Dori won't be home until tomorrow. We could have all night together," he said hopefully.

It was tempting. But still Clary rejected the idea. "As much as I want to do that, I hate being the source of gossip around here. I don't like everyone knowing my business."

He kissed her forehead, lingering with his lips pressed there. "All right, I'll let you go. But not yet."

Clary was only too willing to accept his postponement, warm and comfortable in his arms in the afterglow of lovemaking.

But when her eyes grew too heavy to hold open she pushed herself out of Beau's arms.

"I have to go," she whispered, as if there were someone around to hear her.

He groaned, but stretched and got up to pull on his clothes while she did the same. "You could cause even me to hate small-town life for this," he muttered.

Just once before they left the house, he pulled her into his arms again, kissing her with a parting abandon that almost led them back upstairs. But Clary held fast, and instead they ended up doing just what she said she was going to—walking down the middle of Front Street—though they were hand-in-hand.

At the door to Izzy and Jack's house, Beau kissed her yet again—long, slow, lingeringly—letting her know clearly how adverse he was to leaving her.

"We should have stayed at my house. Now we're going to give the whole town a lot more to talk about when they find me jumping your bones on your cousin's porch," he told her between kisses and hands that wandered to her rear end to pull her up against him.

But Clary gently pushed him away. "Go home, Doc."

He groaned again, then said, "Don't forget Dori's birthday party tomorrow night."

"Are you still having it?"

"With or without the guest of honor," he said wryly. "Let's just hope it's with."

He pulled her back for another quick kiss and then let her go, as if not to would cost him what little willpower he had left.

"Good night, Parsons," he whispered.

"Good night, Dugan," she said back, smiling.

And then she watched him go, damning this small town that kept her from being at his house at that moment, in his arms, in his bed.

Chapter Eight

Clary was just about to run to the convenience store the next morning, when the doorbell rang. Izzy and Jack were still in bed and she hurried to answer the door, hoping it hadn't already awakened them.

She could hardly believe her eyes when she found her friend standing on the front porch, all six feet of lean, lank, California-blond good looks. "Wolf! What are you doing here? Is everything all right at Biminis?"

"The restaurant is fine. But the buyers came in with an offer for Lois's condo yesterday. I knew you'd accept it and I would need your signature on the contract to go ahead. So I hopped a plane to Denver, rented a car there and here I am."

"I can't believe it."

"That the condo is sold?"

"That you're here. Couldn't you have sent me the papers to sign in overnight mail or something?"

"I suppose I could have, but that would have blown my excuse to come and see you. I know you said you were doing great here, but I've been worried."

He was still standing on the porch, in spite of the fact that she held the screen open for him. He glanced over his broad shoulder at what could be seen of Wellsburg from there, and made an expression that contorted his sophisticated, tanned face. "The trouble is, I bought a return ticket for an early flight out tomorrow, thinking that I could spend the night here and drive back to the airport at dawn to catch my plane. It didn't occur to me that this place would be so small and backward that it wouldn't even have a motel."

Clary was so glad to see him that she just laughed at his disgust. "It doesn't matter. You can stay here with us. I'll take the couch and you can have the guest room. Izzy and Jack won't mind."

"Saved from sleeping in the streets," he said with mock relief. Then he held out his arms for a hug and kiss in the doorway, before picking up his leather suitcase to bring it inside.

"This is a quaint little house," he said, without condescension, as he glanced around. "Didn't you say it was where you grew up?"

"Yes, but my cousin has done wonders with it." She took his suitcase and set it in the living room. "I was on my way to buy some almonds to grind for my special pancakes, to surprise Izzy and Jack when they get up. Come with me, so they don't find you while I'm gone and think you're a burglar."

He grabbed up her hand, clasping his other around it. "Lead the way."

Clary was all too aware of the stares they drew as they walked through town to the convenience store. Wolf didn't seem to notice, partly because his male-model good looks often engendered lingering glances and partly because he was too intent on taking in Wellsburg.

"Good grief, this is like stepping into an old movie. Ben's Grain and Feed, Milly's Wallpaper and Gifts, Home Sweet Home Real Estate ... it's hard to picture you coming from this Podunk," he said along the way.

"It has a certain charm," Clary defended, slightly surprised to find she meant it.

"I suppose so. If you like this sort of thing. Me, I'd die in a week without a deli or an all-night taco stand."

"You're just spoiled," Clary teased him.

He dropped her hand to put his arm around her shoulders and look closely into her face. "So how are you?"

"Just fine. How are you?"

"You're still not sleeping," he said, rather than answering her.

"Who says?"

He trailed a finger under one of her eyes. "You get a faint little line right here. I can always tell."

"Has it occurred to you that whatever lines you're seeing under my eyes are just wrinkles?"

"No. I know better. They always appear when something is keeping you up nights and disappear again when you sleep. So 'fess up—coming here hasn't helped, has it?"

Being in Wellsburg hadn't stopped the nightmares or the insomnia, no. Although, admittedly, some of the insomnia came from thoughts and feelings for Beau. But being here, being with Beau, had offered her an escape from constantly thinking about Lois. "I'm better," she claimed, rather than addressing Wolf's direct question.

"If you're not sleeping the night through, you're not better. And if being here isn't making you better, then come home."

Clary decided to treat this lightly. "I think you just miss me. Admit it."

"I do. Of course, I do," he said, as they went into the store. "But I also think you should just come home and let us work through this together."

"Morning." The clerk came out from a rear doorway just then, greeting them.

Clary returned his good-morning and asked where she could find almonds. He directed her past the only other two people in the store—a woman Clary didn't recognize and a girl who looked to be about Dori's age.

As Clary and Wolf passed them, the teenager was slack-jawed, staring openly at Wolf, while the mother only stole glances, pretending to study milk cartons as if there were a decision involved.

"Honest to God, babe, if I thought you being here was helping, I'd say stay. But those lines under your eyes tell me it isn't. They tell me I was right—running away isn't the answer. It hasn't stopped you from beating yourself up, and I want you to come home with me so I can pound it into your head that you aren't to blame—"

"Let's not talk about this now," Clary cut him off, all too aware of the listeners around them.

Wolf seemed to catch her drift, looking for the first time at the three people who made up his rapt audience. He didn't say anymore as Clary found the almonds she needed, paid for them and they left.

But once they were on their way back, he went on. "Lois was as much my friend as yours, you know. If I don't believe I'm responsible for her death, then why should you?"

"Things were different between her and me. And it was my advice she took."

He suddenly stopped in the middle of the sidewalk and grabbed her shoulders. "I just want to shake you!"

Clary glanced around, acutely aware of the scene Wolf was making. "Okay, but could you do it in private?" she joked. "You have no idea what a stir it would cause around here, to do it on the street."

Wolf let go of her as if she were on fire, and then they started walking again.

"Listen, you're right," Clary admitted. "I am still having nightmares and trouble sleeping. But I didn't come here to run away, no matter what you think. I came to regroup and spend time with my cousin—one more person I've let myself drift away from. And that's what I'm doing. So will you just quit worrying about me?"

Wolf made a face. "How long are you going to stay, then?"

"I don't know," she answered honestly. The only thing she was sure of was that the thought of leaving didn't appeal to her. There was Izzy, and not feeling as if she'd completely made up for lost time with her, but there was also Beau. Being with him had made her feel better than she had in a long time, in spite of everything, and she needed more of that. More of him. Before she could go back to L.A.

She hooked her arm through her friend's and went on. "Now don't bug me about this anymore, and tell me what's happening with you and Biminis."

"Would you please get off the phone, Dori. I want to make a call," Beau said to his daughter, after waiting through three consecutive conversations with three separate friends, thinking that any minute the phone would be free.

She waved him away just as the doorbell rang.

"I'm going to answer that, and I want you off the phone by the time I get back."

Dori just turned to look into the pantry while she went on talking.

It took fifteen minutes for Beau to let in his secretary, Skokie and a half dozen other friends who'd come to help him set up for his daughter's birthday party that evening. He put everybody to work and then went back to the kitchen to find the teenager still on the phone.

"Now!" he told her firmly.

"I have to go," Dori finally said into the receiver.

When she hung up she faced him with a sympathetic expression, surprising Beau, in view of the warfare they'd been waging since the morning before.

"I think you should pretend you're making a house call and get over to the MacIntires' right away," Dori announced.

"Why? Is something wrong with Izzy?" he asked, as he washed the counter of the crumbs Dori had left just in the time he'd been gone.

"Something's wrong all right, but not with Mrs. MacIntire. Clary's boyfriend is there. He got in this morning."

Beau's hand stopped midway to the sink. "Clary doesn't have a boyfriend," he said, finally brushing the crumbs down the drain.

"Oh, yes, she does. You know Rhonda's little brother delivers the paper now—well he saw this guy show up at the MacIntires' house real early this morning and he said he grabbed Clary and kissed her. And then Danielle saw the two of them in the convenience store together and heard him trying to get her to leave town with him, saying how much he missed her and he couldn't live without her."

"Clary told me she wasn't involved with anyone," Beau said, though with a little less conviction than before.

"Well, something is definitely going on," Dori insisted. "This guy said stuff about how Clary should stop beating herself up, that something wasn't her fault, and she shut him up real fast when she saw everyone listening."

Beau couldn't help frowning. "That could have meant anything. It doesn't sound too romantic to me."

"Yeah, but I guess the guy is awesome-looking. Totally hot. And he called her *babe,* and said if she'd just go back with him they could work through their problems together. *And* they were holding hands and he had his arm around her as they walked to the store, and then on the way back she had her arm through his, all like they were definitely *together.* I think you'd better get over there. Fast."

"I can't do that," he said, but not after giving it some thought. Who the hell was this guy, anyway? And if Clary had a relationship with him, why had she said she wasn't involved with anyone?

"Do you want me to drop in over there and see what I can find out?" Dori offered hopefully.

"No, I don't. You stay away from there."

"I could do it real smooth, so they'd never guess what I was up to. I'd say I wanted Clary's advice on what to wear tonight. And then she'd have to introduce the guy to me and I could find out who he is and why he's here."

"No, Dori."

"Then what are you going to do? What if she does what he wants and just leaves with him?"

"She wouldn't do that," Beau said, though the knot in the pit of his stomach told him he wasn't as sure as he sounded. "But I do think I should call and invite him to your party tonight."

"Are you sure you want to invite the enemy into your camp?"

"It's the polite thing to do." Besides, what if he didn't and Clary stayed home with this guy?

Dori shrugged, as if she'd done all she could. "Well, okay, if you say so. I know I can't wait to get a look at him, enemy or not."

"I'm sure he's not the enemy, Dori," Beau claimed. He just hoped to hell it was the truth.

"Are you sure about me coming to this thing," Wolf asked Clary, as they headed to Beau's house for Dori's birthday party that evening.

"You were invited," Clary assured him. "Word spreads fast in a place like Wellsburg. Beau—he's the girl's father—heard a friend of mine had come into town and he called to make sure I brought you."

But he hadn't said much more than that, Clary thought, as she took one last look at the khaki slacks and red silk blouse she wore, smoothing a stray strand of hair back into the tightly wound chignon she'd fashioned for the event.

Beau hadn't even asked who Wolf was. And had she imagined it, or had he been a little cool on the phone?

Maybe that was only because he had a houseful of people there when he'd called. Maybe the formality and brevity of the conversation had just been a way to keep everybody from talking about them. After all, Clary had made it clear the night before that she didn't want to incur any town gossip.

But still she felt uneasy as she, Wolf, Izzy and Jack piled into Wolf's rental car and headed for Beau's house.

It was Dori who answered the door when they arrived. She took one look at Wolf and seemed to forget about the rest of them. Instead, she did a slow assessment of him, as if he weren't quite real, taking in his pale yellow pants, polka-dot shirt and the arms of a yellow sweater tied around his shoulders.

Then the teenager regained her senses and stepped out of the way so they could go in.

Clary felt as if she were entering the house beside some sort of celebrity. Silence fell over the crowd and all eyes turned their way. Introducing her friend to Dori in the hush was more a collective introduction than a private one.

"I can't tell you how happy I am to meet you!" the teenager gushed. She reached a hand out to Wolf, but stopped short of actually touching him. "Would you like a glass of champagne?"

Clary glanced at Wolf, suddenly afraid that under the circumstances he might laugh and insult Beau's guests. But her friend minded his manners and simply accepted Dori's offer with a smile that only hinted at his amusement at the awed response he was drawing.

The teenager led the way through the crowd, which parted like the Red Sea.

"He's a big-time lawyer in California," Clary heard as they passed.

"Been friends with Mattie's granddaughter since she moved to Los Angeles."

"He doesn't do divorce. Doesn't believe in them. He's some kind of business-type attorney."

"Not married. Never was."

"Born and raised in Los Angeles."

"Has a sister who's a minister in some funny church."

Clary forced a smile at a few of the people who spoke, thinking that the gossips had been busy today. She wasn't happy to be reminded of how fast, far-reaching, detailed and not altogether accurate Wellsburg's rumor mill was, and she was glad when they finally reached the bar in the dining room and the guests turned to whispering among themselves and stealing glances rather than outright staring.

The bar held a punch bowl and several bottles of champagne. Dori scooped up two glasses of the bubbly liquid and handed one to Clary and the other to Wolf.

As her friend and the teenager got acquainted, Clary scanned for signs of Beau. She didn't see him and was just considering wandering off to find him, when she heard Wolf say, "I understand you're an aspiring actress. And a good one, too. I have several clients who are agents. If you get to L.A., maybe I can put you in touch with some of them."

Unfortunately Beau came through the swinging door from the kitchen at exactly that moment and heard it, too.

His eyes went rapidly from Clary to Wolf and his brow beetled as he set down a bowl of nuts and joined them.

"Clary," he said in greeting.

Not *"Hello, Clary,"* or *"Hi, how are you, Clary,"* or *"It's good to see you, Clary, I'm glad you came."* Just *"Clary,"* not quite barked out, but certainly clipped and cool and not overfriendly by any means.

"Dad, this is Wolfgang Schmidt—Clary's friend," Dori said, before Clary remembered to perform the introductions.

Beau held out his hand and welcomed Wolf, but Clary saw the formality in the gesture. It lacked all warmth, all of the relaxed friendliness that was Beau's signature.

He looked wonderful in spite of it all, though, she thought. He was dressed in dark blue slacks and a navy-and-green striped sport shirt that accentuated the color of his eyes. But those eyes held no warmth whatsoever.

"Dori, I need your help in the kitchen," he said within five minutes of his introduction to Wolf, and without saying another word to Clary.

When he'd managed to extract his daughter, he disappeared through the swinging door.

In a voice soft enough not to be overheard, Clary said to Wolf, "Please don't build up L.A. or encourage Dori's acting. It's a big bone of contention between her and her father. Try to talk about something else. *Anything* else."

Wolf had leaned very near to hear her. He turned his face so he could whisper in her ear. "Sorry, babe. I'll do what I can." To accentuate his apology, he laid his hand alongside her jawbone and kissed her cheek.

Clary looked up just then to see Dori burst back into the dining room with Beau right behind her. The teenager made a beeline for Wolf again, while Beau was unwillingly drawn away by Skokie, though he glanced at Clary, Wolf and Dori with an ominous expression on his face as he went.

Clary realized at that moment that the evening was not going to be a good one.

And she was right.

Feeling responsible for having brought Wolf in to further complicate matters between Beau and his daughter, Clary decided to stick close to her friend through most of the evening, running interference between Wolf and Dori.

She tried everything she could think of to divert the teenager from Wolf and talking about L.A. She introduced any number of other topics for conversation. She excused them both from Dori, claiming she had to show Wolf the backyard. She sent the teenager on half a dozen trumped-up errands for more champagne and water and anything else she could think of.

But for the most part her efforts were futile. Dori left for only short spans of time, or would just briefly tolerate talk of something other than acting or Los Angeles, before returning or asking more questions that brought the conversation back around to what she had a ceaseless appetite for.

To make Clary's evening even more unpleasant, as time wore on, she also became aware of the fact that she and her friend continued to be the subject-of-choice for talk among the other guests. She grew irritated with the surreptitious glances and the abrupt silences as she drew near.

Would she have had more patience with it, had Beau's attitude not been so cool and aloof? she wondered two hours into the evening. Certainly, the fact that he acted as if he barely knew she was there didn't help her mood any.

She understood that, as host of the party, he was busy with the large number of guests, but it seemed to Clary that even when she and Beau might have stolen a moment alone together here or there, he avoided it. And when she did manage to get within shouting distance of him, he maintained a manner that said he was none too happy with her.

Catching sight of several dirty looks Beau threw at Wolf, she assumed her friend was the source of Beau's displeasure, and probably she was, too, for having unleashed Wolf around Dori. But didn't he see that she was doing all she could to put herself between her friend and his daughter? Instead, it seemed as if all her efforts went unnoticed.

By eight o'clock the dining-room table was laden with a buffet that drew everyone from the rest of the house to line up there. As she had throughout the evening, Clary positioned herself to separate Wolf and Dori. Wolf was ahead of her, while Dori was behind.

With his plate full, Wolf headed away from the table, but Clary and Dori were stalled by Miss Crown, who needed to slip in front of them for the utensils she'd forgotten and a second hot cross bun.

"Oh-oh," Dori said under her breath to Clary. "I don't know if it's a good idea for my dad to talk to your boyfriend."

"My *boyfriend?*" Clary repeated dimly.

The teenager pointed to where Wolf approached Beau who stood opening another bottle of champagne. "I better get over there."

Boyfriend? The word echoed in Clary's mind. Surely Beau didn't think that, did he? The rest of Wellsburg might be imagining her relationship with Wolf to be different than it actually was, but not Beau.

And yet, as she reviewed the evening, it suddenly came into perspective for Clary.

Following close on Dori's heels, she decided to take the bull by the horns.

But the bull was being particularly slippery and excused himself moments after she joined him. It took her all through dinner and until everyone crowded into the living and dining rooms to watch the teenager open her gifts before Clary finally cornered Beau in the kitchen.

"I want you outside with me right now," she told him, as if she were a drill sergeant.

He nodded in the direction of the outer rooms. "I have over fifty guests to take care of."

But Clary wasn't accepting any denials. "In the first place, they all act like they're right at home anyway. If they want something they'll help themselves. And in the second place, the whole lot of them are clustered around Dori like a hundred doting grandparents. Nobody will even notice you're gone. Besides, I'm not taking no for an answer."

She slipped an arm through his and guided him out the back door, where she kept on going until she'd reached the waterfall in the corner of the yard. Several lamps were strung from the house out to the tree branches, casting a buttery light all around. "It's time we have a talk" she said when they came to a stop.

"I repeat—I have a house full of people."

"And a bad attitude."

He scowled at her, but didn't deny it.

Clary looked him in the eye, trying to keep a straight face as she said, "Are you staring daggers into Wolf's back because you think he's my *boyfriend,* or because he's filling Dori's head with the wonders of life in L.A.?"

"Both," Beau answered bluntly.

"I told you I'm not involved with anyone."

"The way I hear it you came here to heal a broken heart, when you and this Wolf character split up. But now he's followed you to mend fences. And from the looks of all the touchy-feely-kissyface stuff that's been going on, the fences are definitely mended."

Clary rolled her eyes. "Wolf is a very demonstrative person. It doesn't mean anything. He's my friend, but there is nothing romantic between us at all. Not now, not ever."

"You expect me to believe that little whispering-in-the-corner scene a while ago was just friendly?"

"As a matter of fact, I was warning him to tone down the L.A. accolades and the acting talk with Dori." She mimicked one of his scowls. "Now, will you knock off this jealousy thing. It's nuts."

He studied the waterfall and for a moment the only interruptions to the silence he left were the rush of that water and the muted sounds of his party coming from inside the house.

Lord, but the man had a gorgeous profile, Clary thought as she waited, realizing at the same time how much she preferred his rugged good looks to Wolf's refined ones.

Then Beau sighed and relented. "So why is Mr. California here, if not because he's in love with you?"

Clary ignored the *Mr. California* barb. "He came to get my signature on some papers."

"And how long is he sticking around?"

"Just until tomorrow."

One of Beau's eyebrows arched in what looked like the renewal of suspicion. "Where is he staying the night?"

"With us, where else? I'm giving him the guest room and sleeping on the couch."

"What a gentleman."

Clary gave in to a laugh, at the ridiculousness of Beau's jealousy. "You'd have to know Wolf. He has a heart of gold, but he's very persnickety about his sleeping and personal habits. When he found out there was only one bathroom for the four of us he nearly got in his car and ran back to civilization on the spot."

"But you persuaded him otherwise."

Clary punched him in the arm. "Cut it out. Yes, I persuaded him otherwise. He's my friend. And he's leaving tomorrow at the crack of dawn."

"He'll be out of here at the crack of dawn?" Beau repeated, clearly liking the idea.

"He has a lunch date at noon with a senator," she reassured.

A roar of laughter rose from inside the house, and something about it reminded Clary of the gossip that had been rampant, probably since the instant Wolf's rental car hit the city limits. It tempered some of her own amusement considerably.

"They all think he's my *boyfriend*, don't they?" she said, showing her irritation over being grist for Wellsburg's rumor mill.

"Everybody is friendly around here, Clary, but they don't whisper in each other's ears or walk around town holding hands. How would it look to you?"

She conceded the point. "What all has the good, old Burg been saying?"

He shrugged, crossed his arms over his chest and leaned against the fence, studying her suddenly. "A lot of garbage that's too strange to repeat. And then, again, I've heard a few things I believe. Like, in view of your sleepless nights and exaggerated worry over Izzy's pregnancy and crying over a fetal heartbeat, I'd guess that there's some validity to a conversation you and Mr. California are said to have had in the convenience store this morning. I understand he told you to stop beating yourself up, that you weren't at fault for something."

That sobered Clary considerably. "They didn't miss a thing, did they?" she said disgustedly.

"What does it mean?"

She hesitated, debating about whether or not to skirt the issue. But this was Beau, after all, and as insistently as she guarded her privacy with everyone else, she realized she didn't really want to keep secrets from him. Not anymore, anyway. "You're sure you want to hear it?" she asked him.

"Don't doubt it."

She took a deep breath, sat on the edge of the brick wall that formed the base of the waterfall, and explained that the woman who was her closest female friend in L.A. had had an affair with a married man.

"I hated that Lois was doing it, but I kept it to myself. Then he told her that there was no way he was divorcing his wife, and she came to me about it. I knew she had been counting on him getting divorced and marrying her, and that she wanted to have kids more than anybody I've ever known, so I advised her to break off with him." Clary shrugged helplessly. "She took my advice, but unfortunately I'm afraid she thought that once he was faced with losing her, he'd actually leave his wife to keep her."

"And of course he didn't."

"No. He accepted the end of their affair without a squeak, wouldn't take her calls when she tried to get hold of him again, returned her letters unopened, essentially closed the door completely, as if he was glad to be rid of her. After that she was really down."

Clary hadn't talked about this in any detail with a single soul. Wolf, being friends with Lois, too, had known what was happening as it occurred. Recounting the whole thing now raised a wave of Clary's feelings that threatened to drown her. Fighting it, when she went on her tone was tight, quiet, guilt-ridden.

"I'd been through broken hearts with Lois before—she wanted to get married and have kids so badly that her whole life centered on meeting a man. But she always bounced back and got right back on the trail of a husband. I guess this time was different. More serious. But I didn't see it. I was in my usual mode—trying to take care of everything at the restaurant myself, working fifteen-hour days, sometimes sleeping on the couch in my office rather than going home—"

"You are doing a pretty good number of beating yourself up, aren't you?"

"Only because it's true. Being friends with Wolf is easy. He lives in the condo next to mine. We share a landing, I see him coming and going, over coffee. And his office is a block away from Biminis—he drops in for lunch a couple of times a week. But when it comes to what isn't right under my nose..." Her eyes filled with unwanted tears and she blinked them back.

Beau came to sit beside her. He took her hands and clasped them in both of his. "You're too hard on yourself, Clary."

His deep voice was quiet and yet anchored her enough to enable her to go on. "Anyway, I wasn't as conscientious as I should have been about keeping tabs on Lois, comforting her and supporting her. I called every day for the first week, made sure we had dinner and went to a movie over the weekend to distract her. But then a few days passed before I phoned again. Then a few more . . . a couple of waiters quit. My chef went on a bender and didn't show up for work. There were some delivery foul-ups, my car broke down, I had some plumbing problems. . . ."

Clary took a breath and curbed the self-disgust in her tone. "I let a whole week pass without getting in touch, and when I finally tried to reach her there was no answer. When there was still no answer all that night and the next day, I went to her place. Her drapes were pulled, there was no sign of her. I thought she must have gone away to think—she sometimes did that. So I went home and the next day I called her work. A woman there said no one knew where Lois was. That she hadn't asked for time off, hadn't let anyone know she wasn't coming in and hadn't answered any of their calls, either."

Clary took a steeling breath. "I got scared and went back to Lois's place. I had a key—she'd given me one in case of emergency—so when she didn't answer the doorbell or my calling her name, I used it."

"Clary?" Beau urged gently, rubbing the back of her wrist with his thumb when she stalled, closing her eyes against the mental image that only being with him had chased out of her mind in the past month.

"Lois was dead. She'd hanged herself," she said very, very softly.

His grip around her hands tightened. "And you feel responsible."

"She'd left me a note saying that she couldn't keep as busy as I do, to stave off the loneliness." Clary bit her lip. "If I had just made more time for her—."

"What would you have been able to do?" he asked gently, reasonably. "Could you have solved her problems? Made the man not be a weasel? Taken away her feelings, her depression?"

"I don't know!" she barked back. "Something. I should have done something!"

"To commit suicide, Clary, is a sign that she was much more troubled than any friend could have fixed. Sometimes more than any professional can fix. If you had devoted twenty-four hours a day to her, chances are you couldn't have prevented her from killing herself, if that was what she'd made up her mind to do."

Wolf had said essentially the same thing to her in the past month, but there was something about it coming from Beau that finally brought the truth of it home to Clary. And there was such comfort in his body, as somewhere along the way he'd put his arm around her and pulled her close against his side. In fact, Clary felt more soothed than she had since finding Lois.

"So you came here to see Izzy?" Beau asked after a while.

"I couldn't change anything with Lois, but her death made me take a close look at the way I treat all of my relationships, at how much I bury myself in my work. I realized I didn't want to go on the way I have been for so long. I love Izzy like a sister, and yet I started to add up how many times I'd actually seen her in the last fifteen years, how many letters I hadn't answered, how many phone calls I'd meant to make and hadn't—"

Clary shook her head. "It's not that I think Izzy will kill herself because she hasn't heard from me. Or that the sound of my voice on the other end of a telephone will save anybody from doing something like this. But I cared about Lois. She was more important than waiters quitting, or car repairs, or plumbing problems, or missed deliveries. Only I didn't prove that to her, I put those other things ahead of her. I guess you could say I've made a reassessment and put my priorities in the order they should have been in all along."

"And your friend's death—is that what's put you so on edge about Izzy's pregnancy?"

She shrugged. "It made me realize how really fragile life is. And as for the heartbeat scene—I just had this flash of how much Lois had wanted kids, and it was like a floodgate opened up inside of me."

Beau stood then, taking her with him so he could pull her into his embrace. He held her pressed against him so closely Clary felt melded to him, and it was just what she needed at that moment. She wrapped her arms around him and held on, listening to the steady beat of his heart beneath her ear, drawing from his strength. And for the first time since Lois's death, she felt free of the burden she'd carried with her.

"I'd give just about anything in the world to sneak away right now and be alone with you," she said. "I don't suppose you could say you have an emergency and we could disappear?"

"I'd like to, you'll never know how much," he answered, his voice a deep rumble in his chest. "But I can't do that. Besides, my being the host, in Wellsburg it would only be a matter of time before everyone knew there wasn't really an emergency and we'd just ditched the festivities for some illicit romance.''

''Mmm. My favorite kind,'' she said, managing a lighter tone with some difficulty.

He let go of her with one arm, tilting her face up to his with a knuckle under her chin. In his smile she saw that the tension that had marred his handsome features earlier was gone.

He leaned down far enough to take her lips with his. Parted, warm, loving. He tasted sweet and the scent of his after-shave, the feel of his big body against hers, of his hands on her back, of the roll of his muscles beneath her palms, all worked to awaken her senses, to shoot streaks of desire through her that finished to release her from the demons she'd been suffering.

Beau must have felt the same surge of passion, because he groaned huskily and deepened the kiss, opening his mouth wide, plunging his tongue in to search for hers.

But just then a rousing round of applause sounded from the house, reminding them that it was just a matter of time before they'd be missed and someone would come looking for them.

Beau ended the kiss with a few short, chaste ones and raised his head, dropping it backward to study the night sky and take a few full draws of air.

Clary looked up at him, finding his jaw clenched tight. All she could think was that she wanted to kiss her way around that sharp bone, down the pale skin on the underside of his chin, past his Adam's apple to the hollow of his throat hidden in the shadow of his shirt collar.

''We have to go in,'' he said, as if reading her mind.

Then he opened his arms from around her and took her hand, tugging her back toward the house.

And as Clary reentered his party, with all eyes turning to them in questioning stares that made Clary feel exposed, she remembered all too well the feeling of living in a fishbowl—one of the reasons she'd wanted to leave Wellsburg fifteen years ago.

Chapter Nine

Beau wondered if he'd lost his mind.

It was five-forty-five in the morning and he was sitting in his car, parked in front of the lot he owned next door to the MacIntires' house, watching for signs of Clary and Mr. California.

He'd had to make a middle-of-the-night house call on a suspected appendix attack that had proved to be stomach flu instead. As he'd left his patient he'd remembered Clary saying her friend was leaving before dawn, and that was all it had taken to keep him from getting anymore sleep once he was home again.

So, here he was, with a picnic breakfast packed in a basket in the back seat, watching for her, hoping she'd come out to see off this Wolf character, so Beau could whisk her away for a little while before his office hours.

Or at least that was how he was going to explain it to Clary—the condensed, carefree version.

But his being there wasn't that simple or that carefree, because it wasn't only his desire to spend a little time with her that had brought him out before even the chickens were up.

Not that he didn't want to see her. He did. In fact it wasn't only a matter of *wanting,* it was a matter of need. Not seeing her put him on edge, made him feel incomplete, left him almost incapable of thinking about anything but how to arrange to see her again.

But this morning there was more than that going on inside him. This morning he was worried, too. Worried that she might have decided sometime after the party the previous evening to just go back with Mr. California, the way her friend wanted her to.

And Beau wasn't happy about the feelings that thought brought with it.

Why the hell was he putting himself through this?

"She'll go back sooner or later," he said out loud, as if the truth of it might carry more weight that way.

And in spite of all his previous decisions to live for the moment, to enjoy what time he had with Clary, he again told himself that a smart man would accept that there was no future in this relationship and put some distance between them even before she left. A smart man wouldn't keep adding fodder to the feed bin to keep these feelings alive and growing. A smart man would stop seeing her, stop thinking about her, stop torturing himself with fantasies of taking her to his new house, of having babies with her, of growing old with her.

So why, knowing he was only torturing himself and asking for more of the same later on, didn't he just cut his losses, put some distance between them and forget her?

"Because it's too late."

He wasn't just falling in love with her. He'd already fallen. He hadn't meant to. But he had. The indisputable truth was that he loved Clary with an all-encompassing passion that had a will of its own. And no amount of common sense made it any different than it was. He loved her. He loved her in a way that he'd never loved another soul.

And he didn't know what he was going to do when she left.

Not when he couldn't even go a few hours without craving to see her, the way a normal man craved food and water. Not when his bed seemed desperately empty without her, more even than it had right after Gina had died. Not when he already knew that TV, radio, nothing filled the silence, when he wanted to hear the sound of Clary's voice, her laughter. When not even an icy cold shower took away wanting her, and when sometimes his hands actually itched with the need to touch her, to hold her.

But sooner or later she would go back to L.A. There wasn't a doubt in his mind about that. She'd be a thousand miles away. He wouldn't be able to trump up a reason to drop in on her. It wouldn't be a matter of just anxiously watching the clock, knowing that it would only be a few hours until he could be with her.

And when that happened, it was going to kill him.

But right at that moment all he could do was hope that today wasn't that day.

Clary couldn't stifle a yawn as she pressed a cold washcloth to her face to wake herself up. The first night in a month that she'd been able to easily fall asleep and stay that way without the torment of her nightmares, and she had to get up to say goodbye to Wolf. Ah, the fates were having a little fun with her.

But, oh, how good it had been to sleep! Peacefully. Without jolting awake with adrenaline pumping through her from a dream that put her back in Lois's doorway, re- living the scene she'd come upon the day she'd found her.

Still, sleepy or not, Clary felt a world better than she had since then. And she realized, as she brushed her hair, that not having insomnia or the nightmare wasn't the only re- lief she'd found. Somehow, even thoughts of Lois's sui- cide seemed more in perspective since talking about it with Beau. She even felt absolved of a major portion of the guilt she'd put herself through since then.

She didn't understand why. Maybe it was his expertise as a doctor that allowed her to finally believe what he'd said about her not being able to save her friend. Maybe it was his support and compassion and acceptance of what she'd found impossible to accept of herself.

Or maybe it was the strength and healing she'd drawn from the haven of his arms.

She stopped brushing her hair in mid-stroke as some- thing occurred to her. Beau gave her things she'd never felt before. A sense of belonging, of being appreciated for just what she was, without criticism or even any apparent awareness of her faults. He gave her a feeling that no mat- ter what she ever did, or whatever happened to her, he would be her ballast and her sanctuary. That he could heal all her wounds.

And what she felt for him swelled so big inside her that it frightened her a little.

Wolf tapped faintly on the bathroom door just then, bringing her out of her thoughts. "I'd better get going, babe," he whispered.

"I'll be right out," she whispered back, quickly pulling on hot pink sweatpants and a matching sweatshirt that buttoned up the front.

Wolf was waiting for her on the porch when she went out, looking very dapper in a Savile Row suit. He picked up his suitcase in one hand and wrapped his other arm around her so they could walk to his car that way.

"This flight was pretty empty when I made reservations on it. You could probably still get a seat," he said in the first normal tone of voice either of them had used since they'd gotten up.

Clary glanced in the direction of Front Street, thinking about Wellsburg and being the brunt of so much gossip the day and night before. Leaving that aspect of the small town behind again wouldn't be a hardship at all, she realized.

But in spite of that, she said, "I'm not ready yet. I'm enjoying my time with Izzy too much."

"And with your doctor," Wolf finished for her as he slid his suitcase into the passenger seat.

"And with Beau," she agreed. Wolf had asked her about him after the party the night before and Clary hadn't denied that she was involved with Wellsburg's doctor. Wolf knew her too well for her to believe she could fool him.

The streetlights and the porch lamp were the only illumination in the still dark sky, but Clary saw her friend's blond eyebrows draw together slightly anyway. "You'll take care of yourself while you're here?"

She laughed. "Of course."

"And you won't stay too much longer?"

Thinking about that gave her a strange mixture of feelings that surprised her. There was actually some regret at the thought of leaving Wellsburg itself, over and above Izzy and Beau. But there was also a new anxiousness to go home, to get back to her real life, as if she could handle it all again now.

She didn't say that to her friend, though. Instead, she answered, "No, I won't stay too much longer. In fact, another day like yesterday, of being the main topic of conversation, and I may run home right away.''

"Maybe I should stick around awhile and cause it, then."

"What, and miss your lunch with the senator, just to stir up more scandal in boring, old Wellsburg? I know, you aren't *that* desperate for my company."

"I'm pretty desperate. I could go into Mexican-food withdrawal at any time, without you to go eat it with me."

They rounded the car to the driver's side.

"I'll probably just stay until Izzy's baby comes—she's due in less than a week,'' she assured him. "And then I'll be back with bells on, glad to be just another face in the crowd again."

"Promise?"

"Promise."

Wolf pulled her into a big bear hug. "I'll call if there's anything you need to know about the sale of the condo."

"And don't forget to keep an eye on Biminis for me."

He loosened his grip and kissed her forehead. "Be well, babe,'' he said as he got in the car and rolled down the window.

Clary leaned over to look inside. "Have a good trip and take a couple of deep breaths of smog for me."

"Nah, I'll just save you a jar." He started the engine and craned his head out, puckering up for another kiss.

Clary obliged and then stepped away. "Talk to you soon," she said, waving to him as he backed out of the driveway.

He was only a few houses down the street when car lights turned on from the other direction and another engine interrupted the silence of the early morning, catching Clary's attention. Glancing up, she couldn't believe she was actually seeing Beau's four-by-four rolling toward her and pulling into the spot Wolf had just vacated.

"What are you doing here?" she asked when she went to the car, thinking that the pleasure of seeing him was out of proportion to the length of time they'd been separated. He had on jeans and a black polo shirt, and his hair fell loosely over one side of his brow as if it had only been haphazardly combed. And just one sight of him had her heart racing.

"I had to make a house call a couple of hours ago, couldn't sleep and remembered that Mr. California was leaving at dawn. I thought maybe I could catch you and talk you into a sunrise picnic." He nodded at a basket in the back seat.

Clary smiled at the idea. "So, what have you been doing—sitting out here watching the house?"

"Only for a few minutes. What do you say, are you game?"

"Just let me pull the front door closed."

Clary hurried to the house, as if taking her time might make him rescind the offer. When she got in his four-by-four, she said, "I hope you had the lake in mind."

He winked at her and backed out of the driveway. "That's the best place."

The lake was on the eastern outskirts of Wellsburg. The sight of any number of parties, picnics, fishing expeditions and festivals, it was two miles around and about thirty feet deep in the center. More of Wellsburg's elm trees surrounded it, with a few pines edging up to its southernmost shore.

Beau pulled all the way to the lake's edge, near the wide wooden dock, and stopped the car. But rather than getting immediately out, he angled in the seat, stretched his arm along the back and grinned straight into Clary's heart. "Good morning."

His smile felt like warm honey and she returned it. "You're a man with some pretty good ideas. Did anyone ever tell you that?"

He brushed the backs of his fingers down her cheek. "I have inspiration." Then he reached into the back for the basket. "Come on, Parsons. How long has it been since you watched the sun come up?"

Clary slid across the seat to get out on his side. "I'm already at work by that time every morning, getting ready for the breakfast crowd."

"You're right, you do work too much."

He flipped the blanket open on the grassy shore, set the basket in one corner, and they sat cross-legged in the middle, facing each other.

"This was impromptu, so I only brought what was in the fridge." He began to pull food out. "Grapes. Strawberries. Sliced peaches. Cheese and crackers. A thermos of coffee. A jar of orange juice. And a bottle of champagne from last night—I thought I'd ply you with a Mimosa."

"Perfect. Ply me." As Beau opened the wine, it reminded her of his party. "I'll bet your house looks like a cyclone hit it."

He poured himself straight orange juice and touched his glass to hers in a silent toast. "Actually, I was up late cleaning, so it isn't too bad." The sky had brightened to a pale blue and there was enough light from it to see a frown pull his handsome features. "Dori and I had another big fight after everyone left, and I was too wound up to go to bed."

A stab of guilt struck Clary. "Did your fight have anything to do with Wolf?"

"Not directly. Dori was just spouting a lot of what he'd said, and I lost my temper. It went from there."

Clary reached for his hand and squeezed. "I'm sorry. I probably shouldn't have brought him."

Beau turned his hand in hers so he could hold it. "Then I wouldn't have gotten to see you. And I'd have gone crazy thinking about you staying home with that guy."

Clary smiled at the shadow of his jealousy and took her hand out of his to feed him a grape. "Well, he's gone now, so you can relax."

Beau bit a strawberry in half and then followed her example and fed her the other half.

Clary imagined that it tasted of him and it set her stomach aflutter. "Did you get any sleep at all?"

"About two hours. How about you?"

"Funny you should ask. For the first time in a month, I slept like a baby. I think it has something to do with you."

"I could understand that, if I'd been around to wear you out before you went to bed, but under the circumstances, how did I accomplish that?"

She shrugged. "You're just good for me."

He reached his palm to the side of her neck, big and warm and strong but oh-so-gentle. "I'm glad."

Then he took his hand away, and Clary had the strongest surge of regret at losing his touch.

For a moment they sipped their drinks and ate, without saying anything, watching the sky open up with the faintest hues of yellow. Then Beau said, "I have a confession to make. I was a little worried that you might change your mind and leave with Mr. California this morning."

"He wanted me to," she admitted. She took a peach slice and dipped it in the Mimosa before taking a bite just to see how it tasted.

Beau's gaze followed the fruit from her glass to her mouth. "Why didn't you?" he asked in a hushed, shaky voice.

"What, and miss sitting on a blanket beside a lake watching the sun come up?" she teased, hearing a lower timbre in her own tone. "Here, taste this. It's really good," she offered, dipping a second peach slice in her drink and feeding it to him.

His lips barely brushed her fingers as he took it into his mouth, but the contact sent sparks flying up her arm. And when he sucked the fruit in, something tightened deep in the pit of her stomach.

She moistened her lips and studied strawberries, as if intent on deciding which one to choose just to distract herself. "What would you have done if I'd come out with my suitcase?"

"Slit your tires?" he joked.

When Clary glanced back at him he was studying her. She had the fleeting thought that she could feel his eyes on her, and it set off a tingling sensation that coursed across the surface of her skin. Then he seemed to capture her gaze and hold it, while the corners of his wonderful mouth slid up in a lazy smile.

He took her glass and set it with his in the grass beyond the blanket. Then he got on his knees, put his hands on the ground on either side of her hips and nearly pressed his nose to hers. "Or maybe I'd have run up to you, thrown you on the lawn and given you a reason to stay," he said, easing her backward until she braced herself on her elbows.

Clary smiled. "I thought you brought me out here to watch the sunrise, not to seduce me."

"Maybe I lied," he said. Then he glanced over his shoulder. "Take a look. Beautiful, isn't it?"

She craned to see past him. The sky was alive with bursts of persimmon, hazes of yellow and tinges of orange. "Gorgeous," she agreed. Then she settled on her elbows again.

"Have you seen enough?" he asked.

She looked pointedly down at the opening of his shirt collar, where just a few curly hairs peeked out. "Of the sunrise, yes," she answered, giving in to the impulse to press a kiss to that spot at the base of his throat.

That was all the invitation Beau needed. He took her mouth with his, lowering the weight of his body to her as he eased her to lie flat on the ground.

Clary reached her arms around him, suddenly aware of how hungry she was for his kiss, for his touch, for the feel of his hard muscles, his big, strong body, his smooth skin. For him.

Feeling braver than the first time, she slid her hands under his shirt to soothe one of those cravings, running her palms from the narrowness of his lower back up the widening V to his broad, powerful shoulders.

Still kissing her, wide open and seeking, he rolled more to her side and went to work on the buttons of her sweatshirt. Clary felt her nipples harden, even before he bared them to the cool morning air and his hand, kneading, squeezing, giving her the magic of his touch before he slipped her top off completely.

That was when he abandoned her, tearing off his own shirt and tossing it away. Then back he came, kissing her a few urgent times before trailing a path down her throat, across her collarbone and finally down to her breast, taking her nipple fully into his mouth just as he'd taken the peach slice earlier, sucking, nipping, drawing her into the dark, velvety depth and tightening a cord that ran through her center to the spot between her thighs that was already awake and yearning.

Clary's back arched and a tiny moan escaped as evidence of all he was arousing inside her.

Beau's hand cupped her bare side, working her flesh there for a moment before trailing his palm to her stomach and then lower, inside the waistband of her sweatpants. She could feel his fingertips just barely reaching the cliff's edge of intimacy and she thought she might die if he didn't go the rest of the way and actually touch her.

She curved her leg over the back of his, searching, seeking. And finally, with torturous languor, he slipped inside her, driving her wild with wanting even more of him.

Her hand was on his shoulder and she pressed it down his bulging bicep, skipping over to his side and continuing the descent until she found the front button of his jeans. She slipped it out of its fastening and then slid her own fingers in between the denim and his flat belly.

This time it was Beau who groaned, flexing his hips against her, urging her on.

But Clary didn't need much encouragement. She craved knowledge of him and she sought it, taking the long, thick hardness of him into her hand. Silky, strong, she learned the most intimate details there were to learn about him, reveling in every one of them, feeling her own desire build as she did.

Then, suddenly, he slipped away and made quick work of ridding them both of what remained of their clothes. Coming back to her, he nudged her thighs apart and found his way inside her at the same moment his lips captured hers again and his tongue made the first thrust.

But it was his hips that made the second one, embedding him so deeply in the core of her that she instinctively arched up to meet him.

Together they moved, ebbing and flowing, meeting and matching each movement. Faster, harder, until she couldn't keep up and merely clung to him, letting him raise them both to the pinnacle they sought, reaching it in one great, glorious explosion that fused them, body and soul and heart.

And when it was complete, Beau closed his arms tightly around her and rolled them until she was lying on top of him, still cradling his body inside her.

"I love you, Clary," he said, his voice raspy and rough. "God, how I love you."

She kissed his bare chest and then pressed her forehead to that spot. "I love you, too. So much it scares me."

He ran his hands down her back, to her derriere and then up again, squeezing her so tightly it was as if he wanted to absorb her body into his. "I think being awake most of the night is catching up with me," he said in a voice that sounded thick.

"Mmm," was all Clary could answer. There, in his arms, she had never felt so complete, so safe, so wonderfully tired.

She rode the tide of a deep breath he took and heard him sigh it out as his arms relaxed slightly around her, telling her he'd fallen asleep. And then she gave in to the blissful fatigue that weighted her, the warmth of the just-risen sun on her naked back, and followed him.

"Oh, boy. I think we blew it."

Beau's voice woke Clary. She opened her eyes to bright morning sunshine and then squinted them closed again quickly. "What time is it?"

"Fifteen minutes past when my first appointment was due at the office."

"Terrific," Clary said as they both jolted into action, pulling on their clothes in a hurry. "I was hoping we could sneak back into town before anyone was around. Now Wellsburg will be talking about us all week."

Beau swatted her playfully on the rump. "Just get a move on."

They made quick work of gathering their picnic things and tossing them onto the back seat. Once they were in the car and Beau had started the engine, Clary said, "Just go straight to your house so you can change and get to the office. I'll walk home from there."

He glanced at her as he turned onto the road back to town. "Are you sure you don't want to hide under the blanket in back? I could pull up into Izzy's driveway and you could slink in and hope nobody sees you," he teased her.

"Wouldn't make any difference. There are spies everywhere," she joked back. Instead, as they turned onto Front Street, she smiled and returned the wave of Wellsburg's plumber, who was just stepping out of the coffee shop.

Clary felt as if she were in a parade, as Beau sped down the main drag. And she might as well have been, for all the attention, stares and waves they drew. She didn't have a doubt that it was going to be a long walk home as word spread and three people out of every four stopped to chat, in hopes of finding out what she and the good doctor were doing together at that time of the day, when he was suppose to be in his office.

Then Beau pulled onto his street.

"What the hell?" he said.

Clary turned from looking out her side window to glance through the windshield at Beau's house, where Dori was just walking out the front door. She was carrying a suit-case in each hand.

Beau pulled into the driveway and barely stopped the car before lunging out.

"What's going on, Dori?"

Clary got out of the car, seeing the teenager's chin raise in defiance as she did.

"I'm going to L.A."

Beau jammed his hand through his hair, but before he could say anything Dori went on.

"School is out for seniors, all that's left is the gradua-tion ceremony and I don't care about that. I'm eighteen now and I can legally do what I want. So I'm taking the money out of my savings account—it'll buy me a bus ticket to L.A., and be enough to pay for food and a place to stay for a while. By the time it runs out I'll just have to have a job, whether it's acting or something else."

"Dammit!" Beau ground out through clenched teeth.

Clary didn't want to be involved in this confrontation, and since Beau and his daughter were head-to-head with each other, she decided the best thing for her to do was to just slip away. But she only made it as far as the back of the four-by-four before Dori's voice stopped her.

"Tell him, Clary," she shouted. "Tell him you stayed in Los Angeles and did all right. Tell him it isn't some hor-rible place where I'll be making the mistake of a life-time."

Clary turned back to them, holding her hands up, palms outward. "Please don't draw me into this."

Beau had swung around to look at her and either didn't hear what she said or didn't care. "No, Clary, tell her what she's getting into. Tell her how tough it will be for an eighteen-year-old kid to live in L.A. on pennies. Tell her what kind of housing, what kind of neighborhood she'll be able to afford, waiting tables or cleaning motel rooms or working as a clerk in some store. Tell her how hard it is to get a job—any job—out there, let alone in acting. Tell her what she's getting herself into.''

"It doesn't matter what anyone says!" Dori railed at her father before Clary could get a word out. "It doesn't matter any more that your refusing to support me. I won't stay here! I hate everything about this place and I'm going to be an actress!''

"You don't know what you're talking about," Beau shouted back.

"I know I hate that I have to look at the same faces day after day, year after year. That I have to eat the same foods, do the same things, hear the same voices. I hate that the sidewalks are rolled up after ten o'clock at night, that I can't even take a walk without having to talk to a dozen different nosy neighbors and then have them turn around and talk about me when I leave. I hate that everybody from the vet to the mayor knows every intimate detail of my life. I hate that right now half the people in this stupid place are listening to what we're saying and can't wait to tell the other half.''

"It isn't all that bad, Dori, you're exaggerating.''

"I'm not exaggerating. I'm suffocating! You just think I'm exaggerating because you don't care about those things. You *like* them. But I don't. And I'm going to be an actress! I don't need a college degree to do that—not from Greeley and not from UCLA. I'm already good at it and all I need now is my chance. So I'm going! No matter what you or anybody else says! I'm getting out of this place I can't stand and going where I can do what I want.''

Clary looked from the teenager to Beau, and her heart broke for him. She knew this had to be tearing him apart.

But at the same time, she understood all that Dori said, in a way that Beau never could, because Wellsburg didn't give him the same claustrophobic feelings that it did Clary and Dori.

"Nobody can tell you anything, can they?" Beau yelled at his daughter. "You think you know it all. You're so damn stubborn. Well, go then. You think living here is that bad, see what it's like out in the world on your own. Go for it."

"I will!" Dori stepped around him, and he just stayed standing there like a statue, not even watching her go.

"Beau, don't let her leave this way," Clary said, unable to stop herself.

He spun on her. "What the hell do you want me to do?" he demanded, throwing his hands up in the air. "Shall I write her a check and give her a thumb's up on the dumbest mistake she'll ever make? I only want what's best for her, dammit! I'm not being unreasonable!"

"No, you're not," Clary assured him, taking no offense from his wrath.

"What's best for me is to go to L.A. and act," Dori put in from where she'd stopped just beyond Clary, as if hiding behind her.

"Then give me one year—hell, one damn semester at Greeley and you can transfer to UCLA and go on with the original agreement," Beau tried. "Then you'll have safe housing, a home base, you'll be building a foundation for your future at the same time you can try your damned acting, without having to work."

"No," Dori answered so resolutely it was clear she wasn't going to give an inch. Then again, "No."

Clary glanced over her shoulder at the teenager and then back to Beau. Father and daughter stared at one another, at a stalemate. She didn't know what to do, torn with concern for them both.

"I'm going. Now," Dori announced.

And she was, Clary didn't doubt it. Reasoning with Beau was the only hope, she realized suddenly. "Can you rest knowing she's in L.A. without money or a place to stay? Will you ever forgive yourself, if something happens to her because of it?"

Beau turned his angry eyes Clary's way again. "So you do think I should write her a check," he accused.

"If she won't give you a year, then you give her one," Clary suggested softly into the tension-filled silence that punctuated Beau's frustrating defeat. "Support her for just that long. She can stay at my place, I have an empty bedroom. I'll keep an eye on her. And after a year, if she hasn't made it as an actress and still refuses to go to college, then put her on her own. Just don't do it now. Like this."

Beau stared at her. He looked as if she'd struck him. "You'll keep an eye on her," he repeated.

He didn't have to say what he was thinking for Clary to know. No matter what he'd said, on some level he'd hoped she wouldn't go back to L.A. That she would stay in Wellsburg. And this was a rotten time to be forced to acknowledge the truth.

Clary wanted to rush to him, to feel his arms around her, to comfort him, support him, swear she wouldn't leave the way Dori was. But she couldn't do that. She couldn't do that, because she was going to leave Wellsburg. Just the way Dori was. And with the exception of the acting part of it, for just the same reasons.

Wellsburg had been what she needed to nurse herself through the guilt and grief of Lois's death, but she didn't believe she could live here again. And because of that all she could offer Beau at that moment was a calm, quiet voice assuring him she'd make certain his daughter was taken care of when she left him behind, too.

"Please say yes, Dad!" Dori pleaded from behind Clary.

Beau's eyes were locked onto Clary's and they didn't move, not even when his daughter spoke.

"I'll stay for the graduation ceremony," Dori began to bargain. "I'll even wait to leave for L.A. until Clary is ready to go back. And if I'm not a working actress at the end of the year, I promise to go to college just the way you want."

Still Beau stared at Clary and she willed him to understand. To forgive her.

"Please, Dad," Dori repeated in a voice that sounded much like a little girl's.

And then, from up the street, came the sound of a horn honking as a car raced toward the house. The MacIntires' car.

Jack was at the wheel and he screeched to a halt in front of the house. "Is something wrong with your phone? I've been calling and calling—" he said frantically, leaning out the window. "Izzy woke up an hour ago in a puddle of water and her pains are coming real fast and real hard, and she's swollen up bad!"

Clary shot a glance at Beau, but he had snapped to and was running for the four-by-four. As he did, he shouted to his daughter, "Go inside. We'll finish this later." Then, to Jack, "I'll meet you at the house."

"I have to go, too," Clary told the teenager, wishing she could glue the girl in place until this could be finished with Beau.

But at the moment it was worry over her cousin that pulled at Clary and made her run to the nearest car—Jack's—to climb in a split second before her cousin-in-law pulled the fastest U-turn in history and raced back the way he'd come.

Chapter Ten

Clary had never known such a short drive to feel as long as the one from Beau's house to Izzy's. Her heart was in her throat, and neither she nor Jack said a word as she worried that she was about to lose her cousin on top of just having lost her friend.

The neighbor ladies from both sides and behind were with Izzy when Clary, Beau and Jack rushed into the house. They came out of the bedroom as Beau and Jack went in to Izzy, and, with heartfelt expressions of concern, they asked Clary to keep them informed and left her to pace.

Five minutes. Ten. Twenty, passed before Beau came out of the bedroom and went straight to the telephone. He didn't say a word to Clary as he dialed and told his receptionist without preamble to put his nurse on the line.

Standing a few feet from him, Clary listened unabashedly as he told his nurse to ready the outpatient surgery suite. "Between the onset of toxemia and the advanced stage of labor we're going to have to do a quick cesarean—there isn't even time to wait for a helicopter transport to Greeley. But get it here so we can airlift Izzy and the baby as soon as the delivery is complete."

"You told me Izzy's blood pressure and swelling were no big deal!" Clary said the minute he hung up.

"They weren't then. But they are now."

He went out to his four-by-four and Clary followed on his heels. "Will she be all right?"

"I won't kid you, Clary, toxemia is dangerous. We have to act fast," he answered, as he opened the rear door on the vehicle and pulled out two long poles rolled in canvas. Taking them with him, he ran back to the house.

Only a few minutes later Beau and Jack came out of the bedroom, bearing Izzy on the army litter. Clary held the front door open for them and then caught up just as they were about to slide her cousin into the back of the four-by-four.

"Everything will be okay," she called to Izzy, hoping to God it was the truth.

Jack got in beside the litter, taking his wife's hand. Beau closed the tailgate and Clary ran to the passenger's side, sliding onto the seat just before Beau slipped behind the wheel and started the engine.

"Do your breathing, Iz," he counseled as he hit the gas and raced out of the driveway.

The office's front door was open when they drove up. Beau backed right onto the sidewalk, stopped and within a few minutes he and Jack were rushing Izzy in.

Clary followed, but got only as far as the surgical suite before the receptionist stopped her.

"Need any help?" Skokie called in to Beau.

It was the first Clary realized that the dentist was standing behind her.

"Thanks," Beau answered, his calm, confident tone not easing Clary's fears at all, "but I think we'll be extracting a little more than a tooth in here. Just keep Clary company, will you?"

And then the receptionist pulled the door closed.

Skokie took Clary's elbow. "Come on. Let's get you a cup of coffee."

"No, thanks," she said, only reluctantly allowing the dentist to lead her into his private office, where he pressed her into one of the chairs that faced his desk.

"How about tea, then? You need something, you're white as a ghost. Do it for me, just to make this seem sociable, since I'm here on my day off."

"Okay, tea," she answered, staring out his door at the closed panel of the surgical suite at the other end of the hall. "What are you doing here, if it's your day off?" she asked him, only half thinking about making conversation.

"I was over at the doughnut shop and I heard about Izzy. I just wanted to be here."

Clary shook her head disgustedly, accepting the tea he handed her. "I can't believe how fast the grapevine is."

"It's pretty efficient," the dentist agreed.

Clary's attention wandered back down the hall to the surgical suite. "Damn this town for not having a hospital."

"Relax. Beau's made sure he's well-equipped. He could perform anything short of heart surgery here."

"What if something happens? What if the baby needs special care?"

"The helicopter is waiting just outside of town—can't you hear it?" Skokie joined her in the second patient chair, blocking most of her view. "You know," he said conversationally then, "you and I gave Wellsburg a bad rap when we were kids, both of us wanting out as if it was some kind of jail."

"That's definitely how it seemed to me," she answered, craning to see around him.

"A small town has its limits, but it has advantages, too."

"I imagine so," she answered distractedly.

"I did my time in the big city. All the hustle and bustle and short-fuse tempers, the traffic and lines and crowds, living among a bunch of strangers who couldn't care less about you. No thanks. The old Burg looked pretty good to me after a few years of that. I couldn't wait to get back. Now I see living here as the best of both worlds. I have the advantages of a small town, and when I start to feel penned in, well, hell, I'm not a kid anymore. I hop in my car and take off. Greeley is close by. Denver isn't faraway. I get my fill of the city and then come home. It's great."

"That's nice . . ." Clary couldn't sit still any longer. She set her mug on his desk, stood and went to the door. "How long do you suppose this will take?"

"Not long, I think. The wife of a friend of mine in Denver had triplets by C-section a few years ago. Apparently it's a big deal to get in, take the baby and get out as fast as possible, because the doctor who did it was bragging about how quick he was. It took him under three minutes for each baby, if I remember right. Then, of course there's the closing—"

Skokie went on talking. Clary knew he was just trying to keep her mind off the surgery in the next room, but she couldn't concentrate on what he was saying. Instead, she made an occasional noncommittal comment, all the while staring down the hall at the door that cut her off from Izzy.

And then that door finally opened and Beau stepped out, his green gown blood-splattered.

Clary lunged down the hallway.

"It's a girl," he announced, as if nothing had been amiss.

"Izzy?" Clary demanded.

"She's fine. The baby's fine. Even Dad is fine."

He seemed so relaxed. "What about the toxemia?" she asked, as if it might have slipped his mind.

"Delivery is the cure. It just has to be accomplished before the blood pressure hits the ceiling. As soon as the baby is out of there, the pressure drops and that's that."

"Really?"

"Really."

Relief made Clary wilt. She wanted to close the few feet between herself and Beau, to feel his arms wrap around her, to draw from his strength and support. She stepped toward him, but he only reached out a hand to her shoulder, much as he might have to the waiting family of any patient.

Then he looked at Skokie. "Lend us a hand getting Izzy and the baby to the helicopter, will you?"

"Beau?" Clary said, though she didn't want anything from him except to close the distance he was keeping from her, the same distance he'd kept when she'd first come back to Wellsburg.

Whether purposely or not, he interpreted her query to be in regard to her cousin again. "Everything is fine, but a C-section is still major surgery. Izzy will have to spend some time in the hospital. I'll be going with them to see that they make the trip all right. Will you let Dori know— if she's still around?"

"Of course," Clary answered, softly, hating that straight arm of his that kept her at bay.

Then he let go of her and turned away. "Great. Thanks." And he was gone, with Skokie following in his wake.

Between the drugs Izzy had been given and the emergency delivery, she was dopey and barely awake when Beau wheeled her out on an ambulance stretcher. Jack walked along beside, holding his wife's hand, and Skokie carried the baby, all bundled up in a surgical blanket.

Clary kissed her cousin on the forehead and then went for a peek at the baby. Skokie opened the blanket to show the beet red face, all scrunched up and mad-looking.

Clary wasn't sure if it was relief or sentimentality, but at that first sight of her, tears filed her eyes to the brim. "She's beautiful," she managed to tell her cousin.

And then she realized that Beau was staring at her. Hard. His expression was dark and questioning, his brow furrowed. But all he said was, "We need to get to the helicopter."

Clary stepped out of the way and then followed behind. As she went outside it surprised her to find that a crowd had gathered. Friends and neighbors stood all along the sidewalk, around Beau's four-by-four, up and down the street and across it, waiting and clearly worrying much the same as Clary had.

"We have a girl!" Jack announced proudly, and a spontaneous cheer went up as if the home team had just won the game.

Skokie held the baby slightly aloft to show her off, and like Clary's, some eyes were misty and a few sniffles sounded.

It struck her at that moment how like a big family these people were, and that gave her an odd pang of something she couldn't quite put her finger on.

With the stretcher in the back of Beau's car once more, Jack climbed in, accepting the baby from Skokie, and Beau went up to the front and got in. Part of the crowd eased between Clary and the car, straining to call in their congratulations and good wishes, unintentionally forcing her back. And as she stood watching, cut off from it all like the outsider she was, she realized that pang was just a little envy of the closeness they all shared.

"So everything is okay?" a young voice said from behind her.

She turned to find Dori there, as removed as she was. "That's what your dad says. I suppose you heard—the baby is a girl."

"Yeah, I heard. From Mason, the guy who picks up the trash. He rang the doorbell a few minutes ago to tell me, and wanted to discuss all the details." Dori made a face. "We might as well all just walk around naked. I swear every person in this town knows how many times every other person goes to the bathroom. It's so sickening."

Clary was at a loss as to what to say at that moment, because her own feelings were so mixed, and so she didn't respond.

Dori nodded in the direction of Beau's car as it pulled away. "Did my dad say anything to you about me?"

"Just to let you know that he was going to Greeley in the helicopter with Izzy and the baby."

The teenager visibly deflated. "Oh. Then he didn't say if he was going to do what you said he should and help me out with money?"

"Sorry."

It was clear in the young girl's expression that the issue of finances was weighing on her more than she wanted anyone to know. "Yeah. Well. I guess I'll just go home and see what he has to say when he comes back."

"Dori—"

"Not that it matters. I'm going, even if he won't pay anything," she announced in a fresh wave of bravado that told Clary the teenager wouldn't listen to anything else she had to say.

So Clary swallowed the cautionary words she'd been about to offer. "I'm glad you'll at least wait for him to get home."

Dori just shrugged before leaving Clary to stand on the sidewalk, awash in confused feelings of her own.

It was late that evening before Beau could hitch a ride back to Wellsburg in the helicopter. Ducking out from under the rotating blades, he waved to the pilot and by the time he reached his car the aircraft had lifted off again.

Beau got in the four-by-four, but he didn't start the engine right away. Instead he sat there, staring at the flat farmland stretched out before him, the sun just setting in the west and casting a rosy glow to the cloudless sky.

It occurred to him that he'd started this day watching that same sun rise, and all that had transpired in the interim weighed heavily on him.

What was he going home to? he wondered. Had Dori run off? Or had she stayed to see if he would follow Clary's advice and subsidize a year of trying to be an actress?

Hell, for all he knew, the two of them could already be on their way to L.A.

But deep down he didn't believe that. Clary wouldn't leave without a word. And Dori would be waiting, to see if he was going to help her.

Was he? he asked himself.

He rolled down the car window and angled his elbow out into the cooler night air, thinking about the situation, about his options.

As much as he hated to admit it, Clary was right about Dori. She was going to put acting ahead of college, no matter what he said or did or refused to do. There was no stopping her. Now it was only a matter of how she did it. And what he was left worrying about.

The money was not an issue. It had just been a tactic he'd hoped would keep her from forsaking the rest of her education. From making what he considered to be a mistake. But when all was said and done, he had to concede that it was her mistake to make.

He dropped his head back against the seat and closed his eyes.

"It's her life," he told himself.

And the time had come for him to let go. Just the way he'd had to give in to nylon stockings when he'd wanted her to wear tights, to lipstick instead of Chapstick, to hair spray, to driving, to later curfews when he'd wanted her in the house where he knew she was safe.

But, damn, there was nothing easy about it.

She was going to leave him. She was going out into the world to do what she wanted, headlong and hell-bent. And Clary was also right that he wouldn't be able to rest, if she did it scratch-and-scrabble, living somewhere cheap and maybe dangerous, working God only knew where to make ends meet.

So whether he agreed with Dori's decision or not, whether he liked it or not, there was really only one choice he could make.

Beau tilted his head out the car window to stare at the stars and try to make peace with his defeat. "I'm sorry, Gina. I tried," he said.

And then he took a deep breath, sighed it out and there in his thoughts appeared Clary.

She was leaving, too.

And beyond all reason, her saying it, making plans for it, had been a blow to him.

He'd known she wasn't going to stay. He'd known she was only in Wellsburg for a visit. He'd known she had a life she liked in California. He'd known she had every intention of going back to it.

Hell, he'd warned himself that their relationship was only a temporary fling from the beginning. He'd tried to fight the attraction because of it. Then, when he couldn't, he'd given in to having her for the time being, knowing all the while that she wasn't going to be within arm's reach for long.

And still, somewhere deep inside, he'd denied it all. Why else would it have felt like a knife slicing his heart out to hear her say she'd look after Dori in L.A.?

"Damn."

But in spite of everything, he loved Clary. Lord, how he loved her. And that love didn't care about logistics. It only made him know that he wanted her in his life.

He wanted to build his house with her. He wanted to have babies with her—even though it would hurt as much when those babies grew up and left the nest as it did to have Dori do it now. He wanted to go through the rest of his life with Clary, good and bad. He wanted to marry her.

Would that make a difference to her staying or going?

He was afraid it wouldn't.

But he couldn't be sure. It might.

He sat up straight and finally turned the key in the ignition. "Well, there's only one way to find out."

He had to ask.

Clary had paced until her legs ached, she realized as she stopped to turn on the lamp in the living room now that darkness had crept in. She'd spent all afternoon worrying. About Izzy and the baby, about Beau and Dori. And even though it seemed as if she'd answered the telephone and the doorbell a hundred times, she hadn't heard a word about anything.

Well, she couldn't take it anymore.

She went to the phone in the kitchen, dialed the operator and put a call in to the hospital in Greeley. When she asked for news of the MacIntires, her call was forwarded to a room and within moments Jack's voice came on the line.

"Clary, I was just going to call you."

"Is everything okay?"

"Everything is great! Izzy and the baby have both been checked out by specialists here and they're fine. It's just taken us forever to wade through hospital red tape and finally get them into a room. I would have called, but I was afraid if I left them along the way, to get to a phone, I'd never be able to find them again."

"But they're all right? Izzy's blood pressure went back down and the baby—"

"Honestly, they're fine. Wonderful. Couldn't be better. I'd let you talk to Izzy yourself, but she's learning how to nurse at the moment."

"That's okay. I don't want to bother her. I was just going crazy wondering what had happened to you guys." And Beau, but she paused before asking if he was there with them.

"Oh, no, he left a couple of hours ago. The helicopter took him back. He's pretty worried about Dori—I imagine he went straight home to deal with all of that."

"I imagine," Clary agreed, knowing that the situation with the teenager had to be Beau's first priority, but wishing he'd call or come over so they could talk, too.

"I won't keep you," she told Jack then. "What about you? Do you want me to drive to Greeley to pick you up?"

"No, I'm getting a room in a motel here so I can be with Iz and the baby until they're ready to go home. You don't mind, do you? I mean, being at the house alone?"

"Don't worry about me. Just tell Izzy I love her and I'll call tomorrow."

Clary hung up and went back to pacing. She was relieved that her cousin and the baby were doing well, but somehow that relief didn't do much for her overall tension.

What about Beau? she kept asking herself as she traced a circular path from the living room, through the dining room, into the kitchen, down the hall to the entryway and around again.

Was he angry over her suggestion about Dori? Had the offer to let the teenager stay at Clary's condominium made a bad situation worse? And what about being slapped with the realization that Clary wasn't staying in Wellsburg? How badly had that hurt him?

She had just made the turn into the kitchen when the doorbell rang. If this was another neighbor wanting to know about Izzy and the baby, she'd scream, Clary thought as she beat a hasty path through to the hallway that was a straight shot to the front door.

But the face on the other side of the screen was the one she wanted to see most in the world—Beau's. Only his very serious expression slowed her down some.

"Hi," she said, too brightly. She wasn't anxious to learn what was behind that somberness.

He returned her greeting as he stepped in through the door she held open for him.

"I just talked to Jack a few minutes ago," she went on as if nothing had happened beyond the birth of her cousin's baby.

"I suppose he told you Izzy and the baby came out in good shape, then?"

"He did. I was glad to hear it," she said.

Beau wandered into the living room and Clary followed him, drinking in the sight of his broad back and narrow hips. She couldn't forget the distance he'd forced between them after the delivery, and it kept her several feet away from him as he came to a stop beside a tall wing chair, looking out the picture window rather than turning to face her.

"Dori's still at home," he said then, without much tone in his voice. "She opted for waiting until I got back, to find out if I was going to take your suggestion."

"Are you?" Clary asked softly.

"Yeah. I am." He glanced at her over his shoulder. "You're a smart lady. You were right that I wouldn't have been able to rest, knowing she was trying to scrape by in L.A. I'll support her, and in return she assures me that if she hasn't made it as an actress at the end of a year, she'll go to college. I don't know if that's true—she's already reneged on one college promise—but I guess I can hope."

Clary wanted to go to him, to wrap her arms around him and comfort him in this, which she knew was difficult for him. But she refrained and instead said, "How are you doing?"

"I'll live." Then he turned, crossed his arms over his chest and leveled those green eyes of his on her. "But I'd rather you weren't there for her to live with."

"It isn't an inconvenience. I really like Dori and I have the space and I'd welcome the company...when I'm home, and—"

"That isn't what I meant. And I think you know it," he said quietly, his deep voice a low rumble in his chest. "I'm asking, Clary—stay in Wellsburg with me, marry me, raise a family with me here."

Her hands were shaking and she grabbed onto the back of the sofa to still them. "I love you, Beau," she said. "And there isn't anything I'd like more than to marry you and raise a family."

"But?" he prompted when she stalled.

"But not in Wellsburg."

He looked away from her. "Wellsburg isn't such a bad place."

"Maybe it isn't. But between the gossip about Wolf and me, and listening to Dori spout all my own complaints about life in a small town this morning, I remembered why I left in the first place."

She took a step around the couch and toward him, but when he pinned her with his eyes again she stopped short. "I like L.A. I have a life there, friends, a business. You're a great doctor, you could do good work there. And be with Dori every step of the way no matter what she does, too. Couldn't that be a possibility?"

"You want me to leave Wellsburg and go to California with you?"

"Why not?"

He shook his head. "It's not that easy. It's not even possible."

"Why not?" she repeated, her voice slightly raised in frustration.

"There isn't anything you have in L.A. that you either don't already have here or couldn't have. But beside the fact that I love this little town, I have responsibilities, Clary. If I leave, the people here have no medical care. I'd be abandoning eight pregnant women—like Izzy—without anyone to deliver their babies, if they can't get to Greeley. And that's only the tip of the iceberg. This isn't just a job. I've made a commitment to this town, to family and friends we've both known all our lives. I can't walk out on that. I won't.''

This time he took a step toward her, but he only came halfway before stopping himself. ''I don't think you're giving yourself enough credit for maturity, for being able to make the best of circumstances that might not be ideal. There are drawbacks to living in a big city. And hassles and inconveniences and annoyances. They may be different than what you don't like about Wellsburg, but they exist, don't they?''

''Of course.''

''And you deal with them.''

She shrugged her agreement.

''Well, why couldn't you make small-town life work for you, too? Why couldn't you just deal with whatever bothers you about it, the same way?''

''It's different, Beau.'' Her tone beseeched him to see that. ''The hassles and inconveniences and annoyances are just that—minor nuisances. They don't stifle me or close me in or suffocate me, the way living in Wellsburg did.''

''*Did*—that's the operative word here. You haven't felt that way since you've been back. Or if you have, you've done one hell of a job of hiding it.''

''Okay, so I haven't felt that way—well, not as badly as I did before. But only because I've known all along that this was just a vacation, that I wasn't stuck here for good.''

''You say that as if Wellsburg is some kind of prison. It's just a small town, Clary, with a highway into and out of it.''

''It's a small town I've already lived in and hated, just the way Dori does,'' she shot out in frustration.

"And what about Izzy?" he asked, clearly reaching for straws, in frustration of his own. "You came back to reconnect with her, to stop neglecting your relationship with her—staying here would accomplish that. But if you go back, won't you fall into the same pattern that caused you to drift apart before? You said you needed to change your priorities—what better way to do that than to come back to a place where most everything takes a back seat to the people and the relationships, because there isn't much else to life here?"

"I know you can't understand how I feel about Wellsburg, Beau, because you see it differently than I do."

"You might see it differently, too, if you gave it half a chance, if you looked at it through the eyes of an adult rather than through those of a teenager—either Dori or yourself fifteen years ago. You could make the best of it, Clary. *We* could make the best of it, dammit."

"It isn't that simple. I was looking at it through the eyes of an adult yesterday and last night and, believe me, it didn't look any better than it did fifteen years ago. And seeing how much Dori hates it here, how much she wants out, is just too vivid a reminder of how Wellsburg made me feel. I can't ignore that. Not even if the feeling isn't strong right at this moment. I can't stay here. I just can't," she said with finality.

Beau's jaw clenched, his back straightened and the look on his face made Clary feel as if he were ripping her heart out. "And I can't leave," he said, with just as much finality, sounding angry and resolute.

Clary raised her chin to him, but her voice was weak as she asked the question that deep down she knew the answer to. "What do we do?"

His kiwi green eyes pierced her. "We say goodbye."

There was a challenge in his tone, in his expression. They stood those few feet apart, staring at one another, and Clary knew he was waiting for her to give in.

But she couldn't. Any more than a claustrophobic could step into a closet and close the door.

And then he walked out.

Chapter Eleven

By noon the next day Clary's bags were packed and loaded into the trunk of her rental car. As she waited for Dori, she double-checked Izzy's house to make sure she hadn't left the coffeepot on, or the back door unlocked, or water dripping anywhere.

The teenager had called the night before, not much more than an hour after Beau left, to tell Clary that her father had given her the go-ahead for the move to L.A., without even asking that she stay for the graduation ceremony.

It hadn't taken Clary long to give in to Dori's anxiousness to leave. With Izzy's baby born and Jack taking the next month off work to help out, the last thing the little family needed was a house guest. Besides, the thought of staying in Wellsburg with Beau so near and yet out of reach to her was Clary's idea of torture.

So she'd managed to book two seats on an evening flight, which gave her and Dori time to stop in Greeley to leave Jack and Izzy their car, and visit, before going all the way to Denver and the airport.

When she'd made sure the house was ready to be left vacant for a few days, she went into the living room to watch for Dori. The only sounds coming in from outside were the soft twittering of birds in the trees and the distant hum of a lawn mower.

Across the street, Maeve Brown was kneeling on the ground to tend her bright yellow and purple pansies, wearing an ancient, limp straw hat and gray gardening gloves like those Clary remembered her own grandmother having. A few houses down from that, old Mr. Morse was atop a ladder painting the shutters on his house and a small boy Clary didn't recognize rode his tricycle happily along the sidewalk, without a parent in sight, but under the watchful eyes of both adults as they went about their chores.

Beau was right about wanting to raise a family here, Clary thought as she took in the sight. A child alone on the streets of just about any big city was in considerably more danger, both from traffic and people. In Wellsburg, the kids could run as free as kids had since Clary was a child, without being at risk for much beyond falling off their bikes.

Beau's four-by-four turned the corner just then and Clary forgot about everything else. Taking a deep, strengthening breath, and forcing a smile that quivered into existence, she went out onto the porch as he and his daughter drove up.

Dori waved wildly, as Beau pulled into the driveway behind the rental car and Izzy and Jack's compact, but her father didn't take his eyes off what he was doing.

He left the engine running, got out and took the teenager's bags from the rear as Dori nearly jumped to the ground in her enthusiasm. "Shall we put my stuff in your car or the MacIntires'?" she asked.

"Mine," Clary answered, watching Beau only peripherally. "Even though you'll be driving Izzy's, we might as well save ourselves the trouble of having to switch your suitcases at the hospital. Hang on a second and I'll get the keys—I didn't think to leave it open after I put my things in."

Clary was back within seconds, finding Beau standing at the rear, waiting for her with his daughter's bags on the gravel drive at his feet. Their eyes met only briefly, but it was long enough for Clary to see the dark, troubled expression there. Then he looked away, picking up the suitcases as if there were an immediate need to do so.

Clary unlocked the trunk and he loaded it. Without so much as glancing at her, he said, "I'll be sending Dori enough money for room-and-board. I appreciate you letting her stay with you. I'll rest a lot easier, knowing you're keeping an eye on her."

His formality struck Clary like an Arctic wind. "I'm looking forward to having her," she answered, none too casually herself.

With the suitcases loaded, Beau slammed the trunk closed again and turned to his daughter.

Clary had never seen a more forced smile and it told her how hard this was for him. "I'll just get my purse and lock the front door," she said wanting to leave them alone to say their goodbyes.

As she turned toward the house, she saw that both Mr. Morse and Maeve Brown had stopped what they were doing to watch, as if what was going on in the driveway was for their entertainment alone. It irked her unreasonably. Couldn't they see this was a private moment? Didn't they care that they were intruding on it?

She was tempted to shoo them away like stray cats. But a glance back at Beau and Dori told her that she was the only one who had noticed the audience, and she refrained, going into the house instead.

By the time she came out again, Dori was in the driver's seat of Izzy's car and Beau was leaning over to talk to her through the window.

Clary went to her own car, opened the door, but didn't get in. Instead she watched Beau, drinking in the sight of his jean-clad hips and the curve of his broad back inside the white shirt he wore.

Then he straightened, hit the roof of the car, said a final goodbye and stepped away. Clary's rental was between him and his four-by-four and he had to pass by her to get to it.

She saw him hesitate for a moment when he realized that. But then on he came, his eyes locking with hers as if he couldn't keep them from doing anything else.

As he drew up alongside her, she waited for him to say something. Anything. But all he did was nod. Just once. And Clary couldn't stand it.

"I'll take good care of her," she said, hating the crack in her voice and the hope in her heart that he would stop, that he would take her in his arms, kiss her, make everything all right.

But "Thanks" was all he answered. His brows pulled into a deep frown and she had the sense that for one split second he considered saying or doing more, after all. But in the end he walked past and got into his own car.

The sound of his slamming door sank her heart.

She hadn't realized it, but deep down she'd been hoping that when he was actually faced with both her and his daughter leaving he might reconsider his decision to stay in Wellsburg. It had been foolish of her, she knew with instant clarity, but that didn't make it any easier to watch him back out of the driveway.

Clary had the unholy urge to call to him to wait, to run to him. But what would she say once she'd stopped him? What could she say? And so she just watched him go, fighting hard to keep the moisture in her eyes from spilling over.

"Do you want to follow me, or shall I follow you?" Dori asked then, craning her head out the window.

Clary dragged her eyes from Beau's departing car and had to swallow hard to get words to pass through her throat around the lump that was there. "I'll follow you. I'm not sure I remember how to get to the hospital once we reach Greeley," she finally managed.

Then she got in her car, strapped herself into her seat belt with a vengeance and backed out of the driveway.

Izzy and Jack had finally decided on a name for the baby. They were calling her Anna, and once Clary and Dori had both exclaimed over how cute she was, Izzy handed her over to Jack.

"Why don't you take her to the nursery for a diaper change. And I'll bet Dori could go along to see the slew of other babies out there, just so she'll know Anna is the prettiest."

It wasn't a very subtle way of getting a few minutes alone with Clary, but Jack and Dori were good sports and left.

Once they were gone, Clary sat on the edge of her cousin's bed and took her hand. "You're looking pretty good, Mom," she said, forcing gaiety she didn't feel.

Izzy waved away the compliment. "I want to know what happened to persuade Beau to let Dori go to L.A."

Clary told her the whole story.

"Okay, but what's the rush?" Izzy asked when she'd finished. "Why isn't Dori at least waiting to go through graduation? With as quick as the two of you are getting out of town, a person would think you'd robbed the bank."

Clary shrugged. "You know how much of a hurry Dori's in, to get to L.A. She didn't care about the ceremony, and I guess when Beau gave in to letting her go, he must have given in to everything."

"Seems to me he'd have used the ceremony to buy himself a few more days with you, if not with Dori."

Clary glanced at a flower arrangement on the table beside Izzy's bed. "We sort of came to a parting of the ways ourselves."

"I was afraid of that. What happened?"

It was a little more difficult for her to tell that part of what had gone on in the past twenty-four hours, but with some effort she managed.

"Oh, Clary," Izzy sighed. "Are you sure about this? I thought you and Beau had found something really good together."

"It was really good. It just wasn't in the right place."

From the look on her cousin's face, Izzy was about to give her a tongue-lashing, but Jack and Dori came back just then and saved Clary.

"We should get going," Dori announced, her excitement bubbling like soda pop.

Clary stood. "You're right, we should."

Izzy's expression still managed to relay her disapproval, as Clary bent over to hug her.

"Poor Beau," Izzy said then. "He must feel awful to have you both going away at once. Shame on you for deserting him."

Clary knew her cousin's barb was aimed at her, but apparently Dori took it personally because it dampened the teenager's enthusiasm considerably.

"He'll probably be too busy to miss us," Clary rejoined brightly.

"Yeah, and when he isn't, we'll do what we can to fill the gap," Jack put in, apparently oblivious to the undercurrent of this exchange.

"I'll call you when you get home, in a couple of days," Clary promised, squeezing Izzy's hand before she and Dori left.

The elevator ride down to the hospital lobby was silent, and Clary could see that Izzy's comment had struck a sharp chord in the teenager. As they got in the rental car in the parking lot, it occurred to her that she might be having second thoughts.

"If you've changed your mind I'll take you back to Wellsburg," she offered, almost hoping Dori might take her up on it, so she could see Beau one more time.

But Dori shook her head resolutely. "I don't *ever* want to go back to Wellsburg," she said, almost spitting the town name out.

Clary didn't say another word. She just started the car and headed for Denver, knowing only too well all of what the teenager was feeling.

It was only a matter of days in L.A. before Dori claimed she was in heaven. What with palm trees, sandy beaches, ocean waves, Disneyland and acting agents, the city was all she had thought it would be. She settled into Clary's condominium, loving it, as well as the attention she drew from the "hot men" who were the sons of several of Clary's neighbors. The teenager also liked Biminis and Clary's idea to put her to work there as a hostess.

Clary wished Dori's high spirits were contagious. She could have used a little. Actually, she could have used a lot.

She felt as if leaving Beau had taken the wind out of her sails. But because she had Dori living with her Clary put on a happy face, to hide the fact that she'd never felt more miserable in her life.

"Come on, babe, let's cash it in early today and have a drink in your office before I head for my poker game," Wolf said when he arrived at the restaurant just after five in the afternoon on Friday of Clary's second week back.

"Sorry, Wolf, but I have work to do before the dinner rush hits, and I need to get Dori home to dress for a date tonight. Give me a rain check."

"No can do." He took her hand and pulled her as far as the bar, pausing there to order them both a glass of wine. Then, as if he owned the place, he informed the restaurant, in general, to pretend no one knew where Clary was and pulled her the rest of the way to her office.

He closed and locked the door before crossing to sit on the mauve couch, where he patted the cushion next to him. "Sit."

"Feeling bossy today, are we?" she joked as she did.

"I'm worried about you."

"Haven't I heard that before?"

He touched her glass with his. "To friends paying attention to what's going on with friends," he toasted.

Clary watched him take a drink of his wine as she sipped hers.

Then Wolf went on. "We both might have neglected Lois and overlooked just how serious her depression was, but I don't intend to make the same mistake with you."

She waved away his concern. "I'm fine."

"You've gotten even more lines under your eyes since you came home from Podunkville, you're losing weight and you are definitely not fine. And I want to know what's going on with you. You said you'd gotten over your feelings of guilt about Lois, so if that's not it, then, what is?''

She hadn't told her friend much about Beau, mainly because talking about him, thinking about him, was so painful for her. But maybe confiding in Wolf would do her some good. Maybe it would be cathartic.

She took a deep breath and explained the whole situation, including that Beau had asked her to marry him and move back to Wellsburg, and the reasons she'd turned him down.

''Well, you're certainly not happy in L.A. any more,'' he said when she'd finished. ''I don't want to lose you, but given the choice, I'd rather have you happy in the boonies than unhappy here.''

''That's just the point—I don't think I could be happy in the boonies.''

''I know I couldn't be,'' he said with a full measure of his distaste for small-town life ringing in his voice. ''Isn't there any chance that the good doctor would move here? I mean, now that both you and Dori are gone and he's had a chance to miss the two of you, maybe his mind can be changed.''

Clary shook her head. ''I don't think so. It isn't only a matter of him wanting to stay there, he also feels responsible for the town. Without him, they'd be doctorless, and the odds of luring another well-qualified M.D. are slim-to-none.''

''So what are you going to do, babe?''

''Hope I get over him?'' she suggested.

Wolf looked dubious, but before he could say anything Dori knocked on the office door.

"I'm sorry, I know Wolf said not to bother you," she said in a tentative voice from the hallway outside. "But my date is supposed to pick me up in less than half an hour..."

"Go ahead and punch out. I'm on my way," Clary called back.

Wolf stood with her. "Well, I was a lot of help, wasn't I?" he said snidely.

Clary touched his arm. "It's nice to know you care."

He covered her hand with his, patting it. "You know I do. I just wish I could come up with a solution. How about a satellite dish for a wedding present, to keep you in touch with the outside world? Think that would help?"

Clary laughed. "It wouldn't do a thing for the living-in-a-fishbowl element, but it might help the claustrophobia of small-town life."

"So that's it, then? What's going on with you is just that you need some time to get over him?"

"I guess so." She went to her desk and took her purse from the bottom drawer.

"Well, I'm here if—"

"It goes without saying. Don't look so concerned. I'm not going to do what Lois did."

Wolf gave her a quick hug. "I know that." Then they headed for the door and he changed the subject. "How are you doing as a parent?"

"I'm trying to behave more like a roommate. I've set a few house rules, but for the most part I mind my own business. Not only is Dori eighteen, but the last thing in the world I'd want is to be as restrictive as my grandmother was with me."

"Might make her feel right at home," he commented as they walked out of the office.

Dori was waiting a discreet few feet outside. She fell into step with them as if she'd been a part of the threesome forever.

"Did that repairman who came yesterday fix the dishwasher all right?" she asked Wolf.

"Works like a charm. I really appreciate you sitting at my place all morning waiting for him."

"No problem. I liked listening to your compact-disc player. You have some great music...for an old guy," she teased.

Wolf grabbed her in a playful headlock in the parking lot, and the teenager tickled her way out of it.

Walking along, Clary smiled at them. Lord, what she wouldn't give to feel that good again!

Clary and Dori left Wolf at his car and crossed the lot to theirs. As Clary drove home Dori worked the radio, continuing to sing one of the songs as she unlocked the door on Clary's bright, airy condo while Clary stopped to collect the mail.

By the time she went in, Dori had hit the play button on the answering machine and it was Beau's voice leaving a message for his daughter that greeted Clary. But for one irrational moment she thought he was there, in her living room, waiting for her, and her pulse kicked up with such joy it winded her before she realized what she was really listening to.

Dori didn't seem to notice that she'd frozen on the threshold and so Clary went the rest of the way in, closing the door behind her and trying to act as if she couldn't care less about the sound of Beau's deep, rich voice filling the place and her heart at once.

It wasn't as if Beau hadn't called in the past two weeks, but each time he had, Dori had just coincidentally answered the phone.

If her reaction to Beau's voice on tape was this strong, Clary thought, what would have happened if she had picked up one of his calls and found the real thing on the other end of the line?

With her pulse still racing and a sick ache suddenly in her stomach, Clary went through the living room to the small combination kitchen/dining room. She could hear Dori placing a collect call to Beau, and within seconds the teenager connected.

She tried not to eavesdrop, but Dori's enthusiasm made her voice too loud to miss. Not that she was saying anything Clary shouldn't hear and didn't know about already, but there was something about knowing Beau was on the other end of that phone that put a vise grip around Clary's heart.

Suddenly, the image of Beau stamped itself on her brain. In her mind's eye she could see his mink-colored hair, those chiseled features, his bright green eyes and his fine, masculine mouth, bracketed with deep creases that rippled out around the corners when he smiled.

Since getting back to L.A. she'd been fighting so hard not to think about him, not to be tortured with this mental image of him, and yet there it was, so vivid he could have been in the room with her. And never in her life had she felt such a powerful mixture of longing and regret as she did at that moment.

Maybe Wolf was right and she should get on the phone and ask Beau again to move to L.A. Maybe he was feeling the same thing she was and this time he'd agree.

But a moment after she offered herself the option, reason took over. She knew that even if he was feeling the same things, he wouldn't give up Wellsburg and his commitments there. He couldn't.

Clary wrapped her arms around her middle, squeezing hard, and leaned back against the counter. She closed her eyes and willed away his image, taking deep breaths and listening to the pounding of her heartbeat in her ears. How could something as simple as a visit to Izzy have turned her whole life upside-down?

"Clary? Are you all right?"

Startled, Clary opened her eyes and stood up straight, wondering when the teenager had gotten off the phone. "Sure. I'm fine," she said too quickly.

"Are you sick?"

"No, my eyes just burned a little. The pollution must be high today."

Dori stared at her much the same way Wolf had earlier, as if she didn't believe a word of it, but didn't know what else to say.

Clary saved her the trouble. Glancing at the slate clock on the wall, she said, "You'd better hurry and change. Your date will be here any minute."

"I don't have to go out. We could have dinner together," Dori offered compassionately.

The idea was incredibly tempting, as Clary realized at that moment that the thought of a long, lonely evening was pretty unappealing. But she didn't give in to it. "Don't be silly. You've been looking forward to this date all week. Besides, I really only came to drop you off. I have to get back to Biminis and finish the book work Wolf interrupted."

Then, as if to prove this hadn't been a spur of the moment idea to escape her own feelings, she went around Dori and headed for the front door. "Have a good time tonight," she called as she went out.

In her car, Clary paused to take more deep breaths and swallow back some of the emotions that had assailed her in the past few minutes.

And then, once she had everything under control again, she made a beeline for the safety net of Biminis.

In the hour that Clary had been at the restaurant, Beau and Wellsburg had been on her mind more than business. And along with that had come the realization that in the two weeks since she'd come home, she'd yet to find the time to call Izzy.

So following Wolf's example, she let it be known that she wasn't to be disturbed, went into her office and locked the door for the second time that day.

A woman answered Izzy's phone but Clary had no idea who it was, so she merely asked for her cousin. When Izzy came on the line, Clary said, "I wasn't sure I'd dialed the right number."

Izzy laughed. "That was the mayor's wife. I was in the middle of changing Anna's diaper."

"Shall I call back?"

"No, no. The mayor's wife came to watch the baby while I go for a walk to get some exercise. She's playing with her, so I'm sure she won't care if I waste a little time on the phone before I go."

"So how is everything?" Clary asked, though her cousin sounded so bright and cheery it seemed unnecessary.

"Great! I'm good, Jack is good and Anna is wonderful."

"You don't even sound tired. How can that be, with a new baby in the house? Don't tell me she's so perfect she even sleeps through the night?"

"No, but I get a nap every day. Wellsburg is a town full of surrogate grandmothers, grandfathers, aunts and uncles. I have more baby-sitters and offers for help than I can use. In fact, I'm being so pampered by everyone else that Jack went back to work instead of taking off all the time he was going to. I just didn't need him.''

Clary smiled genuinely for the first time since she'd gotten home, picturing so many doting baby-lovers vying for some time with the newborn. ''That's nice to hear. Usually, when I ask a new mother how she's doing, she's exhausted and blue and feeling cut off from the rest of the world.''

''Wellsburg is already sort of cut off from the rest of the world,'' Izzy joked. ''Although I have to admit it's a little embarrassing to have the whole town talking about my sore nipples,'' she added with a laugh. ''I guess you have to take the bad with the good.''

''But with the exception of sore nipples you're feeling okay?''

''Good as new. How about you? How are you and Dori doing?''

''Fine. L.A. is hog heaven for Dori. She loves it here.'' Clary paused a moment, knowing she was only salting her wounds to ask about Beau. But she couldn't resist. ''Is Beau adjusting to his empty nest?''

''He seems okay—not great, but okay. He's putting some effort into keeping himself occupied, mainly by finally taking notice of my assistant principal and asking her out to dinner a few times.''

''A few times in just two weeks?''

''It surprised me, too. I tried fixing them up when I first hired her, but he wasn't interested.''

''Well, he must be now, to take her out three times in only two weeks.'' Each time Clary repeated it, it came out sounding a little more extreme.

"It was you who turned him down, remember?" her cousin pointed out, obviously hearing the jealousy in her tone. "Maybe the time you spent together reminded him how nice it was to have a close relationship. Eve thinks you just warmed him up for her."

"Just what I always wanted to be—the opening act," Clary grumbled.

"They broke ground on his house next door last week, so that's underway," Izzy said then.

Clary knew it was irrational but, to her, Izzy's casual change of subject made it seem as if Beau's future with the other woman was a *fait accompli*.

Her cousin went on, "Sonny Dagliani is building it and he says the place should be ready to move into by the fall. Who knows, maybe Beau won't be moving into it alone, after all."

Clary heard an undertone of amusement in her cousin's voice. "Are you just trying to get to me?"

"Yes, I'm trying to get to you, but it's all true. You should know that Beau isn't letting any grass grow under him, in case you might be thinking twice about the wisdom in rejecting him."

"Izzy—"

But Clary could hear the baby crying in the background and her cousin cut her off. "I better go check on things. Can I call you back tomorrow?"

"Sure."

"Think, Clary. Really think," her cousin advised and then hung up.

Clary stared at the phone, but that wasn't what she saw in her mind. The image there was of Beau and the assistant principal. And it ate her heart out.

"Why couldn't he just move to L.A.?" she groused.

But she knew why. She even had to admit that he was right—his leaving Wellsburg would be a much bigger deal for more people than her leaving California. And she wouldn't want Izzy and Jack and the baby to be without a doctor.

So that only left one alternative, if she wanted him.

But could she stand to go back to Wellsburg? To a claustrophobic life in a fishbowl? she asked herself.

Okay, to be honest, for the most part, she hadn't found it as intolerable as she had as a kid growing up there. But was that only because she'd known she was there for a visit and not for the rest of her life?

Maybe.

Or maybe not.

There had been some things she genuinely appreciated—like the friendliness and closeness of the small community, the feeling of safety and the knowledge that there would be any number of helping hands should the need for them arise, the sense of the place as a big family that sincerely cared about one another.

But all that friendliness, closeness and sense of family also translated into minding one another's business.

Clary made a face just thinking about that element.

But what had Izzy said about taking the bad with the good? Could she look at it that way? The way her cousin did? Taking it in stride?

Maybe. Not happily, but maybe.

And what about the claustrophobic aspect? Could she take that in stride, too?

She suddenly had a flash of something Skokie had said when she was waiting through Izzy's cesarean and only half listening to him—something about not being a kid anymore and just getting in his car and heading for the city whenever Wellsburg felt too closed in.

Clary gave serious consideration to that. For the first time, it occurred to her that being a child without the wherewithal to leave the small town, and on top of that, living under the confining restrictions of her grandmother, might have gone a long way in contributing to the claustrophobic feelings of living in Wellsburg.

But she wasn't a kid anymore. And she had a car. Both of those things translated to a freedom that could very well have been why she hadn't felt so stifled and closed in while she was there. They might even be able to keep her from feeling those things if she lived there.

In fact, looking at it from that perspective, she admitted that Skokie might be right. It was possible that living in Wellsburg could actually be the best of both worlds; it offered the advantages of a small town, with nearby bigger cities to escape to whenever she felt the urge.

But more importantly—most importantly—Wellsburg offered Beau.

And she suddenly realized that when she'd decided the bad outweighed the good about the small town, she'd only been thinking about Wellsburg itself. She hadn't factored in Beau. Or her feelings for him.

And those feelings were too powerful to ignore. She loved him with every ounce of her heart and soul.

Wouldn't that love help cushion anything? Wouldn't it make the negatives more bearable?

Suddenly, she believed it would. Because her life wouldn't just be in Wellsburg. It would be with Beau.

Chapter Twelve

It was the middle of a lazy afternoon when Clary arrived in Wellsburg three days later. Sunshine through the elm leaves dappled the small town, and this time when she drove down Front Street nearly everyone who glanced toward her car waved as if she'd never left at all.

If only Beau would be as welcoming.

There weren't any parking places just outside of the medical building, so she had to take one several doors down and walk up. As she did, Clary couldn't help worrying just a little if Beau had really discovered some latent attraction to the assistant principal.

It didn't help, at all, to find the woman walking out of the office as Clary approached it.

An afternoon tryst? she wondered. Maybe they'd had lunch together. What if he'd taken her out to the pond? To the very spot where Clary had shared breakfast, a sunrise and a lot more with him. And what if they'd spent the time the way he and Clary had?

She suddenly lost her courage and paused on the sidewalk in front of the medical building.

But what was she going to do? she asked herself. Was she going to run back to L.A.? Was she going to give up the man and everything she'd just discovered she wanted with him, because he'd had a few dates with someone else? A few dates didn't necessarily mean anything. Even if they did happen before her tire tracks had faded.

She straightened her shoulders, pasted on a smile and went in.

The waiting room was empty, except for the receptionist sitting behind the desk and Skokie leaning against it. Neither of them hid their surprise when they looked up to find Clary. Her first inclination was to wonder if Beau's new relationship with the assistant principal had anything to do with that.

"Hi," she said, hating that it came out sounding as if she were unsure of herself. Which she was. But they didn't have to know it.

"Clary! What are you doing here?" Skokie said, perking up from leaning against the desk.

She just shrugged. "Is Beau around?" she asked, rather than answering the dentist's question.

"He's with a patient," the receptionist put in.

"That's all right," Skokie said. "I'm sure he'll want to be interrupted for this." Taking Clary's elbow, the dentist maneuvered her behind the desk and into the hall that stretched out behind it.

He opened the door to the first examining room just enough to poke his head in. "There's someone who needs to see you right away," he said, clearly enjoying himself.

"Put them in the next room. I'm finished here and I'll be right there."

From inside, the door opened farther then, and a woman steered out a small boy with a fresh cast on his right arm, thanking Beau as she did. That was when he looked up from washing his hands and caught sight of Clary.

"Is something wrong? Nothing's happened to Dori, has it?" he demanded with undisguised concern, grabbing a towel as if he might need to rush out.

"No, she's fine," Clary assured him in a hurry. "I left her in good hands—Wolf is right next door and they've really hit it off, I think he's getting a charge out of playing stand-in father or big brother or sort-of-guardian..." She was babbling and she forced herself to stop. And when she did, she became very aware that Skokie, the receptionist and the nurse were all standing just a few feet away, watching and listening.

"Could we talk?" Clary asked under her breath, still in the hallway, because she didn't feel free to just charge into the examining room uninvited.

"Sure," Beau said, with a slight tinge of sarcasm in his tone. He motioned her in as he began to leisurely dry his hands.

Clary glanced back at her audience and gave a little wave, before stepping just inside the door and closing it.

For a moment, Beau didn't say anything and Clary couldn't think of a good way to begin. Instead, she glanced around, pretending not to notice that he was scrutinizing her, and wishing that instead of nearly lunging out of her car in her hurry to see him that she'd paused to run a brush through her loose-hanging hair, or retouched her blush, or checked to make sure her purple blouse was still tucked into her black stirrup pants.

Then Beau's deep, commanding voice broke the silence. "What are you doing here?" he asked her without preamble.

But before Clary would say what she'd come to, she had to clear something up. She nodded toward the front of the office. "I...uh...just saw the assistant principal leaving. Is she sick?"

"Eve? Not that I know of. I think she had an appointment with Skokie to have a cavity filled this afternoon."

Clary couldn't help blurting out what had been eating away at her since she spoke to Izzy. "I hear you're seeing her."

"We've had dinner together. Did you come all the way from L.A. to ask me that?"

His weight was slung on one hip, he still held the towel dangling from his right hand, while the left was stuck in his back pocket, holding his lab coat open to gray slacks, a pale pink shirt and matching tie. His green eyes were shaded by the pull of a frown that moved his brows closer together. His features were sober, almost stern, and Clary was struck all over again by how handsome he was in spite of it.

But he'd asked her a question. "No, I did not come all the way from L.A. to ask you about having dinner with *Eve.*"

"Then why did you?"

"I came because you ruined California for me."

"How did I do that?"

"By not moving there."

He just stared at her, waiting, those eyes of his holding her pinned in place.

Clary took a breath and forged on. "Dori is in her element, she couldn't be happier—just the way I was, when I first moved to L.A." She hesitated, shrugging and going on in a softer, more tentative voice. "But I just love you too much to be there without you now."

His features relaxed some. "Is that so."

"It is."

"And you know what the alternative is?"

"Wellsburg."

"Wellsburg," he confirmed, his tone a challenge.

She told him all she'd thought about and realized in the past few days. "I just decided small-town life might not be so bad, if being married to you came in the bargain. Even if the whole population does end up talking about my sore nipples."

He cracked a smile. "At the moment, I think it's Izzy's that are being discussed."

"In great detail, I have no doubt."

"And you think you can stand to have yours be the topic of conversation?"

She cringed slightly at the thought. "I'm willing to try."

His smile stretched into a full-fledged grin. He tossed the towel aside and crossed to her, pulling her to him, letting his forearms ride her hips as he clasped his hands on her rear end. "And what about Biminis?"

"My manager has been saving to invest in her own restaurant. I think we can agree on terms for her to buy me out. Izzy seems to think I could make a go of reopening Sylvia's Kitchen here. I might give that some thought."

But thinking was hard to accomplish, with Beau kissing her neck. "Whatever you want. I'll do everything I can not to let the Burg seem too confining," he promised in a moment's pause before nibbling on her chin.

Then he reached around behind her, locked the door and began to unbutton her blouse.

"Here?" she whispered.

"Here," he confirmed. "Let's give them something really juicy to talk about."

But Clary stopped the descent of his hands by pressing her palm to the next button down. "I don't know. I haven't heard anything about your intentions. Town trollop is not what I'm back to become."

"Town trollop?" he repeated with a laugh. "No, that would never do. I guess I'll just have to marry you and make an honest woman of you."

"Well, you don't have to. I could always go back to L.A.," she threatened, taking a turn nibbling on his chin, flicking at the dent there with her tongue.

He gave up on her buttons, bracketed her hips and pulled them against him. "Not a chance. I'm never letting you go again. In fact, I may keep you barefoot and pregnant for the rest of your life just to make sure."

"Is that the hillbilly way of saying you love me?"

"I beg your pardon. I am not a hillbilly. But I do love you." He cupped her derriere with one hand, to keep her close, while he went back to work on her buttons with the other.

"I love you, too," she nearly moaned as he reached inside her blouse, slipped beneath her bra and found first her breast and then her nipple, rolling it gently between his fingers.

"Not sore, is it?" he asked.

"Not yet."

"Let's see what we can do about that, shall we?"

"Mmm," was all she could answer, as his mouth came down over hers.

Then in one fell swoop he lifted her into his arms and swung her around to the examining table, pulling one of her legs up to wrap around him once he had her sitting there. "Welcome home, city girl," he said in a passion-raspy voice as he pressed the hard ridge of his desire into her much softer flesh.

"Glad to be here, Dugan," she purred, just before giving in to the wonders of his mouth and hands, and the love that was definitely good enough to counteract everything else.

And in that instant she realized that she hadn't been exaggerating—she really was glad to be there, in Beau's arms, in Wellsburg. Where she belonged.

*   *   *   *   *

THE DONOVAN LEGACY
from Nora Roberts

Meet the Donovans—Morgana, Sebastian and Anastasia. Each one is unique. Each one is . . . special.

In September you will be *Captivated* by Morgana Donovan. In Special Edition #768, horror-film writer Nash Kirkland doesn't know what to do when he meets an actual witch!

Be *Entranced* in October by Sebastian Donovan in Special Edition #774. Private investigator Mary Ellen Sutherland doesn't believe in psychic phenomena. But she discovers Sebastian has strange powers . . . over her.

In November's Special Edition #780, you'll be *Charmed* by Anastasia Donovan, along with Boone Sawyer and his little girl. Anastasia was a healer, but for her it was Boone's touch that cast a spell.

Enjoy the magic of Nora Roberts. Don't miss *Captivated, Entranced* or *Charmed*. Only from
Silhouette Special Edition. . . .

Take 4 bestselling love stories FREE

Plus get a FREE surprise gift!

NORA ROBERTS

Love has a language all its own, and for centuries flowers have symbolized love's finest expression. Discover the language of flowers—and love—in this romantic collection of 48 favorite books by bestselling author Nora Roberts.

Two titles are available each month at your favorite retail outlet.

In November, look for:

For Now, Forever, **Volume #19**
Her Mother's Keeper, **Volume #20**

In December, look for:

Partners, **Volume #21**
Sullivan's Woman, **Volume #22**

Collect all 48 titles
and become fluent in

THE LANGUAGE of LOVE

Silhouette®

Silhouette
Christmas
Stories 1992

Experience the beauty of Yuletide romance with Silhouette Christmas Stories 1992—a collection of heartwarming stories by favorite Silhouette authors.

JONI'S MAGIC by Mary Lynn Baxter
HEARTS OF HOPE by Sondra Stanford
THE NIGHT SANTA CLAUS RETURNED by Marie Ferrarella
BASKET OF LOVE by Jeanne Stephens

Also available this year are three popular early editions of Silhouette Christmas Stories—1986, 1987 and 1988. Look for these and you'll be well on your way to a complete collection of the best in holiday romance.

Plus, as an added bonus, you can receive a FREE keepsake Christmas ornament. Just collect four proofs of purchase from any November or December 1992 Harlequin or Silhouette series novels, or from any Harlequin or Silhouette Christmas collection, and receive a beautiful dated brass Christmas candle ornament.

Mail this certificate along with four (4) proof-of-purchase coupons, plus $1.50 postage and handling (check or money order—do not send cash), payable to Silhouette Books, to: **In the U.S.:** P.O. Box 9057, Buffalo, NY 14269-9057; **In Canada:** P.O. Box 622, Fort Erie, Ontario, L2A 5X3.

ONE PROOF OF PURCHASE

Name: _____
_____

Address: _____
_____

City: _____

State/Province: _____

Zip/Postal Code: _____

SX92POP

093 KAG